"Tell me again you don't want me," he whispered against her hair.

Savannah was drugged with passion. When Travis pulled her close, she could hear the thudding of his heart. "I don't…I can't…" The raw ache within her burned traitorously and her thoughts centered on making love to this very special man.

"Tell me you never loved me."

"Travis…please," she gasped, trying to make some sense of what was happening. She couldn't fall under Travis's spell again, wouldn't love him again, and yet her body refused to push him away.

"Don't ever be ashamed of anything that's happened between us. Whether you believe the truth or not, the fact is that I loved you more than a sane man would let himself love a woman. We were caught in a web of lies, Savannah. Lies spun by the people we trusted."

Coming soon from
LISA JACKSON
and
MIRA Books

A TWIST OF FATE

June 2003

LISA JACKSON

Mystic

MIRA

ISBN 1-55166-957-9

MYSTIC

Copyright © 1986 by Lisa Jackson.

Visit us at www.mirabooks.com

Printed in U.S.A.

Mystic

Prologue

Savannah slowed the mare to a walk and patted Mattie's sweating neck. Her breath was as short as that of the mare; the sprint through the open pastures had been exhilarating. A soft breeze rustled through the branches of trees along the fence and made the July afternoon tolerable as it cooled the trickle of sweat running down her back. She pushed her black hair away from her face and squinted against the hot sun in the northern California sky.

"I guess it's time to go back home," she said reluctantly as she reined the mare toward the gate at the far end of the field. Mattie flicked her ears forward expectantly.

Looking east, Savannah noticed a tall broad-shouldered figure near the gate. She squinted as she approached and tried to place the man repairing the sagging fence. *Must be a new hired hand,* she thought idly, fascinated nonetheless.

She pulled Mattie up short, several yards away from the man, and waited in the dappled shade of an old apple tree. Unable to get through the gate until he was finished with his work, she leaned back in the saddle and observed him.

He was wearing only dusty jeans and boots. His shirt had been tossed over a post, and his deeply muscled back, tanned and glistening with sweat, was straining as he stretched the heavy wire around a new wooden fence post.

I wonder where Dad found him, Savannah mused, admiring the play of rippling muscles and straining tendons of his shoulders and back as he worked. His hair was dark with sweat, and the worn fabric of his jeans stretched taut over lean hips and muscular thighs.

"That should do it," he said, rubbing the small of his back as he straightened and admired his work. His voice was strangely familiar.

Then he dusted his hands together and turned, as if he'd felt her staring at him. Shielding his eyes against the lowering sun, he looked in her direction and every muscle in his body went rigid. "Savannah?"

The sight of Travis's eyes fixed on her made her stomach jump unexpectedly. Savannah urged her horse forward and stopped the mare only a few feet from him. "I...I didn't know you were back on the farm," she replied, blushing slightly at being caught staring at him. *It was Travis for God's sake. Just Travis!*

His amused smile stretched over the angular features of his face. Wiping the sweat from his forehead, he stretched his aching back muscles. "The prodigal son has returned, so to speak."

"So to speak," she whispered, her throat uncomfortably tight as she stared into his steel-gray eyes. The same gray eyes she'd seen most of her life. Only now, they seemed incredibly erotic, and the corded muscles of his chest and shoulders added to his intense masculinity—a sensual virility she'd never noticed before. He'd always just been Travis, almost a brother. "I thought you had a job in L.A."

"I do." He leaned insolently against the post and the hard line of his mouth turned cynical. "But I thought I'd spend the rest of the summer on the farm before I get stuck in the rut of three-piece suits and three-martini lunches."

"So you're staying?" *Why was her heart pounding so wildly?*

"Until September." He glanced around the farm, taking in the whitewashed buildings, the rolling acres of pastureland, and the dusky hills in the distance. "I'm gonna miss this place, though," he admitted, his gaze darkening a bit as it rested on the scampering, long-legged foals in the next field.

"And we'll all miss you," Savannah replied, wondering at the unusual huskiness in her voice.

Travis's head jerked up and he stared at her for a moment. His brows drew together in concentration before he cleared his throat. "Not much to miss, really," he argued. "I haven't been around much."

"That's what happens when you go to school to become a politician."

"Lawyer," he corrected.

Savannah shrugged. "That's not the way I heard it. Dad is already planning a future for you in politics." She cocked her head to the side and smiled. "You know, I wouldn't be surprised if someday you become a senator or something."

"Not on your life, lady!" Travis let out a hollow laugh, but his gray eyes turned stone cold. "Your old man is always scheming, Savannah. But this time he's gone too far." He reached to the ground and picked up a bottle of beer that had been hidden in the dry grass.

"But your father—"

"Was a senator from Colorado, and now according to the press, the old man might not have been as lily-white as the voters thought." Travis scowled, swore under his breath and kicked at the fence post with the toe of his boot. "But then you already knew that." Eyeing her over the top of the bottle, he lifted his chin and took a long swallow of beer, then tossed the empty bottle to the ground. With a sound of disgust, he wiped the back of his hand over his mouth and then raked tense fingers through his hair in frustration. "It seems to be the popular thing to do these days, digging up the dirt on dead politicians."

Savannah didn't know what to say, so she looked away and tried not to notice the way the afternoon sun played in Travis's rich, chestnut-colored hair. Tried not to notice the

ripple of his shoulder muscles as he shoveled a last scoop
of dirt around the post, or the fact that the curling hairs over
his chest were dark with sweat and accentuated the flat con-
tour of his abdomen.

"I can't worry about it, anyway. What's done is done.
Right?"

"Right."

He looked up at her again and she couldn't help but stare
at his mouth. Thin lips curved slightly downward in vexa-
tion as he noticed the intensity of her gaze.

He pretended interest in his work and avoided her eyes.
"Still going with that boy...David what's-his-name?" he
asked.

"Crandall. And no."

"Why not?"

She lifted one shoulder and shifted uncomfortably in the
saddle. For the first time since she could remember, she
didn't like Travis poking his nose into her private life. "I
don't know. It just didn't work out."

His jaw tightened a bit. "Want to talk about it?"

"No, uh, I don't think so."

"You used to tell me whatever was on your mind."

"Yeah, but I was just a kid then."

"And now?" He slid a glance up her body.

"And now I'm seventeen." She tossed her black hair
away from her face and sat up straight in the saddle, shoulders pinned back, unconsciously thrusting her breasts forward.

Travis sucked in his breath and frowned. "Oh, I see; all
grown up."

"Just like you were when you were seventeen." She
arched a disdainful eyebrow, hoping to appear more sophisticated than she felt sitting astride Mattie. Her T-shirt
and cutoff jeans, wild black hair and freshly scrubbed face
didn't help the image. She probably looked the same as she
did when she was a skinny kid of nine.

"Seventeen. That was so long ago, I can't even remember."

"I do. That's how old you were when you moved in with us."

"You remember that far back?"

"Give me a break, Travis. I was nine, and I've got a great memory. I thought you were so...I think the word they use today is 'awesome.'"

Travis shook his head. "I was a rebellious brat."

"And I was impressed by your total disrespect for anything."

Travis winced. "Reginald wasn't."

"Dad is and always has been the ultimate authoritarian. That's why I thought you were so...brave." She laughed and some of the growing tension between them dissolved. "And now you're an old man of twenty-five."

"Yeah, I guess so." He leaned against the wooden post and crossed his arms over his chest as his smile faded. "And it's time to quit sponging off your dad and try and make a living on my own."

"You've never sponged off Dad!" Indignation colored Savannah's cheeks. "Maybe some people don't know it, but I do."

"He took me in—"

"And you worked. Hard. On this farm. For nothing. Just like you're doing now! As for your education, you had a trust fund. You didn't exactly come here as a pauper, you know!"

"Whoa!" He laughed deep in his throat. "I didn't know I had such a bulldog in my corner."

"Just stating the facts, counselor." She smiled and blushed a little under his unyielding stare. The warm familiarity that had existed between them just seconds before suddenly vanished.

"You never cease to amaze me, Savvy," Travis said, using the nickname he had given her all those years before. His voice was barely above a whisper as his flinty gaze locked intimately with hers. Savannah's heart began to pound in the thickening silence, and Travis's eyes narrowed.

A stallion whistled in the distance, and Mattie snorted, breaking the silence. Travis gave his head a quick shake, as if to dislodge an unwanted thought. "Remind me to hire you when I'm having trouble getting the jury to see my client's side of the story," he joked, picking up his shirt, empty bottle and shovel and carrying them to a Jeep parked on the other side of the gate.

"I doubt that my testimony would make an impact."

"I don't know," he said, rubbing his square, beard-shadowed chin thoughtfully. His gaze inched up her bare, suntanned legs before lingering slightly on her waist and breasts and then finally reaching her eyes. She felt as if she'd just been stripped bare, and her cheeks burned under his assessing stare. "I just don't know."

Somehow she understood that he wasn't referring to his fictitious courtroom scenario, and her heart fluttered. To save herself from further embarrassment, she kicked Mattie and the game little mare broke into a gallop. Savannah leaned forward in the saddle and raced away from Travis and the odd feelings he'd unwittingly inspired.

The next five weeks were torture. Savannah saw Travis every night at dinner. Every night, that is, that he wasn't with Melinda, his fiancée. Why his engagement to Melinda Reaves bothered Savannah now, eluded her. Melinda was a nice enough girl—make that woman, she corrected herself—and Travis had dated her for years. It was only natural that someday Travis and Melinda would marry. Right? Then why did she feel sick inside every time she thought about Travis and Melinda together?

During the days, Savannah ran into Travis working around the farm. In the stables, in the tack room, at the lake, in the stallion barn, everywhere. There didn't seem to be a place she could hide without experiencing the sensation that he was watching her. She had even caught him staring openly at her more than once, though he'd always looked quickly away when she caught his gaze. Though Savannah had tried to be discreet, she was fascinated by him. She'd watch him work and her mind would create deliciously wanton fantasies about him.

"Don't do this," she warned herself on more than one occasion when she found herself dressing with more care than was her custom. "This is Travis you're thinking about. Travis!" But the pain in her middle wouldn't go away, nor could she keep her eyes from straying to his face, his hands, his lips, his thighs. Oftentimes she found herself wondering just what it would feel like to have Travis touch her with those large, work-roughened hands, what it would taste like to have his sensual lips brush against hers…how it would feel to become his lover. Just the thought of his hard, male physique pressed hungrily against her body made her break into a nervous sweat and her heart beat savagely.

"You're out of your ever-lovin' mind," she told herself.

"What's wrong with you, Savannah?" David asked as they were driving back to the farm.

The date with David had been a disaster from the start, and she knew now that she never should have agreed to it. Though she'd tried not to think about Travis, she hadn't even tasted the gourmet food or paid any attention to the movie that David had taken her to.

"Nothing's wrong with me." *Except that I took this date out of spite, because Travis is with Melinda again.* She felt uneasy, and some of the uncomfortable feeling was from guilt. She'd used David to lash back at Travis. Not fair. David was a friend, a good friend. And Travis hadn't even noticed.

"Give me a break. You've been brooding all night. Why?"

"I'm not brooding."

"Look, just tell me, was it something I did?"

Savannah smiled and shook her head. "No, of course not."

David sighed in relief and parked the car behind her house, near the back porch. He cut the engine and switched off the headlights. The breeze that filtered through the open windows of the car was little relief from the stifling night. Savannah felt hot and sticky as she reached for the handle of the door.

"Wait." David's hand touched her on the shoulder and she stopped. His brown eyes searched hers. "There's someone else, isn't there?"

"No," she lied. Her feelings for Travis were just schoolgirl fantasies and she recognized them as such.

"Then, what, Savannah? Don't you know I love you?"

It was the last thing she wanted to hear. "David, you're a good friend and I like you very much—"

"And I sense a big 'but' coming here," he complained.

"Can't we just be friends?"

"'Friends?'" he repeated. "Friends. Savannah, for crissake, didn't you hear me?" He placed a finger under her chin and forced her to look into his intense gaze. "I *love* you."

"David—"

But she couldn't stop him as his arms tightened around her and he kissed her with more passion than she'd ever thought possible. When he lifted his head, her lips were throbbing painfully. "David, please, don't," she whispered, trying to pull away from him.

"You used to like me to kiss you," he rasped in disbelief.

"I told you…I just want to be friends."

"Like hell." He pulled her close to him again and this time when he kissed her she felt his tongue press against her teeth and his sweaty hands reach below the hem of her sweater to touch her naked abdomen and inch upward to her breasts.

I can't! she thought desperately. *I just can't let him touch me!* Gathering all her strength, she wrenched one arm free and slapped him across the cheek. It had the effect of a bucket of cold water. He drew back his head and his eyes glittered frightfully. "Don't push me, Savannah," he ground out.

"And don't push *me*!"

He released her then and his face slackened. "I just don't understand. Why did you go out with me?"

"Because I like you. I thought you were my friend."

"There's that word again," he said, rubbing his cheek. "I never thought I would hate being called a friend, but I do." He placed his hands over the steering wheel and let his head fall forward. "There is someone else, isn't there?"

She understood his despair. Wasn't she in the same position herself?

"I don't know, David," she said, tenderness softening her voice. "I...do care for someone else...." He flinched. "But believe me, he doesn't know I'm alive.... I'd...I'd better go."

"I'll walk you to the door."

"No! It's okay. Really. I can make it."

This time she got the door open.

"Savannah—"

"Yeah?"

"I'm sorry."

Tears stood in her eyes. "I know, David." She didn't wait for any further confessions from him. All she knew was that she'd probably lost a very good friend and she'd humiliated him in the bargain. She got out of the car and slammed the door shut.

"I can't seem to do anything right," she thought aloud as she climbed the two steps to the porch. She heard David's car start and listened as he drove away. "Thank God," she whispered and realized that she'd started to cry.

Reaching into her purse for her keys, she heard a sound: the heel of a boot scraping against the flagstones. She nearly jumped out of her skin. Swallowing back a small lump of fear she turned and faced Travis, who was sitting in the shadows of the porch in a rocking chair. *Oh, God...*

"You should be more careful about who you go out with," he said, his voice cold.

"And you should be more careful about sitting in the dark. You nearly scared me to death."

"I thought you weren't dating David."

"I'm not."

Silence. Savannah could hear her own heart pounding.

"You're leading him on," he accused and Savannah heard the irritation in his voice, though she could barely see his face.

"You should mind your own business."

"Then maybe next time, you'll have the decency to roll the windows up." With a sinking sensation, Savannah realized that Travis had heard all of her conversation with David. She was mortified and kept rummaging in her purse. *Where was the damned key?*

"Maybe next time *you'll* have the decency to mind your own business and not eavesdrop."

"I wasn't eavesdropping."

"Than what're you doing out here all alone? Where's Melinda?"

"At home." His voice sounded dead.

"Oh."

Her fingers found the key ring, but it was too late. Travis was on his feet and walking toward her. As the gap between them closed, her pulse began to race wildly. He stopped only inches from her, close enough that she could feel the heat radiating from his body, see the pain and concern etched over his harsh features. "I'm serious, Savannah. You shouldn't lead that boy on. And that advice goes for any other man as well."

"I told you, I wasn't leading him on."

"He cares about you, and when a boy, a young man, cares about a woman, sometimes he gets carried away. He can't help himself. He stops using his brain and starts thinking with his— Oh, hell, I'm making a bloody mess of this!''

"You sound as if you're speaking from experience."

His muscles became rigid. "Maybe I am."

Savannah thought of Melinda and felt like crying all over again. Travis leaned a shoulder against the wall and she felt his eyes staring at her mussed hair and flushed face.

"Just be careful, Savannah," he said tenderly, touching the edge of her jaw. "Don't get yourself into a situation that you can't get out of. I won't always be here to take care of you."

The feel of his fingers on her skin made her pulse jump. The heat of his touch seemed to scorch a path to her heart. "A lot of good it did having you here."

"I didn't want to butt in. It really wasn't any of my business. But, believe me, if David hadn't come to his senses when you slapped him, I would have jerked open that car door and beat the living hell out of him."

"David wouldn't hurt me."

"I didn't know that."

The thought of Travis willing to fight to protect her virtue was pleasant and she couldn't help but smile.

"This is serious business, Savannah."

The finger at her jaw moved slowly to her throat and Savannah felt herself melting inside. A warm ache stretched deep inside her and it was hard to keep her mind on anything but Travis's warm finger and his dark, searing gaze. It took her breath away.

"I...I know."

"Just don't make the same mistake Charmaine did."

Savannah felt herself color. Her sister, Charmaine, had gotten pregnant the year before and was now married to Wade Benson, the father of her little boy. "I don't need a lesson in sex education," she tossed back.

"Good." He let his hand drop and even in the hot night she shivered. "'Cause I'm sure as hell not the one who should be giving you one."

"What's that supposed to mean?"

He closed his eyes. "Oh, Savannah, you just don't have any idea what you do to a man, do you?" Opening his eyes, he looked at her lovingly for a fleeting moment. "Just don't underestimate your effect on men or overestimate a man's self-control."

Her throat was dry, but she had to ask the question. "All men?"

"All men."

"Does that include you?" she whispered.

"All men," he repeated and opened the door to the kitchen. "Now go upstairs to bed and get some sleep before I forget the fact that I'm supposed to be a brother to you, that I should be looking out for your best interests."

"I don't need a keeper, Travis," she said, placing her fingers on his arm.

His eyes were cold and assessing as he measured the innocence in her gaze. "Well, maybe *I* do." He took hold of her wrist and his face became expressionless as he forced her hand away from him. "You've heard the old expression, 'Don't play with fire unless you're ready to get burned'?" he said, his jaw tight. "Think about it."

And then he strode away, into the dark night.

For five days Savannah didn't see Travis, and she discovered that it was more difficult to work on the farm when he was absent than when he was there. Just how much of the conversation with David had he heard, and how much had he pieced together? Had he realized that he was the man she cared for? Savannah wondered.

That she loved Travis McCord came as an unwelcome and painful realization. The fact that he loved another woman made the situation all the more intolerable.

Just two more weeks, Savannah thought as she lay on the top of her bed, staring at the ceiling, wondering where Travis was at one in the morning. *Just two more weeks and then he'll be gone.*

At the thought of his leaving and marrying Melinda Reaves, Savannah's heart wrenched painfully. She rolled over and looked at the clock, just as she had every two minutes for the past half hour. "This is crazy," she told herself.

For nearly as long as she could remember, Travis had been a part of Beaumont Breeding Farm. When his parents had been killed in a plane crash, her father and mother had taken him in as if he were their own. Savannah had always looked up to the rebellious young man as the older brother she'd never had. Never in her wildest dreams had she imagined that she would fall in love with him. Well, not "in love" exactly. She loved him. He still thought of her as a kid sister and it was probably best that way. If she could just make it through the next two weeks without letting him know how she felt about him, everything would work out. Travis would marry Melinda, and Savannah would go to college. *If she didn't die first!* Her small fist curled and pounded the unused pillow on her bed.

Her restlessness finally got the better of her and she threw off the covers, grabbed her robe, slipped on a pair of thongs and sneaked down the hallway. The only sounds in the house were the soft ticking of the hall clock and the hum of the refrigerator. One of the steps squeaked as she hurried down the staircase. She froze, but no one in the house stirred. Taking a deep breath, Savannah quietly hurried down the rest of the stairs, softly opened the front door, slipped outside and closed the door behind her.

The night was illuminated by a lazy half-moon and a sprinkling of stars that peeked through the wispy, dark clouds. The smell of honeysuckle and lilacs filled the air and the soft croaking of frogs was interrupted by the occasional whinny of a mare calling to her foal. Other than those few noises, the night was still.

Savannah walked down the worn path to the lake almost by instinct. She climbed over the gates rather than risking the noise of unlatching them. When the scrub oak and pine trees gave way to a clearing and the small irregular-shaped lake, Savannah smiled, slipped out of her thongs, tossed her robe to the ground and waded into the water. It felt cool against her skin and she dived to the bottom before surfacing.

She had been swimming about fifteen minutes when she realized that she wasn't alone. Her heart nearly stopped beating and she braced herself for one of her father's stern lectures.

"Dad?" she called unsteadily at the figure of a man leaning against the sturdy trunk of an oak tree. "Dad, is that you?"

For the first time in years, Travis had consumed more alcohol than he could handle, and he intended to clear his head with a long walk. The argument he'd had earlier in the evening with Melinda was still ringing in his mind. She'd accused him of being aloof, disinterested in her, and maybe she was right. Because for the past few damning weeks, he'd been thinking solely of Savannah Beaumont. *Reginald's daughter, for God's sake!* And the thoughts he'd had about her were far from brotherly.

From the first time he'd seen her, half-dressed, her firm breasts straining against a T-shirt, her supple legs wrapped around that bay mare, he'd been out of his mind with lust. The burning desire had tortured him with wildly erotic fantasies that took away his sleep.

He'd even had to leave the farm for a couple of days to get his head back on straight. The last thing he needed was to get involved with a seventeen-year-old girl, the daughter of the man who'd raised him. But it was confusing. Confusing as hell. And he didn't blame Melinda for being angry. Since he'd seen Savannah again, he hadn't been able to concentrate on Melinda at all—to the point that his interest in making love to her had all but disappeared.

He let his shirt gape open, hoping that the cool air would help clear his head. Leaning against an oak tree, he heard the splashing in the lake. His head was spinning crazily, but even in the darkness he recognized Savannah and the fact that she was swimming nude in the inky water. His fingers dug into the rough bark of the oak tree for support. *Oh, God,* he thought, trying to think straight. *Give me strength.*

Then she called to him. "Dad?" Silence. Travis's heart thundered in his chest. "Dad, is that you?"

"What the devil are you doing here?" Travis asked, barely trusting his voice.

Not Travis! Savannah's heartbeat accelerated when she recognized his voice. *Not here!* "Minding my own business," she managed to choke out.

Silvery light from a iridescent moon rippled on the water, alternately shadowing and highlighting the firm white swell of her breasts and the dark tips of her nipples. Her black hair was slicked away from her face and her chin was thrust forward defiantly. Drops of water clung to her lashes and slid down her cheeks and a traitorous ache began to throb in Travis's loins.

"You shouldn't be here," he said, his throat uncomfortably tight. "Someone might see you."

"*Someone* has."

"You know what I mean." Travis fought to clear his head and he battled against the fire radiating from his loins. Shifting against the tree, he willed the natural reaction of his body to subside. And failed. *Leave right now,* he told himself, *before you say or do something foolish.*

"Where's Melinda?" Savannah asked, swimming nearer to him.

He heard the tremor in her voice, saw the quiet suffering in her eyes. *Go away, Savannah, don't look at me like that.* "I don't know." He closed his eyes and tried not to watch the gentle water caress the satin-white skin of her body. "I don't think we'll see each other again."

"But you're engaged."

"Not any more." He fished in the pocket of his jeans and retrieved the diamond ring. Holding it up to the moonlight, it winked mockingly at him. His fingers curled around the cold metal and stones before he cursed and hurled the ring into the water. It settled into the lake with barely a splash.

"You shouldn't have done that," Savannah reprimanded, edging closer to the bank, but she couldn't hide the pleasure in her voice.

"I should have done it a long time ago."

"You're drunk."

"Not drunk enough."

"Oh, Travis," she said with a shake of her head. "If you're not careful, you'll self-destruct."

The comfort in her voice touched a primitive part of him and he knew the battle he was alternately fighting and surrendering to was about to be lost.

He saw her robe near the bank and he pushed himself upright to retrieve it. As he stood, he swayed slightly. Righting himself, he walked over to the bank. "You'd better get out of there," he said. "It's the middle of the night, for crying out loud."

She laughed and dipped back into the water. Knowing that he wasn't tied to Melinda made her feel as if a tremendous weight had been lifted from her shoulders.

"Savannah—"

"Don't worry about me," she said, resurfacing and shaking the hair out of her face.

"Does anyone know you're out here?"

"Just you."

"Great," he muttered, his eyes riveted to the fascinating hollow of her throat and the pulse throbbing there. The reaction that Melinda hadn't been able to stir began just at the sight of Savannah's wet body.

"Oh, all right." She swam to where her feet touched the soft silt at the bottom of the lake and began to walk out of the water. Travis, knowing that his duty was done and that he should walk away, stood fascinated as she slowly emerged from the water.

Savannah knew there was no way she could hide her

body. The best thing to do was get to the robe and cover up as quickly as possible, but she could feel Travis's eyes upon her, two gray orbs sizzling into her flesh.

Travis sucked in his breath as he watched her. Her white skin contrasted to the black night and droplets of water slid seductively down her throat to her breasts. He watched the gentle sway of her breasts as she walked toward him. Her waist was small and her navel a provocative dimple in her abdomen.

Travis's breath was tight in his lungs as her hips and thighs emerged. He tossed the robe to her.

"Put it on before you catch cold." He was forcing himself to walk away and had taken the first step when Savannah, intent on putting on the robe as quickly as possible, tripped against the root of a tree and fell to the ground.

"Savannah!"

In two steps he was beside her. "I'm okay," she said, holding onto the shin she had banged when she hit the ground.

"Are you sure?"

"Yes, yes." She shook her head and covered herself with the robe. "Aside from being mortified, that is."

His hands were on her upper arms, his fingers lingering against the silky texture of her wet skin. He felt her tremble at his touch and when he kissed her comfortingly on her temple she sighed and didn't draw away.

"I don't know what came over me," she said, thinking back to her wanton behavior and trying to ignore his tender kiss. She'd just walked out of the lake, stark naked, straight at Travis. She hadn't even had the decency to ask him to look the other way. She felt like a complete idiot.

Travis wanted to comfort her...hold her...never stop making love to her. *Push me away,* he thought as his physical needs overcame common sense. She looked at him with wide innocent eyes and the moonlight caught in her dazzling gaze. Travis felt his resolve waver as he tried to keep the robe from falling off her shoulders. Though she tried to knot the belt, her fingers fumbled and the neckline continued to gap despite her efforts to cover herself.

"What—" He cleared his throat and tried not to concentrate on the dusky hollow between the two silken mounds. "What were you doing out here?"

"I couldn't sleep."

"Why not?"

She shook her head and the droplets of water in her hair caught in the moonlight and sparkled like fine diamonds. "I don't know." He was so damned close to her. She could smell the scent of brandy on his breath, read the smoky desire in his eyes. Her heart throbbed with the thought that he wanted her and her skin quivered from the warmth of his breath on the back of her neck.

"I'm having trouble sleeping these nights myself."

"Because of…the problems with Melinda?"

He shook his head. "Because of the problems with you."

"Oh."

His fingers traced the pout on her lips. "I haven't been able to think of much besides you lately. And it's driving me out of my mind." His eyes caressed her face and watched as she swallowed when he touched her throat, his fingers inching lazily up and down the soft white column.

"Travis—"

"Tell me to leave you alone, Savannah."

"I…I can't."

"Tell me to take my hands off you," he suggested, but she shook her head.

"Then do something, anything, slap me the way you did that kid that attacked you the other night."

"I can't Travis," she moaned as his fingers slid lower to trace the lapels of her robe.

His face inched closer to hers and the weight of his body leaned against hers as he kissed her, tenderly at first and then with such savagery that it tore through her body.

Her lips were chilled from the water but responded when his mouth settled over hers in a kiss that questioned as much as it claimed. He was asking and taking all at once and she leaned closer to him, her fingers touching the muscles at the base of his neck.

The fires that had started as a dull ache in Travis's loins burned through his bloodstream and destroyed all of his rational thought. When she parted her lips, his kiss became fierce and hungry, his tongue eager as it discovered its waiting mate.

He lifted his head and saw her swollen lips, the seduction in her eyes. "This is crazy," he groaned. "Haven't you had enough?"

"I don't know if I could ever have enough of you," she admitted.

"Don't do this to me, Savannah, I'm not made of stone, for crying out loud! I was just trying to shock some sense into you!" But the painful ache between his legs told him he was lying.

Savannah's arms wrapped around his neck, her fingers touched the sensitive skin over his shoulders and he groaned before lowering himself next to her and kissing her with all the passion that was dominating his mind and body.

She responded in kind. When he rolled atop her, one hand pressing the small of her back upward against him, she felt the hard evidence of his passion. He rubbed anxiously against her and one of his hands slid beneath the lapel of her robe to discover the creamy softness of her breast.

Her body arched up from the ground, molding her flesh to his, fitting against him perfectly.

Stop. Stop me, Savannah, he thought, but he slid lower on her body, his lips kissing and caressing her skin, finding the pulse at her throat, lingering seductively before his hands and mouth parted the robe, inched down her ribs and found the dark, waiting peak of her breast. He rimmed the nipple with his tongue and Savannah moaned his name into the night. Then slowly, with the delicate strokes of a dedicated lover, he licked and suckled at the straining breast until he felt her fingernails digging into his back.

"Oh, God, I should be shot for this," he muttered, attempting to grasp onto some shred of his common sense. But even as he did, he slid his belt through the buckle and kicked off his jeans.

"Just love me," she begged, trembling beneath him.

"I do. Oh, God, Savannah. I do."

He was naked then, his lean body glistening with sweat as he lay upon her. She welcomed the burden of his weight and when he entered her, she felt a sharp jab of pain before she was lost in the brilliant and beautiful bursts of their union. She stroked the hard muscles of his back with her fingers and kissed at his face and chest and heard herself scream as the increasing tempo of his strokes pushed her upward to a precipice and then over the edge in a dazzling climax that sent aftershocks rolling through her body for several minutes. As she fell slowly back to earth, she sighed in a contentment heretofore unknown to her.

With Travis's arms wrapped securely around her, Savannah listened to the sounds of the night—Travis's irregular breathing, the clamoring of her heart, the sound of a fish jumping lazily in the water and farther away, the sound of a twig snapping.

Travis's body stiffened. He kissed her softly on the forehead and drew the robe around her. "Go back to the house," he whispered against her ear and cut off her questions by pressing a finger to her lips.

"But—"

"Shh." He squinted into the darkness. "I heard something. I don't think we're alone. I'll come to you—soon," he promised.

Then soundlessly, Travis was jerking on his clothes. Savannah didn't argue, but followed his instructions to the letter. Holding her robe closed with one hand, her thongs in the other, she ran barefoot along the path, feeling the sharp stones and twigs that cut into her feet.

Breathlessly she sneaked back into the dark house, hurried up the back staircase to her room and waited in the bed, her heart clamoring, her ears straining for any sound of Travis's arrival. She was sure that he would be true to his word and come to her. It was only a matter of time.

When the first gray light of dawn streaked through the room, she realized that Travis had probably been held up by whomever it was who had come to the lake. It didn't matter. She'd meet him later in the day.

Facing her father—or whoever it was who had stumbled upon Travis and her—wouldn't be a picnic, but Savannah was convinced she could handle it. She drifted off to a heavy sleep and woke up much later—sometime after ten. She showered, dressed and went downstairs to discover her father sitting at the kitchen table, stirring a cup of coffee, and reading the morning paper.

"Good morning," Savannah said, eyeing him. Everything looked normal. Obviously, Reginald had been out to the stables at the crack of dawn as was his usual custom. He was clean shaven, his boots were by the door to the porch, and he'd already finished breakfast. His plate still held a few crumbs of toast, though it had been pushed to the side of the table.

Reginald looked up sharply, frowned and put down his paper. "Morning."

"Good morning, dear," her mother, Virgina, said, when she came breezing through the door to the kitchen from the dining room. Her dark hair was perfectly combed, her makeup looking as if she'd just applied it. "You overslept this morning. It's too bad, too. You weren't here to say goodbye to Travis."

"Goodbye?" Savannah repeated, stunned.

"Yes." Virginia poured herself a cup of coffee and then sat down at the table across from Reginald. "Seems he and Melinda decided to get married as soon as possible—and high time, I say. They've been dating forever. The wedding will probably be next week, so he went to Los Angeles to see if he could rent his apartment earlier than he'd originally planned."

Savannah sagged against the counter, her cup of coffee nearly spilling from her shaking hands.

"I guess he got tired of working here at the farm," Reginald said. "Don't blame him a bit. Since he passed the bar exam, there's no reason for him to be hanging around here, when he could be out chasing ambulances."

"Reginald!" Virginia admonished, but Reginald chuckled to himself and Virginia's blue eyes sparkled at the prospect of a wedding.

Savannah felt the tears burn at the back of her eyes. "I'm surprised no one woke me up so that I could say goodbye," she said.

"No reason to." Reginald said with a shrug. "Travis will be back. Bad penny syndrome, you know. They always have a habit of showing up again."

"Father! Listen to you," Virginia said, but smiled.

"Didn't Travis want to—talk to me?"

"I don't think so. He never mentioned it. Did he, hon?"

"Not to me." Virginia saw the hurt in Savannah's eyes and sent her a kindly smile. "But then he's pretty busy, what with the wedding plans and all. You'll see him then."

Savannah felt a traitorous burn in her heart, but she told herself not to believe anyone—not until she heard from Travis.

The problem was, he never called or came back to the farm. And he married Melinda Reaves two weeks after having made love to Savannah by the lake.

"I'll never speak to him again," Savannah told herself angrily on the morning of the wedding. To her mother's disappointment, she refused to attend the marriage ceremony.

"I can't, Mom," she said when Virginia pressed her for a reason. "I just can't."

"Why not?" Virginia asked, sitting on the edge of the bed and surveying her youngest daughter with concern as Savannah stood at the window of her room and pretended interest in the view.

"Travis...Travis and I had a disagreement."

"All brothers and sisters—"

"He's *not* my brother!"

Virginia arched a knowing brow. "Oh, I see."

"I don't know how you possibly could," Savannah said, feeling wretched inside. No one could possibly understand, least of all her mother. So why didn't they all just leave her alone in her misery?

"How involved with Travis were you?" Virginia asked gently.

"I'm not—" Savannah's voice caught. "Oh, Mom," she whispered, her fingers winding in the soft fabric of the curtains.

"It's all right, honey," Virginia consoled, walking over to her daughter and placing a comforting arm around Savannah's shoulders.

The tears that had been threatening for two weeks ran down Savannah's face. *It wasn't all right. Never would be.* She turned and sobbed against her mother's shoulder for a few minutes.

"Loving the wrong man is never easy," Virginia said thoughtfully.

"But how could you know?"

"Oh, I know, all right," Virginia said with a sad smile, as if she wanted to confide in her daughter. "I was young once myself. I've...well, I've made a few mistakes."

"With Dad?" Savannah sniffed, eyeing her mother.

Virginia avoided Savannah's eyes. "Yes, honey. With your father." There was something cryptic in Virginia's voice, but Savannah couldn't think about it, or anything else for that matter. Melinda Reaves was going to be Travis McCord's wife! Savannah felt as if her entire world were crumbling at her feet.

"But I love him so much," she admitted.

"And he'll soon be a married man. There's nothing you can do about it. Not now."

"Oh, yes there is," Savannah said, the tears still streaming down a suddenly thrusting chin. "I'm going to forget about him. I'm never going to speak to him again. And...and I'll never let myself fall for any man again."

Virginia was smiling through her own tears. "Don't be so rash, there's still a few good men out there. David Crandall cares for you."

"Oh, Mom—" Savannah said, rolling her eyes to the ceiling. "David's just a boy...a friend."

"And Travis was more?"

"Yes."

"So it was that way, was it?" Virginia asked quietly. "Are...are you all right?"

"Do I look all right?"

"I mean—"

"I know what you mean," Savannah said softly, reading the worry in her mother's eyes. "You won't be shamed by me."

Virginia sighed. "And you still love him?"

"Not any more," Savannah vowed, her fist clenching in determination. "Not any more and *never again*." Whatever it took, she would throw off the shackles of her love for Travis. He would soon be Melinda's husband and Melinda's problem. As far as Savannah was concerned, she didn't care if Travis McCord lived or died.

She had no idea that nine years later she'd still be trying to convince herself that she despised him.

One

Savannah didn't regret moving back to the farm. The gently rolling countryside northeast of San Francisco had been a welcome sight to her when she'd returned. She hadn't realized how much she'd missed the hazy purple hills surrounding the farm and the fields of lush green grass and grazing horses.

The bustle of the city had been exciting while she was a college student and for a few years when she worked in San Francisco in an investment firm. But she was glad to be back at the breeding farm even if it meant putting up with her brother-in-law, Wade Benson.

In the past few years Wade had given up most of his accounting practice to manage the farm and he was being groomed to step into Reginald's boots, whenever her father decided to retire. That might be sooner than he had planned, Savannah thought sadly, considering her mother's poor health.

It was just too bad that Travis hadn't stayed at the farm and followed in Dad's footsteps, she thought idly and then mentally chastised herself. Though it had been nine years since he had left the farm to marry Melinda, Savannah had never really forgiven him—she'd even managed to avoid him most of the time. Now there were rumors that he would run in the next election for governor of the state of California. Hard to believe.

"Hey, Aunt Savvy, want to go riding?" Joshua, Charmaine and Wade's only child, called as he ran up to her.

Savannah smiled as she looked into the nine-year-old's earnest brown eyes. His cheeks were flushed, his brown hair in sad need of a trim. "I'd love to," she said, and the boy broke into a grin.

"Can I ride Mystic?"

Savannah laughed. "Not on your life, buddy! He's Grandpa's prize colt!"

"But he likes me."

"The way I understand it, Mystic doesn't like anyone."

"Hogwash!" The boy kicked the toe of his sneaker at an acorn on the ground in frustration. "I know I can ride him," Josh boasted proudly, his eyes twinkling mischievously.

"Oh you can, can you?" She smiled at the determination in Josh's proud chin. "Well, maybe someday, if Grandpa and Lester think it's okay, but not today." Savannah eyed the graying sky. "Tell ya what, I'll saddle Mattie and Jones, and we'll take a couple of turns around the field before it starts to rain."

"But they're old nags. They're not even Thoroughbreds!"

"Shame on you. Even old non-Thoroughbred-type horses need exercise. Just like obstinate little boys! Come on—" she gave Joshua a good-natured pat between the shoulders "—I'll race ya."

"Okay!" Joshua was off across the wet grass in a flash and Savannah let him win the race. "You're old, too," he said with a laugh once she had crossed the imaginary finish line at the stable gate.

"And you're precocious."

"What's that mean?"

Savannah's eyes gleamed with love for the little boy. "That no one but an aunt could love you."

He immediately sobered and Savannah realized she'd said

the wrong thing. "Well, no one but Grandma and Grandpa and your mom and dad and—"

"Dad doesn't love me."

"Of course he does," Savannah said, seeing the sadness in the little boy's eyes and silently cursing her brother-in-law.

"He never does anything with me."

"Your father's very busy—" *Damn, but she hated to make excuses for Wade.*

"He's always busy," Joshua corrected, and Savannah rumpled her nephew's floppy brown hair.

"Managing this farm is a big responsibility."

"But you have time to play with me."

"That's because I'm totally irresponsible." Savannah laughed. "Now, quit feeling sorry for yourself and find the saddle blankets."

Joshua, appeased for the moment, found the required blankets as Savannah bridled the two horses and silently told herself to have it out with her brother-in-law. No father should be so indifferent to his only son.

"Stay here a minute," she told Joshua after tightening the cinch around Jones's girth. "I'll see if there's anything to drink in the office. Wouldn't you like a Coke while we ride?"

"Sure!"

"I'll be right back."

She walked through the stable door, down the cement walk running parallel to the clapboard building, and up the stairs to the office located directly over that part of the stables used as a foaling shed. The door of the office was partially open and she heard voices within. Her father and Wade were involved in a heated discussion.

"I just don't think you can count on him," Wade was saying. Savannah took a step forward, intent on telling her brother-in-law to pay some attention to his child, but Wade's next words made her hesitate. "McCord's just about over the deep end and Willis is damned worried about him."

Travis? What was wrong with him? Savannah's heart began to pound with fear.

"Willis Henderson worries about anything that comes along," her father replied calmly.

"Maybe there's a reason for that. He's McCord's law partner for God's sake. He works with McCord every day."

"And he thinks Travis is—"

"Cracking up."

Savannah stifled a gasp. "Nonsense," Reginald said. "That boy is tough."

"Willis says McCord hasn't been the same since his wife's death."

Reginald sighed. "Look, Wade, I'm telling you that Willis Henderson is jumping at shadows! Lawyers tend to do that. Travis McCord will end up the next governor of this state, just you wait and see."

"I don't know. I certainly don't want to bet on it."

"Of course not," Reginald said with audible disgust. "God, you accountants are all so damned conservative."

"There's nothing wrong with that. If you had been a little more conservative in the last five years, we wouldn't be in this mess."

"It's not a mess!" Reginald roared.

"I call zero cash flow a mess."

"You're as bad as Willis Henderson; always borrowing trouble," Reginald muttered. "Lawyers and accountants cut from the same cloth."

Savannah, feeling guilty about eavesdropping, and yet overcome with worry for Travis, walked into the room. Reginald and Wade, both seated at the table, looked up from their cups of coffee. "What kind of trouble are you talking about?" she asked her father.

Reginald scowled into his cup before sending a warning glance to Wade. "Oh, nothing. Wade's a little concerned about cash flow."

"Is it bad?" Her eyes moved to her brother-in-law.

"Yes," Wade answered, his gaze shifting uncomfortably

under her straightforward stare. He tugged nervously at the hairs of his blond moustache.

"No." Reginald shook his graying head and adjusted his plaid cap. "Wade's just being...cautious."

"That's my job," Wade pointed out.

Savannah didn't listen. "What were you saying about Travis?" she asked, walking over to the refrigerator and trying not to look overly interested though she felt a nervous sheen of sweat break out on her palms.

Reginald's jaw worked. "Oh, nothing serious. That partner of his, Henderson, is worried about him. Thinks Travis is...depressed. Probably just letdown from that last case he won. Got lots of publicity with that Eldridge decision and we all know how tough it is to get back into the regular office routine after all that hoopla. It's just letdown. The same way we felt after Mystic won the Preakness."

"So you think he'll still run for governor?"

Reginald smiled. "*I'd* be willing to bet on it," he said, casting Wade a knowing glance.

Savannah grabbed a couple cans of Coke from the refrigerator and closed the door. "Did Willis Henderson call you? Is that how you found out about Travis's 'depression'?"

"No." Her father avoided her eyes.

"I ran into him at the track," Wade said hurriedly. "Just yesterday at Hollywood Park."

Savannah raised a eyebrow skeptically; she could feel that Wade and her father were deliberately hiding something from her, but she couldn't delve into it. Not right now. Joshua was waiting for her in the stables and she wasn't about to disappoint him.

"Since you got back to the farm," she said, looking pointedly at Wade, "have you bothered to talk to Joshua?"

"Huh? Well, no. I just got in last night and then he got up and went to school this morning. Not much time." Wade squirmed uncomfortably in his chair.

"Maybe he needs a little fatherly attention."

"I'll...I'll talk to him tonight, when I'm not so busy."

"I think it would be a good idea," Savannah said, striding out of the room and feeling an uncomfortable tightening in her stomach. She'd known there were money problems at the farm, of course; there always had been, but she didn't like the sound of the conversation between her father and Wade, especially the part about Travis.

"What's the matter, Aunt Savvy?" Joshua asked when she returned. She led the horses outside and tried to concentrate on anything other than Travis.

"What? Oh, nothing, Josh," she said, mounting Mattie and remembering that she had encountered Travis all those summers ago while riding the very same mare. "Let's take the horses over by the lake today."

"But you never like to go to the lake," the boy pointed out after climbing onto Jones's broad back.

Savannah smiled sadly. "I know. But today is different. Come on." She urged Mattie into a trot and Joshua followed behind her on the gelding. The path between the trees was overgrown from lack of use, and the lake, usually calm, had taken on the leaden hue of the winter sky.

"Why'd you want to come here?" Joshua asked, sipping his Coke, oblivious to the cold weather that suddenly cut through Savannah's jacket like a knife.

"I don't know," she admitted, staring at the lake, her thoughts lingering on Travis as raindrops began to pelt from the sky and dimple the dark water. "It used to be a place I liked very much."

Joshua looked at the barren trees, exposed rocks and muddy banks surrounding the lake. "If you ask me, it's kinda creepy."

"Yeah, maybe it is," she whispered, shivering from a sudden chill. "Let's go back to the paddocks." *Maybe then I won't think about Travis and wonder what's happening to him....*

It had all started again a little over a month ago, Travis reflected dourly, when he'd seen Reginald Beaumont and

Wade Benson at the racetrack. That in itself wasn't so un-usual. After all, Reginald's prize three-year-old colt, Mystic, had been running, and Wade was now, under Reginald's guidance, managing the farm. What had been odd was the fact that Reginald was at the racetrack with Willis Henderson, Travis's law partner. Henderson had never mentioned the fact that he was interested in the races and Reginald had no reason to know Willis Henderson, except through Travis. When Travis had questioned his partner, Willis hadn't wanted to discuss his day at the track.

Later, learning that Savannah was now back at the farm with her father and Wade, Travis had begun to think about her.

And now it seemed as if he could think of nothing else.

She just wouldn't leave him alone, even after nine long years. At the most inopportune moments, her image would come vividly to Travis's mind and he would be teased by the memory of her wide, sky-blue eyes, gleaming ebony hair and seductive smile. In the nine years that had passed since he'd found her swimming in the lake, her image still lin-gered.

"Mr. McCord!" The sharp voice of Eleanor Phillips brought Travis back to the present, and the image of Savannah faded quickly. Travis's eyes focused again on the stylish but over-dressed woman sitting on the other side of the desk. "You haven't heard a word I've said!"

Travis offered a slightly apologetic smile and stared directly into her eyes. "Oh, yes I have." He couldn't hide the cynicism in his voice. "You were talking about the woman your husband met in Mazatlan."

"The girl, you mean. She was barely twenty!" Eleanor Phillips said with self-righteous disgust. "You know she was only interested in Robert for his money—my money."

Travis listened impatiently while Mrs. Phillips continued to rant about her husband's indiscriminate affairs. The way his wife told it, Mr. Phillips had the sexual appetite of a man half his age.

As she went on about Robert Phillips's indiscretions, Travis glanced out the window of his office, noticed that it was getting dark and checked his watch. Five-thirty. So where was Henderson, his partner? And why wasn't he handling Eleanor Phillips? Too many things had been happening in the law firm that didn't add up and Travis wanted it out with Henderson.

"So you see, Mr. McCord, this divorce is imperative," Mrs. Phillips said in her high-pitched voice. "I want you to work with the best private investigator in Los Angeles and—"

"I don't handle divorces, Mrs. Phillips. I tried to tell you that on the phone, and when you first came into the office today. You deliberately lied to me—said that you wanted to see me about a take-over bid by a competitor."

She colored slightly and Travis knew he had offended her. The trouble was, he really didn't give a damn about Eleanor Phillips, her husband's sex life, or Phillips Industries. As Henderson had so often accused, Travis was suffering from a serious case of "bad attitude." Thinking about Savannah only made it worse.

"But I've been with your firm forever. You've handled all my legal work," Eleanor complained, fingering the elegant string of pearls at her throat.

"On corporate matters." Travis tried to remain calm. The woman only wanted a divorce from her philandering husband and that in itself wasn't a crime. In fact, Travis didn't blame her for wanting out of an unhappy marriage, but there was something in her superior attitude that rankled him and he wondered if Mr. Phillips was as bad as his wife had insisted, or if her cold, money-is-everything way of looking at life had driven him from her bed.

"Oh, I see," Eleanor Phillips said primly, reaching for her purse and looking around the well-appointed office in disgust. "Since that Eldridge decision, you're too big to take on something as simple as my divorce."

"That has nothing to do with it—"

"Hmph."

"I'm sure one of the associates, or perhaps Mr. Henderson himself, can help you." *If I ever find the bastard.* "I'll speak to him."

"I want you, Mr. McCord! And I think you owe it to me to handle this yourself...after all, I need complete discretion. And you have a reputation that's spotless."

Travis winced at the ridiculous compliment and instead of feeling flattered, he suffered from a twinge of conscience. "I don't handle divorce."

"But you will for me." She smiled knowingly and Travis experienced the unlikely urge to shake some sense into her cash register of a head. *Wealthy women,* he thought cynically, *he'd met enough to last him a lifetime!* He jerked at the knot of his tie. Once again the suite of modern offices seemed confining.

"I've already contributed to your campaign," Eleanor pointed out, raising her brows.

"*What!*"

"My contribution."

"What the devil are you talking about?" Travis's jaw hardened and his eyes glittered dangerously.

For the first time that afternoon, Eleanor Phillips had gained the advantage in the conversation and she was pleased. "It was a very healthy contribution," she rattled on. Travis's eyes narrowed, but the expensively clad woman only smiled to herself. "Mr. Henderson took care of it and promised me that you would handle this divorce personally. He also said that you would be able to assure me that my husband won't get a dime of my money—and not much of his."

Travis's jaw tightened and his lips curved into a grim smile. "When did you talk to Mr. Henderson?"

"Just last week...no, it was two weeks ago, when I called to make the appointment with you."

Two weeks ago. Just about the time Travis had noticed some discrepancies in the books.

Eleanor Phillips rose to her full five feet two inches and focused her frigid eyes on Travis. "I'll be frank, Mr. McCord. I want to divorce my husband as quickly as possible and I expect you to take him to the cleaners." The smile she offered was as chilly as a cold November night.

"Mrs. Phillips," Travis said slowly, as if to a child, as he stood and leaned threateningly over the desk. "I don't handle divorce and I'm not sure what Mr. Henderson told you, but I haven't decided to run for governor."

"Well, I know it's not official—"

"And I haven't seen your…contribution. I wouldn't have taken it if I had." His gray eyes glinted with determination. "But I can assure you of one thing: Willis Henderson will return it to you." *If I have to persuade him by breaking every bone in his feeble little body.*

"Then perhaps you'd better speak with Mr. Henderson. I assure you I gave him a check for five thousand dollars. Good luck, Governor."

Eleanor Phillips walked out of the room and Travis punched the extension for Henderson's office. There was no answer. "You slimy son of a bitch," Travis muttered, slamming down the receiver, grabbing his coat and thrusting his arms into the sleeves, "what the hell kind of game are you playing?"

Before leaving the room he looked around the office and scowled at the expensive music box on the shelf collecting dust; a gift from Melinda. The desk was polished wood, and leather-bound law books adorned the shelves of a walnut bookcase. The liquor cabinet housed only the finest labels. The carpet had been found in Italy by Henderson's interior decorator. And Travis hated every bloody thing that had to do with L.A. and his partnership with Willis Henderson.

"Today, ol' buddy, you've just gone one step too far," Travis said, shaking his head. "It's over. Done. *Finis!*"

He marched into the reception area. "Where is Henderson?" he demanded of the blond secretary.

"I really don't know." She quickly scanned her calendar. "He had an appointment out of the building today."

"With whom?"

"I don't know," the girl said again, obviously embarrassed. "He didn't say."

"Did you ask him?"

"Oh, yes."

"And?"

The secretary shrugged. "He said it was personal."

"Great." The muscles in the back of Travis's neck began to ache with tension. "Great. Just great." He rubbed at the knotted muscles in his back. "Do you have *any* idea where he might be?"

"I'm sorry—" A negative sweep of the short blond curls.

Where the hell was Henderson and why did he take Eleanor Phillips's money? "I know it's late, and you're about to leave, but if he comes back here before you go, tell him to call me."

"I will."

"And I want to speak to our accountant. Call Jack and see if he can come into the office later this week."

"Jack Conrad?" The girl looked confused.

Travis held onto the rags of his thin patience. "Yes, the accountant for the firm."

"But he doesn't handle the books any longer."

Travis had been heading for the door, but he stopped dead in his tracks. The day had just gone from bad to worse. "What do you mean?"

"I, uh, I thought you knew. Wade Benson is handling the books."

"*Benson!*" Travis felt his fingers curl into tight fists.

"Didn't Mr. Henderson tell you?"

"You're sure about this?"

"Yes." She looked oddly at Travis before reaching into a file drawer. "Here's a copy of the letter from Mr. Benson and the response from Mr. Henderson. Mr. Benson's accounting fees are much lower than Mr. Conrad's were."

"But Mr. Benson doesn't take on any clients. He's working for Reginald Beaumont now, as the manager of the Beaumont Breeding Farm." *With Savannah.* Travis smiled twistedly. Hadn't he been looking for an excuse to see Savannah again? It looked like Willis Henderson had just handed it to him on a silver platter.

The young blonde shrugged. "Maybe he decided to do it as a favor to you. You've known Mr. Benson all your life, haven't you?"

"Most of it," Travis acknowledged. *So why hasn't Henderson told me any of this?*

Travis pushed open the glass doors with the gold lettering and strode into the hall, down three flights of stairs and through the lobby of the building. As he walked to his car, a crisp southern California breeze rustled through the palms and rumpled his hair, but he didn't notice.

His thoughts were centered on his partner. *Some partner.* Right now Travis would like to wring Willis Henderson's short, Ivy League neck! Accepting a contribution, legal or otherwise, from Eleanor Phillips wasn't the first of Henderson's none-too-subtle attempts to force a decision from Travis, but it was damned well going to be the last! And this business of switching accountants…

Wade Benson, for God's sake! Travis didn't trust the man an inch. It was bad enough that Benson had married Reginald's eldest daughter, Charmaine, Savannah's sister, and become manager of Beaumont Breeding Farm, but now he was encroaching on Travis's domain. *But not for long!* Travis didn't want anything more to do with Wade, Reginald Beaumont or his raven-haired daughter.

Savannah again. Would he ever be able to get her out of his system?

He smiled grimly to himself. "Your own fault," he reminded himself before concentrating on the problem at hand. Travis had already decided what he was going to do with the rest of his life and it was a far cry from running for governor of California. And if Willis Henderson, Eleanor

Phillips and all the other people who were willing to contribute to his campaign for personal favors didn't like it, they could bloody well stuff it!

Henderson's condominium was across town in Malibu Beach. It would take nearly an hour to get there, but Travis didn't hesitate. If Willis wasn't at home, Travis would wait.

Why did Willis want him to run for governor? Prestige for the firm of Henderson and McCord? Maybe. But Travis couldn't help but feel there was something more to it. It was that tiny suspicion that gnawed at him until he made his way through the snarl of L.A. traffic and reached Willis's home.

Willis was outside, in the driveway, with someone. Travis parked on the street and observed his partner. It was too dark to see clearly, but when the visitor stepped into the light from the street, Travis recognized him. An uncanny premonition of dread slithered up his spine as he stared at Wade Benson.

Swearing softly under his breath, Travis watched the two men. Because his first reaction was to corner Henderson and Benson and have it out with them, he reached for the handle of the door. But there was something slightly sinister in the clandestine meeting and he stayed in the car. "You're losing it, McCord," he whispered to himself, but couldn't take his eyes off the two men in the driveway.

It was bad enough that Wade had suckered Reginald Beaumont into his confidence, but Henderson as well?

The whole setup seemed out of place. Wade was the manager of Beaumont Farm, but the legal work for the farm was handled by Travis, not Henderson. Or was it?

Quietly, Travis rolled down the window, but his car was parked too far away from the condominium to hear any of the conversation.

Wade lit a cigarette and laughed at some comment uttered by Henderson. *Just like old fraternity brothers,* Travis thought unkindly. The anger in Travis's blood was replaced by cold suspicion. He watched as Wade walked back to his

car and tossed his glowing cigarette butt onto the ground
before stamping on it and opening the car door.

So Wade was involved with Willis. What about Reginald,
Savannah's father? Did he know about this meeting? Probably. Travis had seen Reginald and Wade at Alexander Park
with Willis Henderson when Reginald's colt, Mystic, the
favorite, had run and lost. What the hell was going on?

Everything he had seen and heard could just be an unlikely set of circumstances. Henderson had the right to fire
an accountant and he certainly could go to the races any
time he damned well pleased.

*But Willis couldn't take a campaign contribution for a
campaign that didn't exist!*

Unless, of course, Eleanor Phillips had been lying. Travis
wouldn't put it past her.

An ache settled in the pit of Travis's stomach as he
thought about Reginald Beaumont's Thoroughbred farm and
the fact that Savannah was still there, working with Wade.

"Dammit all to hell," he whispered, watching Wade's
car glide out of the driveway.

Pensively rubbing his jaw, he watched as Willis Henderson walked back into his condo and shut out the lights.
Then, Travis slowly got out of the car, stretched and walked
up the concrete walk to Willis Henderson's front door.

Savannah was seated at her father's desk in his study,
sifting through the mail, when the phone rang. "No one's
here," she said to the ringing instrument and eyed the stack
of unpaid bills on the corner of the desk. If the caller was
another creditor...

"Beaumont Breeding Farm," she answered automatically.

"I'd like to speak with Wade Benson. This is Willis Henderson," an imperious voice requested.

Savannah straightened in the chair. Willis Henderson was
Travis's law partner, the man who had talked to Wade at

the racetrack. Her fingers curled more tightly around the receiver and she gave her full attention to Travis's partner.

Maybe something had happened to Travis—an accident. She felt a surge of panic wash over her, but managed to keep her voice calm. "I'm sorry, Mr. Benson is out of town."

A pause. "Then maybe I could talk to Reginald."

"He's also gone for the week. Is there something I can do for you, Mr. Henderson?" Savannah could sense the man's hesitancy to confide in her, so she gave him an out. "Or should I have Wade return the call when he gets back next week?" She eyed the calendar. "Wade should be back by the twenty-third." Two days before Christmas.

"Let me talk to…whoever is in charge."

Savannah bristled a bit, but she smiled wryly. "You're speaking to her. I'm overseeing things while Dad and Wade are away."

"Dad?" Henderson repeated. "Oh, you mean Reginald?"

"Yes. I'm Savannah Beaumont." Savannah settled back in the chair, took off her reading glasses and braced herself for the worst. "Now, what can I do for you?"

Only a slight hesitation. "Ah, well, this has to do with Travis McCord."

Savannah felt her spine stiffen slightly. "What about him?"

"There's been a little trouble."

Her pulse jumped and nervous sweat dotted her forehead. *Trouble.* The second time she'd heard that word in connection with Travis. "What kind of 'trouble'?"

Henderson hedged. "Well, that's why I wanted to talk to Wade."

Savannah frowned at the mention of her brother-in-law. Travis and Wade had never been close. But then, Henderson had bumped into Wade at Hollywood Park…. "As I said, Mr. Benson isn't here and he won't be back until next week—just before Christmas. Now, if Travis is in trouble, I'd like to know about it.''

"Look, Miss Beaumont—''

"Savannah.''

"Yes, well, Savannah then. I don't want to worry you, but Travis…Travis, he's, well, in a bad way.''

Savannah's heart nearly stopped beating and a few dots of perspiration broke out on her back. "What do you mean? Has he been in some kind of accident?''

"No—''

Thank God! Her tense muscles relaxed a little and she fell back into the soft leather cushions of the chair.

"—But he's…well, to put it frankly, Miss Beaumont, Travis has checked out. He's lost all interest in the business, doesn't come into the office, refuses to see me. And all that talk about him running for governor in a couple of years; that's gone, too. He's just not interested. In anything.'' Once the dam was broken, Henderson talked freely, his words spilling out in a gush. "You probably know that he hasn't been the same since his wife died, but I thought he would pull himself out of it. When Melinda passed away he threw himself into his work, especially the Eldridge case and now that that's over, he seems to have lost his will to live, I guess you'd say.'' He stopped abruptly, as if having second thoughts about discussing his partner's personal problems to Savannah. "Well, to put it bluntly, Miss Beaumont, I think he's gone over the deep end.''

Savannah tried to think clearly, but her worried thoughts were centered on Travis—a man she should hate. "I don't understand; Melinda's been dead for over six months.''

"I know. God, don't I know.'' He let out a long sigh. "At first he seemed to snap out of it, you know. But it was all just an act. He had the Eldridge case, you see. And once he won that decision and got all the publicity, well, there was talk, a lot of talk, about him running for governor, but I think he's about to chuck it all. It's gotten to the point where he doesn't bother to show up at the office at all. So far I've been able to cover for him, but I don't know how long I can. And what with all this talk about him running for the governorship...I just don't think we can hide what's going on.''

"We?" she repeated.

"Wade and I.''

Wade again. ''What's Wade got to do with it?''

"Wade and your father are pushing Travis toward governorship—you knew that?''

"I'd heard,'' Savannah admitted sarcastically.

"Well, that's why I'm calling. Travis came by to see me the other night, told me to dissolve the partnership, that he would sell his half to me, and that he was leaving on the noon flight to San Francisco today. I thought he was joking, but when he didn't show up at the office or answer his phone the last couple of days, well, I had to assume that he was serious!''

"Did he say why he wanted out?''

"No...not really, he just said that he was going up to Reginald Beaumont's Breeding Farm. He intended to talk to Wade and Reginald. He asked if I'd have Wade pick him up at the airport.''

Savannah glanced at the grandfather clock in the foyer. It was after eleven. "What time will he be in?''

"I think he said one-thirty. Yes. Flight number sixty-seven on United. Will you see that someone goes to meet him?''

"Of course.''

"And you'll get in touch with Wade?''

"I'll tell my sister, Charmaine. She's Wade's wife. He should be calling tonight and Charmaine will give him the message that you need to speak with him.''

There was a sigh on the other end of the phone. "Thank you, Miss Beaumont,'' Henderson said before hanging up.

Savannah replaced the receiver and thought for a moment. Several of the hands weren't on the farm, and with Reginald and Wade gone, the farm was being run by a skeleton crew. She couldn't afford to let anyone off to drive to the airport.

"It would serve him right if he had to walk here," she muttered, some of the old bitterness she'd felt toward Travis rising to the surface.

"I guess I get to do the honors," she decided before she grabbed her purse, walked out of the den, across the tiled foyer and pulled her jacket off the coat rack. *So Travis was finally coming home. But why and for how long? And how much of Willis Henderson's story was true?*

She walked out of the two-storied plantation-style house, turned her collar against the chill December rain, and half ran down the brick path to the garage. Taking the steps two at a time, she climbed upward to the loft that her sister, Charmaine, had converted into a studio and ignored her tight stomach.

It was pouring and Savannah shivered as she rapped on the door and then pushed it open to find Charmaine wrist deep in potting clay. Charmaine looked up from her work and slowed the foot treadle. The revolving, undulating and as yet indistinguishable objet d'art folded in upon itself into a lump of sloppy gray clay.

"Sorry about that," Savannah apologized, nervously gesturing to Charmaine's work. She hated being in the loft.

"It's okay. Wasn't turning out anyway. Good Lord, you're soaked!" Charmaine observed.

"Just a little." Savannah wiped the drops of rain from her face and tried to forget that this loft had once been Travis's.

"No such thing as 'just a little' soaked."

"Look, I'm going to the airport," Savannah said.

"Like that?" Charmaine asked, eyeing her sister's casual jeans and sweater in disapproval.

"Like this. Can you keep an eye on Mom?"

Charmaine grimaced slightly at her work. "I suppose." She wiped her hands on her cotton smock and stood up from the potter's wheel. "I've got to stick around and wait for Josh's bus anyway. What's up?"

"Travis is coming home."

Charmaine started visibly. "Here?"

"I guess. Anyway, that's what his partner, Henderson, said on the phone just now. The flight arrives in San Francisco at one-thirty, so I've got to run. If Wade happens to call, tell him to phone Henderson or, better yet, have him call back tonight once Travis gets here."

Charmaine scrutinized her sister thoughtfully. "Why is Travis coming back to the farm? Why now?"

"I don't know. But I think I should tell him about Mom, so warn her. He'll be furious when he finds out that she's been ill."

Charmaine agreed. "Good luck. You're going to need it." She pursed her lips. "Do you think that he heard about Mother and that's why he's coming back?"

Savannah was in too much of a hurry to sit around and conjecture, and thinking about Travis always brought out a lot of feelings she didn't want to examine. Though her hostility had lessened in the past nine years, it was always there, just under the surface and she hated to admit it. "Beats me. Henderson said something about Travis needing a rest. He's had a rough year."

As for Henderson's story, it bothered her, but she wanted to make sure it was true before she passed it along to Charmaine or anyone else. Besides, Savannah had never trusted Wade, and Charmaine was his wife. Nervously she shoved her chilled hands into the pockets of her jacket.

Charmaine studied her sister suspiciously. "And that's all?"

"That's all that I know," Savannah lied.

"Hmph." After casting Savannah an I-know-you-better-than-that type of glance, Charmaine capitulated. "Well, I suppose you're right. Melinda's death was a blow to Travis. He loved her very much."

Savannah only nodded but her fingers tightened around the keys in her pocket.

"And now all this talk about him running for governor, right on the heels of that Eldridge decision. He probably does need a rest, but I don't think he'll get much of one here." Still slightly disturbed, Charmaine settled back on her stool and began working the clay. "Sure, I'll look in on Mother."

"Thanks." Savannah left the studio and climbed down the steps quickly. She raced into the garage and hopped into her father's car. As she left the farm her thoughts were centered on Travis. She couldn't remember a time in her life when she hadn't loved him, first as a brother, then as a woman loves a man. Wholly, completely.

Then he'd used and betrayed her.

"Well, that was then," Savannah said with determination. "And I was a fool. A stupid, little girl of a fool. But I'm not about to make the same mistake twice, Travis McCord. You taught me too well. I don't care what's bothering you, I'd rather hate you than fall in love with you ever again."

Two

Traffic was thick near the airport and it took Savannah nearly twenty minutes to park and get into the terminal building. Pushing her cold hands into the pockets of her jacket and telling herself that she had made a big mistake in coming to get Travis, she threaded her way through the crowd until she reached the concourse where Travis's plane was to unload. The seats near the reservation desk were filled with people waiting for their flights. Carry-on luggage, overcoats and brightly wrapped gifts occupied the vacant seats while tired travelers sat reading, smoking or pacing between the rows of uncomfortable chairs. Above the din of the crowd, faint strains of piped-in Christmas music filtered through the terminal.

Peace on earth, good will to men, Savannah thought as she stood at the gate, but she couldn't help feel a premonition of dread. Inside her pockets, her cold hands began to sweat. She tried to relax and forget that Travis had left her without so much as an explanation, that he had married another woman and walked out of her life without bothering to say goodbye, that he had used her because he was angry with himself and Melinda. But the old bitterness still reared its ugly head.

"It's over and done with; you're a grown woman now," she chastised herself. But this was the first time in nine long years that she would be with Travis alone. Whenever she had seen him in the past, there had always been plenty of people around him, and Melinda had been at his side. The crowds had been convenient, and now Savannah wondered if facing him alone was such a good idea.

She looked through the window and watched as the plane pulled into its berth. *Get a grip on yourself, girl.*

Travis was one of the first people off the plane. To her disgust, Savannah's heart pounded traitorously at the sight of him.

He looked older than his thirty-four years; more cynical. Deep lines bracketed the corners of his hard mouth, and smaller lines formed webs at the outside corners of his eyes. His shirt was rumpled, his tie askew, his chin already darkened with five o'clock shadow, though it was early in the day. A black garment bag was slung over one of his shoulders, and he carried a briefcase in his free hand.

It has been two years since Savannah had seen him, but he seemed to have aged ten. Probably due to the loss of Melinda, she told herself. They had been inseparable. No doubt the fatal boating accident that had taken Melinda's life had destroyed a part of Travis as well.

Savannah forced a smile to her face and walked toward him. He stopped dead in his tracks and the look on his face could have turned flesh to stone.

"Hi," she greeted, tilting her face upward and meeting his cold gaze.

"You're the last person I expected to see," he muttered, unable to disguise his surprise.

"Yeah, well, I'm glad to see you, too."

Something flickered in his gray eyes. "You always were quick to rise to the bait."

"Maybe too quick. Willis Henderson called the farm this afternoon. He was looking for Wade or Dad."

Beneath his shirt, Travis's broad shoulders stiffened. His gaze hardened. "Go on."

"They're both gone this week. So," she eyed him with the same cynicism she saw in his gaze, "whether you like it or not, you're stuck with me."

"Great." The brackets around his mouth tightened.

Refusing to "rise to the bait" again, she nodded toward the long concourse. "The car's in the lot. Do you have any other bags?"

"No." He shifted his garment bag. "Let's go."

Without further conversation, they walked with the flow of people through the main terminal and outside to the parking lot. Sliding a glance in Travis's direction, Savannah found it difficult to believe that the man beside her could have been the man she had fallen in love with so desperately all those years before.

A winter-cold wind sliced through her jacket and blew her hair away from her face, chilling her cheeks. She huddled her shoulders together and wondered if she was shivering from the wind or the ice in Travis's eyes.

Henderson was partially right, Savannah thought uneasily. Travis looked tired and beaten; world-weary. But there was still a spark of life in his gray gaze, a flicker of interest that argued with Henderson's theory that Travis was "ready to chuck it all." Travis seemed bitter and cynical, but far from suicidal. *Thank God for small favors.*

Once they had made it to the silver sports car, Travis took one look at the BMW and frowned. "Is this yours?"

"Dad's."

"Figures." He tossed his garment bag into the back seat and slid into the passenger side of the car. Once there he pushed the seat back as far as it would go, lowered the backrest so that he could recline, jerked at his tie and let it dangle unknotted at his throat and then unbuttoned the top two buttons of his shirt. Savannah pretended interest in starting the car, but found herself fascinated, as always, with him. She saw the tufts of dark hair visible now that the throat of his shirt gaped and noticed the angry thrust of his jaw as he raked his fingers through his thick hair.

As Savannah started the engine and drove out of the parking lot, Travis leaned his head against the headrest and closed his eyes. His breathing became regular, so Savannah decided not to disturb him. *Let him sleep,* she told herself angrily. *Maybe he'll be in a better mood when he wakes up.*

It started to rain again and she flicked on the wipers. When she glanced at Travis, she found him staring at her. His gaze was thoughtful as it moved lazily over the soft planes of her face. "Why did you come to the airport?"

"To get you; Willis Henderson said—"

"I don't care what he said. Why didn't you send one of the hands?"

"We're shorthanded."

He let out a sound of disgust and looked out the window. "Not exactly flattering."

She felt her temper begin to ignite. "What's that supposed to mean?"

"I thought maybe you wanted to see me again."

After nine years! The arrogant, self-centered bastard! "Sorry to disappoint you."

"I doubt that you ever could," he muttered. "It just seems strange that after nine years of avoiding me, you came to the airport. Alone."

"I haven't avoided you."

He turned his knowing gray eyes back to her face, silently accusing her of the lie.

"Every time you were at the house…" Her voice trailed off and her fingers clenched around the steering wheel. "There were a lot of people around."

"The way you wanted it. You wouldn't let me near you."

"You were married."

A satisfied smile curved his thin lips and Savannah's anger burned again. "I just wanted to talk to you."

"A little too late, don't you think?" she pointed out, gritting her teeth and trying to concentrate on the road ahead. "Look, Travis, let's not argue."

"I'm not."

"No, you're just being damned infuriating."

"I just thought that since we're alone, I should explain a few things."

"I'm not really interested in any excuses, or apologies," she said "No reason to rehash the past."

His gaze darkened angrily and he shook his head. "Fine—if that's the way you want it. I just thought you should know that I never intended to leave you."

"Oh, sure. But it just couldn't be avoided? Right?" She shook her head and her fingers tightened around the steering wheel in a death grip. The pickup in front of her swerved and the driver slammed on his brakes. Savannah stood on hers. The BMW fish-tailed, but stopped before colliding with the red pickup. "Oh, God," Savannah whispered, her heart thudding in her chest from the tense conversation as well as the close call on the road.

"Want me to drive?" he asked, once the cars started to move.

"No!"

"All right. Then, let me explain what happened at the lake."

Savannah's nerves were shattered. She glanced from Travis to the traffic and back again. "Look, I'd rather not discuss this, not now. Too much time has passed."

"Okay, not now. When?"

"Never would be okay with me."

He cocked a disdainful dark brow and frowned. "I'm too tired to argue. So, have it your way...for now. But we are going to talk this out. I'm tired of being manipulated and forced to live a lie."

"I never—" She started to protest and then snapped her mouth shut. She wasn't ready for a conversation about the past, not yet. She needed time to reassess her feelings for Travis before she let herself get trapped in the pain of that summer. It seemed like eons ago. "So that's the reason you're coming back to the farm."

"One reason," he admitted, staring through the rain-spattered windows to the concrete ribbon of freeway and the clog of traffic. An endless line of red taillights flashed ahead of them and blurred through the wet windshield. "I think it's time to set a few things straight with you—'' Savannah's breath caught in her throat ''—and the rest of the family. Speaking of which, where is Wade?''

"With Dad in Florida. They're considering stabling some of the two-year-olds there in the spring. When Mystic won the Preakness, Dad thought it might be time to move some of the stronger colts to the East Coast.''

"And you disagree?''

"The Preakness was only one race—one moment of glory. After winning at Pimlico, Dad was on cloud nine and he really expected Mystic to go on to win the Belmont.'' She shook her head sadly. "And the result was that Supreme Court, the winner of the Derby, walked away from the field at Belmont. Mystic finished sixth. He hasn't won since. He's back on the farm now and Dad's trying to decide whether to run him next year, sell him, or put him out to stud.''

Travis didn't comment. Instead he slid a glance up her body, taking in her scruffy boots, faded jeans, blue cowl-necked sweater and suede jacket. His cold gray eyes seemed to strip her bare. "That still doesn't tell me why you came to the airport.''

"When Henderson called, there wasn't much time.''

The corners of his mouth turned downward at the thought of his partner. "Good.'' He leaned back against the headrest again. "Maybe it's better if I don't see your brother-in-law for a while. And, as for you—'' he placed a hand on her shoulder, but she didn't flinch; his fingers were strong and gentle, just as they'd always been ''—you may as well get used to the idea that we're going to talk about what happened, whether you want to or not.''

"I don't.''

"And so you came to the airport all alone.'' He let out an amused laugh before dropping his hand. "You're lying, Savannah, and you never were much good at it.''

"I thought you were coming to the farm to talk to Wade,'' she said.

Travis scowled. "Him, too. But he's not gonna like what I've got to say."

"And what's that?"

Travis slid her a knowing look and there was just the trace of bitterness in his eyes. "I think I'd better tell Wade myself."

She frowned as she turned off the freeway and onto the country road that cut through the hills surrounding the farm. Wet leaves piled against fence posts and rising water ran wildly in the ditches near the road. "Do you honestly think I'd worm something out of you and then call Wade?" The idea was so absurd that she almost laughed.

"Don't you like your brother-in-law?"

She pursed her lips, but shook her head. "It's no secret and the feeling's mutual but there's nothing much I can do. He's Charmaine's husband."

"And your dad's right-hand man."

"Looks that way," she said wryly, considering her sister's husband. A first-class bastard, in Savannah's opinion. Unfortunately no one at the farm agreed with her, except maybe her mother, and Virginia wouldn't say anything against Wade.

"So what about you?" he asked quietly.

"What about me?"

"I thought you were going to marry that Donald character—"

"David," she corrected.

"Right. What happened?"

Her shoulders stiffened. "I had second thoughts."

"And cold feet."

For a moment, she felt her temper start to flare, but when she looked at Travis, she saw a glimmer of amusement in his eyes. The old Travis. The man she had loved. "Yeah, cold feet," she agreed. "David wasn't keen on a wife who liked to work with horses. He said he didn't like the smell of them and always had a sneezing attack whenever he was near the stables."

Travis grinned. "Then what the hell was he doing with you?"

"He thought he could change me," she said.

"I remember," Travis replied, thinking back to the night that he'd wanted to kill David Crandall when the kid had pushed himself onto Savannah in the car, all those years ago. Travis's mood shifted again and he felt tense. "Crandall didn't know you very well, did he?"

Savannah could feel his gaze on her face, but she kept her eyes steady on the road. "I guess not."

"Do you still see him?"

"Occasionally. He's married now. Has a wife and two kids." She smiled to herself. "A proper, respectable wife who gave up her career as a chamber musician to be his bride."

"Ouch."

Still grinning, Savannah shook her head, and her ebony hair brushed across the shoulders of her jacket. "It didn't really hurt. Well, maybe my pride was wounded a bit. He married Brenda just three months after we broke up, but it all worked out for the best."

"You're sure?" Travis eyed her speculatively.

"Yep. Can you imagine me living in San Francisco as the wife of an architect?"

"No."

Neither could she. "Well, there you go."

"So you came back to the farm."

After four years of college and three years of working in an investment firm in San Francisco, she'd longed to return to her family and the breeding farm. "I got tired of the city."

Savannah turned off the main road and drove down the long lane leading to Beaumont Breeding Farm. Barren cottonwoods and oaks lined the asphalt drive leading to the main house and garage.

Once Savannah had parked the car in its reserved spot in the garage, Travis gathered his bags, slid out of the BMW and stared at the house. "Some things don't change much," he observed.

Thinking of Virginia, Savannah was forced to disagree. She touched him lightly on the arm. "Maybe more than you know."

He looked at her and his eyes narrowed suspiciously. "Meaning?"

She cleared her throat. "I think you should know that Mom's...not well." He continued to stare at her and the only evidence that he had heard her at all was the whitening of his lips as his jaw clenched. "She's suffered from a series of heart attacks...small ones, but still, she's not well."

"Heart attacks!" Travis looked as if he didn't believe Savannah, but the gravity of her features convinced him. "Why wasn't I told?" he demanded.

"Because that's the way Mom wanted it."

"Why?" His angry glare burned through her.

"Mom didn't want to bother you. You've had your share of problems, y'know." When he didn't seem convinced, she spelled it out for him. "The first attack happened about a week after Melinda was killed in the boating accident. Mom didn't want to worry you."

"That was over six months ago," he said sharply, his voice edged in steel.

"And the next attacks... A series of small ones happened when you were in the middle of that Eldridge case."

"Someone should have told me. *You* should have told me."

"*Me?* I couldn't!"

He leaned against the car. "Just why the hell not, Savannah?"

"Mother insisted on it and Dad—"

"Your father wanted me kept in the dark?"

Savannah shook her head. "He knew how important that case was for your career, he knew that you had been shattered by Melinda's death. He was just looking out for your best interests."

"Like hell!" he roared, grabbing her shoulders in frustration. "I'm a thirty-four-year old man, Savannah. I don't need protection. Especially from your father!"

"But Mom—"

"Where is she?"

"In the house...probably her room."

He released her and controlled his rage. "So level with me—how bad is it?"

Savannah gritted her teeth and decided that despite her mother's request, she couldn't lie to Travis. "It's not good, Travis. Lots of days Mom doesn't come downstairs."

The skin tightened over his face. "Why isn't she in the hospital?"

"Because they can't do anything for her. A private nurse visits the house every day."

"Great," he said with a sigh. "Just great. And no one bothered to tell me." He rubbed the back of his neck in frustration. "I'm going to see her, y'know."

"She'd kill you if you didn't." Savannah offered him an encouraging smile as they entered the house. He took off his jacket and headed up the stairs, his jaw clenched in determination.

Savannah started to follow him, but paused. Virginia would need time alone with Travis. She'd been a second mother to him and Savannah didn't want to interfere in the private conversation. She went back down the stairs and into her father's study, but couldn't concentrate on the stack of bills she'd been sorting earlier in the day. All of her thoughts returned to Travis and memories of that summer long ago filled her mind. "You're a fool," she muttered to herself and tossed the large pile of invoices back on the desk in exasperation.

After pacing in the den for a few minutes, Savannah decided to walk out to the barns and see that the stable hands were taking care of the horses. With the intention of speaking with Lester Adams, the trainer of the farm, she walked outside and turned her collar against the cold, December wind.

Dealing directly with Lester was usually her father's job, but since Reginald was in Florida, Savannah worked with the grizzled old trainer and listened to his complaints about the horses as well as his praise.

"Reginald should have sold this one," Lester said for the second time as he leaned over the fence and watched the colt's workout. "He looks good, but he's hell to work with."

"So was Mystic." Savannah smiled and watched Vagabond run with the fluid grace of a champion. He was a beautiful bay colt with dark eyes that glimmered menacingly and a long stride that seemed effortless.

"He's different."

"Same temperament, I'd say. Besides, I thought you were the one that said you liked a colt with fire."

"Fire, yes. An inferno, no!" Lester shook his head and his gray eyebrows drew together in frustration. "This one, he's got a mean streak the likes of which the devil himself has never seen."

"He could be a winner."

"If he doesn't self-destruct." The old man put his boot onto the bottom rail of the fence as he studied Vagabond's long strides. "He's got the speed, all right. And the stamina."

"And the heart."

Lester laughed and shook his head. "Heart, you call it." He chuckled softly. "Geez, that's kind. I call it blasted stubbornness. Nothing else."

"You'll find a way to turn him into a winner," Savannah predicted as the horse slowed. "Just like Mystic."

The trainer avoided her eyes. "It'll be a challenge."

"Just what you like."

"Hmph." The old man cracked a wise smile. "That's

enough, Jake," he called as the exercise boy slowed Vagabond to a canter.

"Good." The small rider slid down from the saddle, and patted Vagabond's muscular shoulder. Sweat and mud covered the colt's sleek coat. "I'll go clean him up now."

Lester nodded his agreement, pushed his fedora down over his eyes and reached into his breast pocket for a crumpled pack of cigarettes.

"So Travis came back today," he said as he lit up and inhaled deeply. Leaning against the fence, he watched Savannah through a cloud of blue smoke.

"He's at the house now."

"Will he be staying long?"

"I don't know, but I doubt it. He only had one bag with him." She looked past the workout track, over the fields surrounding the farm and studied the craggy mountains in the distance. Snow was visible on the higher slopes, above the timberline. "He wants to talk to Wade."

"About runnin' for governor?"

"I don't know," she admitted. "I never got around to asking."

"I can't figure it out," Lester said.

"What?"

"It just seems strange that's all. Travis, he always did well with the horses. And I know he liked working with them, it was obvious from the start. I had a feelin' about that boy, that he'd...well, that he'd stay on here at the farm. But I was wrong. Instead he goes off to college and becomes a lawyer—hardly ever sets foot on the place again. It just never made much sense, not to me."

He flicked his cigarette onto the wet ground and ground it out with the sole of his boot.

"To top things off," Lester continued, "that sister of yours marries Wade Benson...well, I guess she had her reasons. But Benson, for God's sake, a man I swear couldn't tell a mustang from a Thoroughbred, gives up his accounting practice to work with the horses. It just don't seem right.''

"Wade still does the books for the farm," Savannah said, and then wondered why she was defending the man when she, like Lester, had doubted Wade's motives from time to time.

"Yep, but that ain't all. He's managing the place most of the time.''

"I know. Dad's been thinking about retiring, because of Mom's condition.''

"A shame about your mother," Lester said quietly. His black eyes darkened with an inner sadness.

"Yes."

"A damned shame," Lester muttered before slapping the top rail of the fence and clearing his throat. "I guess I'd better go check on the boys—make sure they're earning their keep and watching over the yearlings.'' He started off toward the broodmare barn and Savannah, her thoughts once again centered on Travis, turned back to the house.

A few minutes later Savannah took off her boots on the back porch, stopped to scratch Archimedes, her father's large Australian sheepdog, behind the ears and went into the house through the kitchen.

Sadie Stinson, who served as housekeeper and cook, was busy slicing vegetables, and the room was filled with the tantalizing scent of roast pork.

"That smells wonderful," Savannah said, peering into the oven and warming her hands against the glass door. "I missed lunch.''

Sadie Stinson clucked her tongue. "Shame on you.''

"Oh, I don't know. From the looks of this, it was worth the wait.''

"Flattery will get you nowhere," the cook said, but beamed under the praise. She eyed Savannah's red face, stockinged feet and damp hair. "Now, you go and get cleaned up. I'll have this on the table in half an hour.''

"Can't wait," Savannah admitted, her stomach rumbling in agreement.

"You'll have to."

"Spoilsport," she teased and Sadie chuckled. "By the way, have you seen Travis?"

Sadie's mood changed and the smile fell from her face. "That I have. He's in your father's study, pouring himself into a bottle, it looks like." She began slicing the zucchini with a vengeance. "Probably won't even appreciate all the work I've gone to."

"I doubt that," Savannah lied and walked out of the kitchen and down the short hallway to the den. Travis was inside, sitting on the broad ledge of the bay window, his legs braced against the floor, his eyes trained on the gathering darkness. He'd changed out of his suit and into worn cords and a flannel shirt that he hadn't bothered to button. His eyes were narrowed against the encroaching night and he held a half-filled glass in his hand. A fire was crackling in the stone fireplace.

Travis glanced over his shoulder and noticed Savannah in the doorway. Her black hair framed her face in wild curls and her intense blue eyes were focused on him. At her studious stare he experienced a tightening in his gut. He'd forgotten how really beautiful she was. "Come in, join me," he invited with a grimace as he lifted his glass.

"I don't think so."

Shrugging indifferently, he turned toward the window and leaned insolently against the frame. "Suit yourself."

"I will." She walked into the room and closed the door before kneeling at the fireplace and warming her hands near the flames. "Did you see Mom?"

The broad shoulders bunched. "Yes." He took a long swallow from his glass and once it was empty, walked over to the bar near the fireplace and poured himself another three fingers of Scotch. "You should have told me."

"I couldn't."

"Like hell!"

"Mom thought—"

"She's dying, dammit." He accused her with cold gray eyes. "I thought that I could trust you, Savannah."

"Me?" she repeated, incredulously. "You thought you could trust me?" *What about the trust I put in you nine years ago? The trust you threw away with the morning light?*

"You know what I mean. When we were kids, we had secrets, but we were always straight with each other."

Except once, she thought angrily. *Except for the one night that you told me you loved me and I believed it with all of my heart.*

"We're not kids any longer and Mom asked me not to say anything," she said. "I keep my word, and besides, Mom said that Dad would tell you when the time was right."

"And when was that?"

"How am I supposed to know?" She shot him an angry glare and then started for the door. "I've got to get cleaned up for dinner. If you don't drink yourself into oblivion, I'll see you then."

"Savannah—"

Her hand was on the brass handle of the door, but she turned to look over her shoulder and for a fleeting second she saw honest regret in his eyes before his expression turned hard. "I'll be at dinner," he said.

"Good." With her final remark, she walked out of the room.

Dinner was tolerable, but just. Virginia was tired and had her meal in her room, Charmaine was brooding over the fact that Wade hadn't called and Travis showed no interest in the spectacular feast that Sadie Stinson had prepared.

Wonderful, Savannah thought sarcastically. *This is just great!*

The only person who genuinely enjoyed himself was Josh, and Savannah was grateful for the little boy's com-

pany and constant chatter. ''So how long are you stayin'?''
Josh asked Travis.

''I don't know.''

''I heard Dad say that you were going to be president or
something!''

''Governor, Josh,'' Charmaine corrected, and Travis
winced before leaning back in his chair and smiling at Josh.

It was the first time Travis had really smiled since he'd
gotten off the plane, and it had a disastrous effect upon
Savannah.

''Is that what he said?'' Travis asked.

''Yep.'' Josh pushed his plate aside and leaned forward
eagerly. ''Dad thinks that's where you belong at the...
wherever the governor is.''

''Sacramento.''

''Yeah, he says that it's best if you're anywhere besides
here on the farm.''

''Is that right?'' Travis drawled, his grin widening and
pleasure gleaming in his eyes.

''Joshua!'' Charmaine said, coloring slightly. ''If you're
done with your meal go upstairs and do your homework!''

''Am I in trouble?''

''Of course not, Josh'' Savannah cut in, giving Travis a
warning glance and pushing aside her chair. ''Come on, I'll
get you started.''

''It's math,'' Josh warned.

Savannah pulled a face. ''Not my forte, but I'll give it a
shot anyway. Let's go.'' She waited for the boy and together
they climbed the stairs. Once on the landing, she hesitated.
''You go and get started,'' she suggested, ''and I'll check
on Grandma. Okay?''

''Sure.'' Josh replied and ran down the hall.

After knocking softly on the door, Savannah entered her
mother's bedroom. Virginia smiled. ''I wondered when
you'd show up,'' she chided.

''Couldn't stay away.'' Savannah walked over to the bed
and took the tray off the bed.

"And how are you getting along with Travis?"

Savannah let out a sound of disgust and leaned against one of the tall posts of the bed. "As well as can be expected considering the fact that he's got a chip on his shoulder the size of the Rock of Gibraltar."

"He's had a rough year," Virginia said, her brow puckering slightly.

"Maybe you're right," Savannah said, deciding it best not to worry her mother unnecessarily. Travis's problems were of his own making and they didn't concern Virginia.

"Then give him a chance, for Pete's sake."

"A chance?"

"To heal his wounds."

"Did he tell you why he came here?"

Virginia's head moved side to side on the pillow. "As a matter of fact, he was rather vague about it. I got the impression that he had some business to conclude with Reginald and that he was taking a rest. It does him good to be here, you know. He always enjoyed working on the farm, with the horses. He can even have the loft again, for an apartment...." Her voice faded slightly.

"Look, I'll take this tray downstairs and see you later," Savannah said. "Right now I promised Josh I'd help him with his math."

Virginia chuckled. "The blind leading the blind..."

Savannah laughed aloud. "No faith in your own daughter. Won't you be surprised when Josh aces his next test?"

"With you tutoring him? That I will be," Virginia said as Savannah carried the dinner tray to the door.

"I'll see ya later," Savannah said before walking down the long hall to Josh's room and finding the boy on the floor, Transformers and Gobots spread out on the carpet in a mock battle.

"Who's winning?" Savannah said with a smile.

"The Decepticons!"

"I thought you were supposed to be working on math."

"Aunt Savvy…" Josh pleaded, turning his bright eyes up at her.

"Right now, mister." She gathered up some of the toys and set them on Josh's already overloaded dresser.

"You could play with me," he suggested.

Savannah sat on the edge of the bed and shook her head. "Maybe later. Right now we've got math to master." She kicked off her shoes and crossed her legs. "Hop to it."

"I hate math," the boy grumbled.

"So do I, but, though I loathe to admit it, arithmetic, geometry, algebra, etcetera are very important. Someday you'll find out."

"Not in a million years." Josh grabbed his book and put it on the desk. Then he took a seat and hunched his shoulders over his homework.

Savannah concentrated on the problems. "This'll be a breeze," she predicted. "Simple multiplication."

A few minutes and several problems later, a soft cough caught her attention and she looked over her shoulder to find Travis lounging in the doorway. One of his shoulders was propped against the frame and his hands were pushed into the pockets of his jeans. How long he had been there, watching her with his slate-colored eyes, she could only guess. "How's it going?"

"It's not," Savannah admitted.

"Horrible!" Josh said.

"Need some help?"

"Yeah!" Josh was more than eager to have Travis help him. Savannah's heart went out to the boy. All Josh wanted was a little positive fatherly attention and he got very little from his own dad.

"Sure. Why not?" Savannah said, "I've got to take this tray down to the kitchen anyway." She stood up and reached for the tray she had set on the nightstand.

"Don't let me scare you away," Travis said, sauntering into the room, his gaze locking with hers.

"You're not."

"And you're lying again," he accused. "Bad habit, Savannah. You'd better break it."

"I guess you just bring out the worst in me," she whispered through clenched teeth, hoping that Travis would take the hint and drop the subject.

"Or the best." His eyes roved down her rigid body to rest on the thrust of her breasts against her sweater.

Under his stripping gaze, anger heated her blood and colored her cheeks, but she kept her tongue still because Josh had turned his head to study her.

"Is something wrong, Aunt Savvy?"

"Nothing," she replied tightly. "I just have a couple of things to do. I'll...I'll see you later." Controlling her anger with Travis took an effort, but she managed to give Josh a genuine smile before leaving the room and telling herself that she would only have to suffer Travis's indignities a few more days, only until Wade and Reginald returned to the farm.

And what would happen then? Savannah grimaced to herself when she realized that she was looking forward to the reunion with both anticipation and dread.

Three

Wade didn't call that night, and Savannah didn't know whether to be thankful or worried.

The next day Savannah tried to avoid Travis, finding it easier to keep out of his way than risk another confrontation with him. It wasn't difficult. Travis spent his time locked in the study, on the phone, or in the loft, which Charmaine had partially cleared out of. Savannah went grocery shopping, then made it a point to work with Lester and the horses during the day, before going up to her room in the evening to shower and change for dinner. She dressed in black slacks and a red sweater and tried to tell herself she wasn't primping as she brushed her hair.

Savannah walked into the dining room and was surprised to see that her mother was already at the table. Seated at the head of the long table and dressed in a rose-colored caftan, Virginia looked healthier than she had in weeks.

Travis sat to the left of Virginia with Charmaine on his other side. His eyes followed Savannah as she walked into the room and took the empty seat across the table from him. Wearing an open-necked shirt and leaning on one elbow, he sipped a glass of wine and appeared relaxed as he talked with Virginia. *Like a vagabond son returning home,* Savannah thought, meeting his interested gaze. Only when she entered the room, did he show any sign of tension.

"Glad you could make it down, Mom," Savannah said, bristling slightly as Travis poured her a glass of wine.

"It's not every day that Travis comes home," Virginia

remarked with a pleased smile. "I'm just sorry he didn't tell us he intended to be here earlier so that we could welcome him properly yesterday."

Properly must have meant with silver, linen napkins, a floral centerpiece, flickering candles and shining crystal, Savannah thought, eyeing the table. The chandelier had been appropriately dimmed, the silver polished until it gleamed. Virginia always had liked to put on a show.

"Not necessary," Travis said, his gray eyes moving from Virginia to Savannah and lingering on the proud lift of her chin.

"Of course it is." Virginia laughed. "You haven't been home for nearly two years!"

Small talk carried Savannah through the meal, though she could feel the weight of Travis's gaze as she ate. He leaned back in his chair and observed her with amused, but cynical eyes that seemed to look into the darkest corners of her mind.

Joshua was seated beside Savannah and he appeared preoccupied. His small brow was creased with worry and he barely touched his food. Any attempt to draw the boy into the conversation met with monosyllabic responses.

Despite the formal decorations and the mouth-watering meal, Savannah felt the undercurrents of tension in the room. *Just like the calm before the storm,* she thought uneasily as she shifted her gaze from Josh's brooding expression to Travis's intense gaze.

"Wade called this afternoon," Charmaine announced, setting her fork on her plate after dessert.

The strain in the room exploded.

"What!" Travis's head jerked toward Charmaine and he pinned her with his angry glare. "Why didn't you tell me?"

Charmaine met his gaze and lifted her chin. "You were in the stables with Lester. I didn't want to bother you. Mother was resting and Savannah was in Sacramento doing the grocery shopping. So I took the call and told him you were here and anxious to speak with him."

Travis scowled, his impatience mounting. "Maybe I should phone him."

"No. He said he'd be home tomorrow. The plane lands about six, and he and father should be here by seven-thirty at the latest." She placed her napkin on the table and pushed her chair back, but didn't stand. "If it's any consolation, he was as anxious to talk to you as you are to speak with him."

"I'll bet," Travis mocked.

Charmaine overlooked his remark and turned to Josh. Her voice was still tight, but she attempted to appear calm. "So Daddy will be here in plenty of time for Christmas. Isn't that great?"

The boy had been pushing the remains of his apple pie around in his plate. He stopped, looked past his mother and shrugged.

"Joshua?"

"I don't want him to come home," Josh mumbled, glancing at Savannah before pretending interest in his plate.

Charmaine, obviously embarrassed, cleared her throat. "Joshua. Surely you don't mean—"

"I do mean it, Mom." Tears had gathered in his eyes, though he was bravely trying to swallow them back. "Daddy hates me."

Virginia gasped. "Oh, dear," she whispered, trying to think of something to cut short the uncomfortable scene.

Stiffening slightly, Charmaine blushed. "You know that's not true, Josh."

"It is, too. And I finally figured it out," Josh blurted. "Some of the kids were talking at school today...."

"About what?" Charmaine asked, dread tightening the corners of her mouth.

"I know the only reason you married Dad is because of me!" he said miserably, guilt weighing heavily on his small shoulders.

To her credit, Charmaine didn't flinch. "I married your father because I loved him."

"Because you *had* to!" Joshua said brokenly, partially

standing, but managing to hold his mother's gaze. "That's what the kids at school said."

"Josh," Savannah cut in, but Charmaine held up her hand.

"This is my problem, Savannah." Then, looking back at her son, she said, "No one *had* to marry anyone."

"Would you have married Dad if you weren't pregnant with me?" He blinked against the tears in his eyes.

Virginia went pale and picked up her water glass with trembling fingers.

"Of course—" Charmaine whispered tenderly.

"No!" Josh screamed, his face red and tear-stained.

Charmaine braced her shoulders. "Joshua, I think you should go up to your room and I'll come talk to you there," she said in measured tones, her voice shaking.

Savannah tried to touch Josh on the shoulder, but he jerked away and Savannah's stomach knotted in pain. "Josh—"

"I don't want to talk," the boy said angrily, his fists balled at his sides. "It's true—it's all true and I don't want Dad to come home! I wish—I wish that I didn't have a father!"

Travis looked from Savannah to the boy and back again, his jaw tight, his eyes filled with understanding for the rebellious youth.

"You don't mean that," Charmaine insisted.

"I do! I do mean it!"

Joshua's chair slid back from the table, scraping the floor. He ran out of the room and clomped noisily up the stairs.

"No," Charmaine murmured, closing her eyes to steady herself.

"I'm sorry," Savannah whispered, knowing there was no way to console her older sister.

"No reason to be," Charmaine said tightly. "This has been coming for a long time. Wade and Josh have never gotten along. Sooner or later Josh was bound to figure out that his dad resents him. I just…never wanted to face it, I guess.''

"I'll go," Savannah offered, fighting her own tears.

"No. This is my problem, a mistake I made ten years ago. I'll handle it." With new conviction Charmaine got out of her chair and hurried out of the dining room. "Joshua," Charmaine called and Savannah had to close her eyes to fight her own tears. "Joshua, don't you lock that door!"

When she opened her eyes again, Savannah found Travis staring at her intently. His jaw was rigid, his gray eyes cold. He finished the wine in his glass and rubbed an impatient hand over his jaw.

"I suppose it had to come to this," Virginia said, breaking the silence and throwing her napkin on her plate in disgust. "I just hoped I wouldn't see the day." She stood shakily from her chair and Travis got up to help her. Virginia, though pale, anticipated his move and waved him away. "I'm all right. I just want to go upstairs for a while. I can make it on my own."

"Are you sure?" Savannah asked.

"I've been climbing those stairs for over thirty years," she said with a worried smile. "No reason to stop now."

With a proud set to her shoulders, Virginia walked out of the room and slowly mounted the stairs.

"When I get my hands on Wade Benson," Travis warned, his voice low, his angry eyes focused on Savannah, "he'll wish he'd had the common sense to stay in Florida or wherever the hell he is." Setting his half-empty wineglass on the table, he stood up and walked out of the room. A few seconds later the front door slammed shut.

Still concerned about Joshua, Savannah helped Sadie clear the table and straighten the kitchen to get her mind off Josh as well as Travis. Then, telling herself that she wasn't looking for Travis, Savannah went outside to the stables, checked on the horses and filed some reports in the office over the foaling shed. Travis wasn't in the yard or the office and Savannah felt a twinge of disappointment when she decided to go back to the house.

"You're a fool," she told herself with a frown. "Stay as far away from him as possible." She stretched before locking the door to the office, then climbed down the stairs. The night was bitterly cold and starless. Huddling against the frigid air, she raced across the parking lot and through the back door of the darkened house.

Archimedes stirred on the back porch and thumped his tail loudly as she kicked off her boots and slipped into the kitchen. The only sound disturbing the silence of the house was the hum of the refrigerator and the ticking of the grandfather clock in the hall.

"God, I'm tired," she whispered, opening the refrigerator. She poured a large glass of milk and slowly drank it while staring out the window to the darkened stable-yard. Thoughts of Travis wouldn't leave her alone and she wondered again where he was and why he had come back to the farm.

After putting the empty glass in the sink, she rubbed a hand over her eyes and walked toward the study to put away the mail.

The den was dark, illuminated only by the light of the dying fire. When Savannah entered the room, she found Travis lounging on the hearth, his fingers clasped around a glass, his back to the blood-red embers, his long legs stretched in front of him.

"What're you doing here?" she asked.

"Waiting."

"For?"

"You." He looked up at her, his intense gaze causing her heart to flutter.

"Okay," she whispered. "I'm here." She planted herself in front of him by leaning against the desk and balancing her hips against the smooth, polished wood. She reached for the lamp.

"Leave it off."

"Why?"

"The room seems quieter that way...less hostile."

Savannah let out a soft laugh. "You should know. Lately I think you wrote the book on hostility."

"Not with you," he said, taking a sip from his glass. "Why'd you interfere with Josh?" he asked slowly.

"I didn't."

A crooked grin sliced across his face. "Call it whatever you want, but it's the second time you've done it."

She lifted a shoulder and frowned, her dark brows drawing together as her thoughts returned to her nephew. "I don't think I'm interfering," she argued. "Sometimes I feel that he doesn't get enough attention or credit around here. Everyone points out his faults, but no one ever seems to pat him on the back."

"Except for you?"

"And his grandfather. Despite what you feel about him, Reginald's been a damned good grandfather, just like the kind of stepfather he's been to you. Just in case you've forgotten."

Travis's square jaw hardened. "What about Charmaine? How does she get along with her son?"

"Josh is a difficult child and Charmaine nearly raises him by herself. Obviously Wade doesn't have much time for the boy."

"Obviously," Travis commented dryly.

"As for Charmaine; she tries. But sometimes she has trouble understanding Josh. You know, she expects perfection and won't let him just be a kid."

"So that's when you step in."

"Only when I think Josh needs a little extra support. It's not easy being the only nine-year-old in a house full of grownups, y'know." She crossed her arms under her chest, unconsciously sculpting her sweater over breasts.

"You love him very much."

"Who wouldn't?" she asked, smiling to herself.

"Maybe Wade?"

Savannah's jaw tightened and she couldn't hide the impotent rage she felt every time she thought about Wade's treatment of his son. "I don't know if Wade is capable of loving anyone, even himself," she muttered. "And Josh is right about one thing: Wade should never have become a father." Then, thinking better of confiding in Travis, she tried to let go of her anger and changed the subject. "Do you know that Josh fantasizes about riding Mystic?"

"And what do you fantasize about?" he asked, his gray eyes focused on the proud lift of her chin, the flush in her cheeks and the elegant column of her throat. Her tousled black curls gleamed against her white skin and brushed the soft red sweater.

"I don't," she replied, slightly unnerved.

He looked as if he didn't believe her. "No dreams, Savvy?" he asked, and his voice caressed the familiar nickname he had given her when he had first come to the farm and she'd been just a skinny kid of nine.

"Not anymore."

He dragged his eyes away from her and stared into his drink. "Because of what happened between us."

"That's part of it," she conceded, feeling the old bittersweet pain in her chest.

He took a long swallow of his Scotch before lifting his eyes to her face. "So tell me, if you're so fond of Josh, why didn't you have any children of your own?"

"Simple. No husband."

"That's always puzzled me."

She shifted her gaze to the fire before returning it to him. His chestnut hair glinted with red highlights in the firelight and his tanned face looked more angular from the shadows. "I thought I explained that. David and I—"

"There were other men. Had to have been. You went to college at Berkeley, worked in San Francisco. You can't expect me to believe that you lived the life of a nun."

She bristled, thinking how close he had come to the truth.

"Not quite. But I guess I never found a man that I thought would be right."

"That was probably my fault, too."

"Don't flatter yourself."

Ignoring her bitterness, he crossed his legs before him and finished his drink. "For what it's worth, you would have been one helluva mother."

"I suppose I should take that as a compliment."

"It was intended as one."

She felt an uncomfortable lump in her throat and tried to use the feeling of intimacy that was stealing into the room to her advantage. "A little while ago you said that we used to share secrets."

"We did."

"So why don't you tell me why you're here. Why now? And why is Henderson, your partner, so upset?"

"I'll tell you when—"

"I know. When Wade and Dad get back. Tomorrow. A good thing, too," she added mockingly.

A muscle in the corner of his jaw began to work. "Why? Are you getting tired of me?"

"No, but you couldn't last here, counselor. At the rate you're going, we'll be out of Scotch in two days."

He cocked his head to the side and a laconic smile sliced across his face. "You think I'm a lush."

"You're doing a damned good impersonation." Standing up and stretching her tired muscles, she kept her eyes fixed on Travis. "Why don't you just tell me why you came back? I already know that you're planning to dissolve your partnership with Henderson and I know that you're probably going to give up on the idea of running for governor, despite the current rumors or any grass-roots ground swell."

"Henderson talks too much."

"He didn't want to."

"But with your powers of persuasion, you convinced a respected member of the bar, a man who had held his tongue in a courtroom when it was to his client's advantage, to bare his soul," he prodded, the corners of his mouth pinching.

She ignored his blatant sarcasm. "Something like that."

"Like I said, he talks too much." His eyes slid slowly up her body, lingering at the swell of her breasts. "And you're too inquisitive for your own good. Always have been." His gaze continued upward, hesitating a moment at the corner of her mouth before reaching her eyes.

Savannah's throat worked reflexively. There was something inherently male about Travis that reached her on a very sensual level. There always had been.

"Why did you come back?" she asked, hoping to break the thickening tension in the room.

"I don't want to discuss it."

"Why not?"

He grimaced into the remains of his drink. "Because I want to talk to Reginald first. Something's not right."

"With what?"

He rubbed the bridge of his nose and closed his eyes. "Oh, Savvy, with everything—the law practice, the campaign. There're a few things that don't add up and—" He stopped himself, realizing that he was confiding in her. "Just trust me on this one, okay? Once I talk to Wade I'll be able to sort everything out."

"What does Wade have to do with anything?" she asked.

"I think he's involved."

"In what?"

A muscle in the corner of Travis's jaw tightened. "I haven't put it all together," he admitted in disgust. "But frankly, I'm not sure that I want to."

"You're afraid."

Travis smiled grimly and shook his head. "I just don't know if it's worth all the trouble."

"Something's eating at you."

"I don't like to be a pawn. That's all." He got up and paced around the room. "Have you ever wondered *why* it's so damned important to your father that I run for election?"

"I guess I really hadn't thought about it."

"Well, he's pushing, Savannah. He's pushing very hard. And the only reason I could see that it would matter to him at all is for personal gain—his personal gain."

"You really have become a cynic, haven't you?" she tossed back, but the seriousness of his expression made her heart miss a beat.

"Think about it. Why would he care? What's it to him—unless he were expecting something from me."

"Like what?"

"I don't know...." He lifted his hand and then dropped it again. "Maybe you can tell me."

"I don't have an inkling of what you're talking about."

"Don't you? I wonder." He slid a suspicious glance in her direction before staring at the fire. "You could be in on it."

"You're crazy!" she said angrily.

He laughed a little, leaned an elbow on the mantel and raked his fingers through his hair. "Far from it, I'm afraid."

"You can't just come back here, to the man who all but raised you as his son, and start accusing him of God only knows what. You, of all people, should know that, counselor!" Savannah's temper got the better of her and she looked at him with self-righteous eyes.

"I haven't accused anyone of anything."

"Yet!"

Travis leaned back and smiled sarcastically. "Okay, let's use logic. The governor has a lot of responsibilities. Surely you agree."

"So?"

"For example: the governor of California is the supreme power behind the California Horse Racing Board. The Governor appoints members to the board and may remove a board member if it can be proved that he's incompetent or negligent. And that doesn't begin to touch what the governor is responsible for in the case of land use, corporations...you name it. The governor has a lot of power—the kind of power that some people might like to abuse.''

"Like Dad?''

"For one. Wade and Willis Henderson wouldn't be standing very far behind him.''

Savannah's eyes widened. Travis really believed what he was saying. "Be careful, Travis. You're talking about my father. My father! A man who has only done what he's thought best for you.''

"Maybe not always.''

"This is all idle speculation—half-baked theories!''

"I don't think so. Four of the board members' terms are up during the next term of governor. Four. Out of seven.''

"And you think Dad cares?'' Savannah was seething.

"Of course he cares! Everyone who owns a race horse in California cares!'' He came up and stood before her. "For all I know, Reginald might want to be on the board himself or try to convince me to appoint the right people, friends of his who could be easily swayed to his point of view.''

"But why?''

"Power, Savannah.''

"That's crazy—''

"Power and money. The two biggest motives mankind has known.''

"Don't forget revenge,'' she reminded him.

"Oh, I haven't.'' A ruthless smile curved his lips. "I visited my partner, Henderson, the other night.''

"The night that you told him you wanted out of the partnership?''

"Right. The same night that he met with Wade.''

Savannah froze. "I don't understand....''

"Wade and Willis Henderson seem to be working together on several schemes.''

"Such as?'' she asked, breathless.

He considered her a moment and then decided it didn't really matter what she knew. "Such as the fact that Wade

Benson is doing the books for the law firm—without my knowledge.''

Savannah couldn't hide her surprise. As far as she knew Wade only did the books for the farm. "So what does that have to do with anything?" she asked.

"In itself, not much. But the fact that Henderson admitted that he and Wade have already been taking contributions for my campaign…" Travis shook his head and the thrust of his jaw became more prominent. "That I saw as a problem. Henderson claims that your father was in on it."

"But you haven't announced your candidacy."

Travis's lips twisted cynically. "And won't." He finished his drink. "You can see my point."

"If what you're saying is true…"

Travis squinted into the fire. "Why would I lie?"

"I don't know," she said, "because I don't know you any more."

"Sure you do." His voice was gentle, as gentle as it had been years ago before the bitterness and pain had settled in his eyes.

"You've changed."

He offered a humble smile. "Not for the better, I assume."

"What made you so callous?" she asked. "Melinda's death?"

"I wish it were as simple as all that," he muttered, finishing his drink. "She wouldn't have liked this, y'know. She expected me to run for some political office and she was behind my ambitions…she and your father." He frowned into his empty glass. "And then there was the Eldridge decision," he said bitterly.

"But I thought you won," Savannah said, reflecting on the newsworthy decision. Travis was the lawyer who had successfully brought a major drug company to trial for the family of Eric Eldridge, who had died from taking a contaminated anti-inflammatory drug.

"So did I."

"What changed your mind?" she asked, knowing that he was carrying an unnecessary burden of guilt.

"Everything," he muttered disgustedly as he strode over to the bar and splashed three fingers of Scotch into his glass. "The law firm made money; the Eldridge's got an award so large that they sent me a magnum of champagne and bought themselves two new cars and a yacht."

"What they did with the money doesn't matter."

He took a long drink. "But it didn't bring their son back, did it?" he asked, shaking his head and closing his eyes. "Grace Eldridge got up on the stand and wept for her lost son," he said, as if to himself. "A month later she came into the office wearing a new fur coat and a Bermuda tan and asked if I thought there was any way to file another lawsuit against the drug company." He studied the amber liquid in his glass. "It left a bad taste in my mouth."

He walked back to her and placed his glass on the desk. "That's what I meant when I said all that matters is power and money."

"And revenge," she reminded him.

He was standing in front of her again, his eyes, luminous in the darkened room, drilling into hers. "Right. Revenge." When his hands came up to take hold of her shoulders she didn't move.

The warmth from his fingers permeated her sweater to spread down her arms. She trembled inside, as much from his touch as from the realization that he was, indeed, suspicious of her father's motives. "So that's what you came here to find out," Savannah whispered. "How my father is involved in your 'campaign' or lack thereof."

"Partly," he admitted, his voice husky.

"What else?" Savannah's heart was pounding betrayingly from the feel of his hands on her arms.

"Just this." He lowered his head and gently brushed his lips across hers, tantalizing her with the feel of his mouth against her skin.

"Don't do this to me," she whispered. "Not again."

Jerking free, she took an unsteady step backward and stared into his eyes. "Tell me…tell me what you think Dad's up to," she said, not wanting to think about the passion behind his kiss or her immediate reaction.

"I'm not sure; I'll need your help to find out."

"No, Travis," she whispered. "You really can't expect me to go against my own father."

"I haven't asked that."

He was so close, so damned close, and all she could think about was the power of his body over hers. "But you're trying to—"

"Find out the truth. That's all."

"Then talk to Dad!" she said desperately.

"I will. When he gets back. Until then, I may need your cooperation."

"I can't help you, Travis!"

"If it makes you feel any better, I hope that this is all a big misunderstanding. I would like to think that Reginald's motives are as pure as you seem to think."

"But you won't."

"I'm too realistic."

"Jaded," she corrected.

"Prove it," he dared, his eyes glinting in the firelight.

"I don't know—" She cleared her throat and tried to stop the hammering of her heart.

"Prove me wrong, dammit! You were the one who pushed me, lady. I didn't want to tell you any of this, but you insisted."

"But you're asking me to prove to you that my father, a respected horse breeder, is…what? Trying to get you elected so that he can defraud the racing public? Is that what you're suggesting?"

"Maybe you can verify your opinion."

"Of course I can! If Dad's so hell-bent to abuse your powers as governor, if and when you're elected, it would only affect him here, in California. Then why would he bother with stabling the horses in Florida? Tell me that!

There wouldn't be much of a point, not when he knew that here, in the Golden State, he could manipulate the racing board at will!''

"You're being sarcastic."

"And you're talking nonsense!" she nearly shouted, angry with herself for even listening to him.

"Prove it," he suggested.

Savannah's blue eyes sparked at the challenge. "I will."

"Good." His grin was filled with ruthless satisfaction as he leaned against the mantel, his narrowed eyes lingering on her lips. "I don't suppose your father ever told you who was at the lake that night nine years ago." He touched her softly on the underside of her chin.

Savannah jerked her head to the side. "He knew?"

"Of course he knew."

"I don't believe it! He would have said something...."

"Why?"

"He wouldn't just forget about it."

"I don't think your father forgets anything."

She took in a steadying breath. "How did he know?"

Travis's smoldering eyes delved into hers. "Because Melinda told him."

"And how did Melinda know? Did you confess?" Savannah asked, hardly daring to breathe as she relived that night so long ago.

"She saw us."

"Oh, God." The memory came back with crystal clarity: a twig snapping, Travis going to investigate. *Melinda had been the intruder at the lake!* Embarrassment poured over Savannah and she started for the door, but Travis reached for her. His hand was incredibly gentle on her arm. "I don't want to hear this," she whispered, refusing to be dragged back to the pain of the past. "It's over—"

"Is it?" In the dim light from the fire, with only the sound of the crackling flames and the wind against the rafters, his gaze scorched through her icy facade and into her heart. "I never stopped wanting you," Travis admitted, self-disgust twisting his mouth cynically.

"There's no reason to lie."

His fingers curled over her arm and he gave her a shake. Raw emotion twisted his face. "Dammit, Savannah. I'm not lying. I hate like hell to admit it, but not one solitary day has gone by that I haven't thought of you...wished to God that I'd never left you that night."

"You could have come back," she whispered, her pulse racing.

"I was married! And you were Reginald's daughter!"

Savannah didn't want to hear the excuses or think about the lies of the past nine years. "There's no reason to discuss this, Travis," she murmured, trying to break free of his embrace, but his fingers tightened painfully.

"I never wanted to love you," he said, his voice rough, his eyes glittering in the fire glow. "In fact, I tried to lie to myself, convince myself that you were nothing to me, but it just didn't work. All the time I was married to another woman, I couldn't forget you. That night at the lake was burned into my mind and my soul like no other memory in my life." He took in a long, ragged breath. "And at night...at night I would lie awake and remember the feel of you and I couldn't stop wanting you, dammit. Melinda was right there, in the bed with me, and all I could think of was you!"

"What's the point of all this?" she asked, her breath tight in her throat and tears threatening her eyes. The words of love she'd longed to hear sounded out of place and disjointed with nine years standing between them.

"The point is that I got used to living a lie. But there's no reason to live it any more."

Savannah's throat ached, but she lifted her head high and shook her hair out of her face. "Because Melinda is dead?"

"Yes."

She squeezed her eyes against the tears and lifted her chin. "I don't like being second-best, Travis. I never have."

"Don't you even want to know why I married her?"

"No! It really doesn't matter. Not anymore...." Her voice cracked with the lie.

The fingers around her arms gripped into her flesh and he pushed his head down to hers. He was so close that she could feel the angry heat radiating from his body, smell the Scotch on his breath, see the rage in his eyes. "It *does* matter. It all matters. Don't you understand? I've come here to break away from the lies of the past...all of them. Including the lie of marrying the wrong woman." His gray eyes delved into hers, scraping past the indifference she pretended to feel. "I *loved* you Savannah and damned myself for it. You were the daughter of the man that raised me— and until that summer I'd always thought of you as a kid sister."

In the thick silence that followed, Savannah stared into his flinty eyes and saw the smoldering passion in his gaze. Her heart throbbed with the thought that once, long ago, he had loved her and that he still wanted her. The fingers around her arms were a gentle manacle, but when she tried to tear away from his grasp, his hands tightened to the strength of steel.

"And you loved me," he finally whispered.

Tears burned her eyes, but she refused to break down. "The man I loved would never have left me," she said, her voice breaking before she took in a long, steadying breath. "He would never have left me without so much as a word of goodbye or an explanation."

Travis's nostrils flared and his eyes narrowed. "I've made more than my share of mistakes, lady. God knows I'm no saint and I should have demanded to see you before I agreed to marry Melinda, but everyone, including your father, thought it would be better if I just left."

Savannah shuddered. "How did Dad find out about us?"

His jaw was tense, the muscles of his body taut. "Melinda went to Reginald with the story that she was pregnant. Or else they worked out the story together."

''I don't understand.'' Savannah felt her knees grow weak, but the grip on her arms held her upright and Travis's features became harsh.

''She claimed that the only reason she and I had argued earlier in the night was because she was frightened. Afraid that I would leave her and the child. Then, she had second thoughts and tracked me down.''

Savannah couldn't believe him. ''How did she know you were at the lake?'' she asked angrily.

''Just a lucky guess. My car was in the garage, but I wasn't sleeping in the loft, or in the office. Melinda knew that I went to the lake whenever I wanted to think things out, so—''

''She found us,'' Savannah whispered, her blue eyes flashing with embarrassment and fury.

''Yes.''

She felt tears touch the back of her eyelids but refused to release them. ''So you married her because she was pregnant.''

''Because she *told* me she was pregnant.''

''And the baby?'' she murmured.

''Probably never existed.''

''What!''

A twisted smile contorted the rugged features of his face. ''Oh, yes, Melinda claimed to be pregnant. I didn't question her and that was probably a mistake.'' His steely eyes inched down her face to her breasts before returning to her gaze. ''Obviously not my first.''

Savannah tried to pull away from him but was no match for his strength.

''Melinda claimed to miscarry about three weeks after the wedding. I didn't doubt her until much later, when I thought that we should have a child in an attempt to save the marriage.'' He read the protests in Savannah's eyes. ''I know it's a lousy excuse to have a kid, but I was desperate. I wanted to make things right between us because all the time that we were married, she knew that I'd never forgotten you.

Do you have any idea what kind of hell she must have put herself through?''

"Or the kind of hell she put you through, because of your guilt,'' Savannah thought aloud.

"She was my wife, whether I loved her or not. Anyway, Melinda wasn't interested in a baby then and I doubt if she ever was. I think Melinda lied to me, Savannah, to force the marriage.'' His eyes darkened to the color of slate. "And your father was all for it.''

Savannah digested his words slowly. "That doesn't make sense.''

"Sure it does. Especially if he believed she was carrying my child.''

"I don't see that what happened in the past changes anything. You could have come to me and explained.''

"And how would you have felt?'' he demanded.

She felt the color explode on her cheeks. "Maybe a little less…used.''

He closed his eyes and dropped his forehead until it rested against hers. "Oh, lady, I never wanted you to feel that I used you.''

"How was I supposed to feel?'' she demanded, her wounded pride resurfacing. "Did you think that one night with you was all I wanted?''

"Of course not! But I thought the less people that knew about what happened between us, the better.''

Anger, nine years old and searing, shot through her. She wanted to strike him, lash out against all the pain she had borne, but she couldn't because he was still gripping her arms. "And what would have happened if *I'd* been the one to turn up pregnant?''

"I thought about that. Long and hard.''

"And?''

"I would have divorced Melinda.''

"And expected me to fall into your arms?'' She shook her head and felt every muscle in her body tense. "I would never have married you, Travis,'' she said through clenched teeth. "Because it would have been a trap, for you and me and the child and in the end we'd end up with a child caught between us, just like Josh is caught between Charmaine and Wade!"

"You don't believe that any more than I do."

"I do," she insisted, stamping a foot to add emphasis to her words. But her gaze was trapped in his magnetic stare. "I would never—"

His head lowered and he smothered her protest by capturing her lips with his. The force of the kiss was undeniable, the passion surging. Savannah wanted to push him away, to walk out of the room with her head held high, but she couldn't resist the sweet pressure on her mouth.

"No," she whispered, but he only drew her closer, crushing her body to his hard, muscular frame. The taste of him lingered on her lips and when his tongue pressed against her teeth, she willingly parted her lips.

The pressure on her arms became gentle and he pulled her body to his. Her breasts crushed against the rock-hard wall of his chest and began to ache for his touch. She felt a warmth invade her body, stealing from the deepest part of her and flowing through her blood.

Travis moaned and the kiss deepened, his moist tongue touching and mating with hers until Savannah felt her knees go weak and her fingers clutch his shoulders. Blood pulsed through her veins in throbbing bursts that warmed her from the inside out.

She trembled when his mouth left hers to explore the white skin of her throat and the lobe of her ear. Unconsciously she let her hair fall away from her face and quivered when his tongue slid along her jaw.

"Travis," she whispered, her breathing more labored with each breath as his hands slipped beneath the hem of her sweater and his fingers found the soft flesh between her ribs. She sucked in her abdomen and felt the tips of his fingers slide beneath the waistband of her jeans before climbing upward to mold around the straining tip of a breast. She moaned when his fingers captured the warm mound.

Fire burned within her body and soul as he toyed with the erect nipple and pressed his anxious lips to her mouth.

Vague thoughts that she should stop what was happening flitted through her mind, but she couldn't concentrate on anything other than the power of his touch. He leaned against the fireplace, his muscled legs spread and pulled her to him, forcing her against the hard evidence of desire in his loins, making her all too aware of the burning lust spreading through him like wildfire.

"Tell me again that you don't want me," he whispered against her hair.

Savannah was drugged with passion. When Travis cupped her buttocks and pulled her close she could hear the hard thudding of his heart. "I don't...I can't..." The raw ache within her burned traitorously and her thoughts centered on making love to this one very special man.

"Tell me that you never loved me."

"Travis...please," she gasped, trying to make some sense of what was happening. She couldn't fall under Travis's spell again, *wouldn't* love him again and yet her body refused to push him away.

The arms around her tightened, and he raised his head to stare into the mystery of her eyes. Gone was any trace of passion in his gaze. If their bodies hadn't been entwined so intimately, Savannah would have sworn that she had imagined the entire seduction. "Don't ever be ashamed of anything that's happened between us. Whether you believe the truth or not, the fact is that I loved you more than a sane man would let himself love a woman."

"But it wasn't enough."

"We were caught in a web of lies, Savannah. Lies spun by the people we trusted. Otherwise things would have been different. I swear that to you, and I hope to God you believe me." His face was drawn, his eyes gleaming with the truth as he saw it.

"It doesn't matter," she said, feeling bereft when he released her.

"Oh, but it does," he argued, pushing his hands into the back pockets of his jeans and trying to compose himself. "It matters one helluva lot!" Striding across the room he stopped at the bar and poured himself another stiff shot. "Because I'm back now and things are going to change in a big way. No one—not you, not Henderson, your father or your brother-in-law, is going to manipulate my life any longer. That's over. When I have it out with Reginald, I'm leaving."

"Running away," she accused.

He lifted a shoulder and smiled at a secret irony. "Just the opposite, lady," he said, the muscles in his face tightening in determination. "For the first time in my life I'm doing things exactly as I please. I'm not running *away* from anything, I'm just burying the past and all my mistakes with it."

"Mistakes like me? Well, bully for you," she hurled back at him, stung by his remark. "And just for the record, *I've* never done anything to manipulate you."

He winced. "Not intentionally, I suppose," he acquiesced. "But you sure have a way of turning me inside out!" With a look that cut her to the bone, he walked out of the room, through the foyer, out the front door and into the night. Savannah stood in the den with her arms crossed, hugging herself. *Oh, Travis,* she thought angrily, *why did you even bother coming back? Why didn't you just run away and leave me out of it!*

Four

Sleep was nearly impossible that night. Savannah tossed and turned, knowing that Travis was only a short walk away. She thought about everything he'd said about his reasons for leaving her all those years ago and wanted desperately to believe that he was, as she, a victim of fate.

"That's just wishing for the stars," she told herself angrily. "If he'd really wanted you, he'd have come back and at least explained, worked things out with Melinda...." *But how?* He'd really believed that Melinda had been pregnant. Or so he'd claimed.

And what about her father? Travis seemed to be on some vendetta to prove that Reginald was a scheming, conniving, power-hungry old man hell-bent on ruining Travis's life.

Savannah closed her eyes and tried to sleep, but was awake when the first pale streaks of dawn pierced through the windows of her bedroom.

Realizing that she wouldn't accomplish anything by tossing and turning in bed, she threw back the covers, got up, took a hot shower and dressed in warm work clothes. She didn't bother with makeup and tied her hair away from her face with a leather thong.

The morning was wet and cold with the promise of still more frigid air to come. The sky, darkened by gray clouds, seemed foreboding, and Savannah shuddered as she walked across the parking lot, past Lester's pickup and up the stairs to the office over the foaling shed.

Pulling off her gloves, she shouldered her way into the

office. The smell of perking coffee mingled with the faint odors of saddle soap and horses when she walked into the small room.

Lester was already inside, sipping a cup of coffee and reading the paper at a small table near the corner window. From his vantage point, he could watch a series of paddocks near the stables.

"Mornin'," he said, rubbing a hand over his chin and looking up at her with worried eyes.

"Is it?" she asked. "You look like something's wrong." She poured a cup of coffee and sat at the table across from the small man. His tanned crowlike features were tight with strain.

"Probably nothin'."

Cradling her cup in her hands, Savannah blew across the hot liquid and arched her black brows inquisitively. "But something's bothering you."

"Yep." The trainer leaned back in his chair and scowled into his cup before glancing up at her. "Just a feeling I've got. Everything was fine when I left here last night."

"I know. I checked the horses after you left."

He brightened. "Did you, now?" Pushing his chair back, he walked over to the wall housing the security alarm. "Then you know about this?"

"What?"

Lester was fingering a loose wire to the control panel. "This must've broken last night."

Savannah felt cold dread slide down her spine and her muscles went rigid. She set her cup on the table and walked over to the alarm system controls. "I didn't touch it last night," she said, studying the broken wire. "I used my key to get into the barns and then I came up here with some files."

"Was the wire broken then?"

"I don't know, I didn't notice." She saw the worry in Lester's eyes and read his thoughts. "You think it might have been cut?"

"Nope."

Savannah relaxed, but her relief was short-lived.

"Pulled maybe, but not cut. The break isn't clean." He rubbed his jaw thoughtfully. "It could've just worn out or it could've been yanked on purpose."

"But why?" She thought about the horses; they were valuable, but it would be difficult to steal any of them. The same was true of the equipment. There was no cash in the office, nor any to speak of on the grounds. And the broken wire wasn't enough damage for vandals. "Have you checked the horses?"

"All safe and accounted for."

"No other damage?"

"None that I've found, and I've looked."

"Then it must have just snapped on its own."

Lester frowned, his lower lip protruding thoughtfully. "But it seems strange it should happen when Reginald is out of town, and just a couple of days after Travis shows up."

Savannah's stomach knotted at the implication. "You think Travis had something to do with this?"

"No." The old man shook his head and scowled. "That boy's straight as an arrow. But there's a lot of people interested in his campaign...or lack thereof."

"I can't believe that a broken wire has anything to do with political intrigue," she said, taking a calming swallow of coffee. Lester came back to the table and stared through the window at the gloomy morning.

"I hope not, Missy," he thought aloud. "I sure hope not." His shoulders bowed as he leaned over his lukewarm coffee.

Savannah glanced at the dangling wire. "Maybe it just wore out," she said again, as if to convince herself. "The system's pretty old."

"Maybe." Lester didn't seem to believe a word of it.

"I'll call the people who installed it and see what they come up with."

"Good idea," he muttered, rubbing his scalp.

"Is something else wrong?" Savannah asked.

"Probably nothing, but I just have this feelin'." He laughed at himself. "Maybe I'm just gettin' old. But when I walked into the stallion barn this morning, I sensed, you know, felt that someone was there."

"But no one was?"

"No." He shifted uneasily in his chair. "The stallions, well, they seemed different, like they'd already seen someone and then I thought I heard a noise, up in the loft. So I checked." He shrugged his narrow shoulders. "Didn't find anything."

"Maybe a mouse?"

"And maybe it was nothin'. I don't hear as well as I used to, y'know."

"Well, just to be on the safe side, have one of the hands search the building for mice, squirrels, rats...and whatever else you can think of. I don't want them eating all the grain."

"Already done," he muttered. "I'll sure be glad when Reginald gets back."

"He'll be home this evening."

"Good."

Lester, who was facing the door, frowned slightly as Travis entered the room. Savannah felt her back go rigid and the argument of the night before echoed in her mind.

"Good morning," Travis drawled, pouring himself a cup of coffee and leaning on a windowsill. He stretched his long legs in front of him and watched Savannah as he took an experimental sip of the hot coffee.

"Mornin' yourself," Lester replied, checking his watch. "I've scheduled Vagabond for a workout in about forty-five minutes. Want to come along?"

"Sure," Travis replied, a leisurely smile stealing across his angular face.

"Savannah?" Lester asked.

She set her empty cup on the table and felt the challenge

of Travis's glare. He was watching her every move, expecting her to find a way to avoid being with him.

"Love to," she agreed as pleasantly as possible, meeting his gaze. "Let's see if he's improved any from the last time I saw him run."

"Getting that one to pay attention to the jockey is like trying to tell a rooster to crow at midnight," Lester grumbled. He pushed his fedora onto his head and walked out of the office, leaving Travis and Savannah alone.

Savannah lifted her eyes and stared straight into Travis's amused eyes. He was leaning forward on his elbows, a small smile tugging at the corners of his mouth. "Is something funny?" she demanded.

"I was just wondering if you were still mad?" Travis asked.

"I wasn't mad."

He laughed aloud, surprising Savannah. "And a grizzly bear doesn't have claws."

Ignoring his remark, she stood and walked to the door. It was too early in the morning to be unnerved by Travis's taunting gaze and Savannah wasn't up to playing word games with him. "I'll see you at the workout track. I'm going to check on the stallions before I watch Vagabond run."

"Any particular reason?"

"I just want to make sure that everything's okay. Lester discovered this." She walked to the alarm control and held up the broken wire and Travis followed. "I just want to double-check on the horses and make sure that the system fell apart on its own and that it wasn't helped along by someone."

He examined the wire carefully. "Do you think it was?"

"No. But I believe in the 'better safe than sorry' theory, especially since Lester thinks he might have heard a noise in the stallion barn this morning." Savannah explained the conversation with Lester to Travis, who listened quietly while he finished his coffee.

The laughter in his eyes faded slightly. "I'll come with you," Travis decided.

"Don't you have anything better to do?"

"Nothing," he said with a lazy grin that cut across his face in a beguiling manner and softened the hard angles, making him seem less distant and allowing a hint of country-boy charm to permeate his tough, touch-me-not exterior. No wonder everyone was anxious to have him run for governor, Savannah thought. If the campaign were decided on looks, virility and charm alone, Travis would win hands down.

"Then let's go," she said a little sharply, angry with herself for the traitorous turn of her thoughts.

"You *are* still mad."

"Just busy." She brushed past him and hurried down the steps to the brick path leading to the stallion barn.

Before she'd gone five steps, Travis had caught up with her and placed a possessive arm around her shoulders. "Lighten up, Savannah," he suggested.

"You should talk."

"At least I don't hold a grudge."

She slid a glance in his direction and found him grinning at her with a smile that melted the ice around her heart. Shivering against the cold air, she tried not to huddle against him. "What're you trying to do?"

"Just prove my undying affection, lady," he quipped, kissing her lightly on the hair.

Just like all the pain of the past nine years didn't exist. Savannah clenched her teeth and walked faster. "So what happened to the outraged, self-righteous lawyer I saw last night?"

"Oh, he's still here," Travis reassured her, "but he's had a good night's sleep and a hot cup of coffee with a beautiful woman."

"I swear, Travis, you could sweet-talk the birds out of the trees one minute, and cook them for dinner the next!"

Travis's laughter rumbled through the early dawn and he hugged her close to his body.

Josh, his shoulders hunched against the rain, was standing at the door of the stallion barn. He'd started toward the house, but stopped when he noticed Savannah and Travis approaching.

"What're you doing here?" Savannah asked when she was close enough for the boy to hear her. "And where's your coat? It's freezing!"

Guilt clouded Josh's young face and Savannah was immediately contrite. Obviously the boy was still brooding about the night before and the last thing he needed was a lecture from her.

"I…I just wanted to see Mystic before I went to school."

"Next time put on a jacket, okay?"

"Okay."

Travis patted Josh firmly between the shoulders. "You like Mystic, don't you?"

"He's great!" Josh said, his dark eyes shining.

"Well, Grandpa would agree with you, and I guess I'd have to, too." Savannah said. "Now, tell me, have you eaten breakfast yet?"

"No."

"I didn't think so. You'd better hurry back to the house and eat something so that you don't miss the bus."

"I don't need breakfast," Josh complained.

Savannah smothered a fond smile for her nephew, forced her features into a hard line and pointed her finger at the house. "Scoot, Josh. You don't want to end up in any more trouble, do ya?"

"I guess not," the boy conceded.

Travis cocked his head toward the house. "Do as your aunt says, and when you get home from school, we'll go cut down a Christmas tree."

Josh, unable to believe his good fortune, looked from Travis to Savannah and back again. "For real?"

"For real," Travis said with a laugh.

"Awesome!" Josh said with a brilliant grin before taking off toward the house at a dead run.

"You won't disappoint him, will you?" Savannah asked, once Josh was out of earshot.

"You know me better than that." Travis hesitated a minute. "Or do you?"

"It's just that I don't want to see Josh disappointed. He's had more than his share of false promises."

"Scout's honor," Travis said, his gray eyes twinkling in the dim morning light. "I intend to take him looking for a tree this afternoon. You can come along if you like." He pulled her into the circle of his arms and kissed her chilled lips.

Savannah wanted to back away, but couldn't resist the sparkle in his eyes. "I would like. Very much."

"Good, now, why don't you tell me about Josh's fascination with Mystic," Travis suggested, holding the door to the barn open for her.

The scent of warm horses and hay filled the air. The stallions stirred, shifting the straw in their stalls and jingling their halters. Disgusted snorts and a soft nicker filled the long barn as the inquisitive Thoroughbreds poked their heads over the stall doors.

"Maybe it's because Wade wouldn't let him get a dog or a horse of his own. A few years ago, I bought Josh a puppy for his birthday and Wade made him give it away. He called the gift inappropriate for a six-year-old with no sense of responsibility."

Savannah frowned at the memory. "And then, Josh happened to be in the foaling shed when Mystic was born. From that point on, he's had a special feeling for the horse, though it scares Charmaine to death."

Travis closed the door and looked around the barn. Nothing seemed out of place. Graceful horses, shining water buckets, fresh hay and grain stored in barrels filled the long, hall-like room.

"Why is Charmaine afraid of him?"

"Mystic's got what's known as a 'bad rep.'"

"Not the most friendly guy at the track?"

"See for yourself." Savannah was walking to the end of the double row of stalls and Mystic's box. As she walked, she scrutinized the interior of the barn and looked at each of the stallions, talking softly to each one.

The black colt stretched his head over the top rail and snorted at the intrusion. His pointed ears flattened to his head and he nervously paced in his stall. Rippling muscles moved fluidly under a shining black coat.

"I can see why Josh thinks he's special," Travis said, leaning over the rail and looking at the perfect contours of the big ebony colt. Barrel chested, with strong, straight legs and powerful hindquarters, Mystic was a beautifully built Thoroughbred. His dark eyes were sparked by a keen intelligence, his large nostrils flared at the unfamiliar scent. Mystic looked at Travis and shook his head menacingly.

Savannah patted the black nose and Mystic stamped a hoof impatiently. "When Mystic was running, Joshua read the papers every day, out loud, to me. And when Mystic lost to Supreme Court in the Belmont, Josh really took it to heart." Savannah smiled to herself. "To hear Josh tell it, Mystic lost because Supreme Court boxed him in on purpose."

"Is that the truth?"

"My opinion?"

"Yep. And it won't go any further than these—" Travis looked around at the whitewashed barn "—four walls."

"Okay." Savannah folded her arms over the stall door and studied the big colt. "Mystic could have won the race, I think, if the jockey had given him a better ride. However, whether Supreme Court's jockey intentionally boxed Mystic in is neither here nor there. He didn't do anything illegal. Maybe it was strategy, maybe just luck of the draw. The point is, Supreme Court won and Mystic didn't. End of story. Except that everyone expected Mystic to win at Belmont.''

Travis slid a glance in Savannah's direction. ''Maybe everyone expected too much. Winning the races he had as a two-year-old and topping it off with the Preakness when he was three was no small feat.'' Travis patted the horse and Mystic backed away. ''Sometimes people expect too damned much.''

''Are you talking about the horse or yourself?''

He smiled crookedly. ''I never could lie to you.''

''Only once,'' she said.

Travis pushed his fingers through his thick hair and shook his head in disgust. ''And that was the biggest mistake of my life. I've been paying for it ever since.''

Savannah felt her throat become tight. If only she could believe him—just a little. ''We can't go back,'' she said, but Travis turned to face her. His hand reached forward and slid beneath her ponytail to caress her neck.

''Maybe we can, Savannah.'' His voice was low and intimate and it made her pulse leap. ''Maybe we can go back, if we try.''

The fingers against her neck were warm and comforting and if she let herself, Savannah could easily remember how desperately she had loved him.

She pulled away from him. ''I think it would be best if we forgot what happened between us,'' she said.

''Do you honestly think that's possible?''

''I don't know.'' She stared up at him, her gaze entwining in the enigmatic gray of his, before she looked away.

''Why do you keep lying to yourself, Savannah?''

''Do I? Maybe it's easier.''

His hand reached forward and twined in the thick rope of her black hair. ''You're afraid of me,'' he accused. He pulled her head back, forcing her to meet the intensity of his gaze.

''Not of you,'' she whispered. ''Of us. The way we feel about each other doesn't make any sense.''

"And everything in life has to be rational?"

"Yes."

"Tell me," he said, eyes narrowed, gaze centered on her lips. "How *do* you feel about me?"

"I think I should walk away from you."

Slowly, gently, his fingers caressed her skin. "Okay, that's what you think. Now, answer my question, how do you feel?"

Her breath was shaky, and the feel of his hands against her neck made thinking nearly impossible. "I should hate you," she whispered through clenched teeth.

"But you don't."

"You lied to me! Used me! Left me! And now you're back." He was toying with the edge of her jacket, his fingers grazing the soft skin at the base of her throat. She tried to jerk away, but his fingers took hold of the lapels of her coat. "I should hate you for what you did to me and what you're insinuating about Dad!"

"I don't think you're capable of hate."

"Then you don't know me very well."

"Oh, I know you, Savannah," he said, his face only inches from hers. "I know you better than you do yourself."

And then he kissed her, long and hard. A kiss so filled with passion that it killed all the protests in her mind and held at bay her doubts. The sweet pressure of his lips crushing against hers helped the years and the pain slip away. The hand on her nape explored the neckline of her jacket and her pulse began to throb expectantly.

She felt his tongue slide between her teeth and she welcomed the sweet taste of him. He drew her close and her own hands were fumbling with the buttons of his suede jacket. She touched the soft flannel shirt that covered the corded muscles of his chest. An ache, deep and powerful, began to burn deep within her.

"I've always loved you, Savannah," he whispered against her midnight-black hair. "God help me, I've always loved you,'' he confessed, ''even when I was married to Melinda.''

''Don't—''

His lips cut off any further protest as he kissed her with the surging passion of nine lost years. His fingers twined in her hair, pulling her head backward and exposing the gentle curve of her neck. ''Being near you is driving me out of my mind.'' he whispered. ''Do you know, can you imagine, how much self-control it took not to follow you into your bedroom last night?''

Easily, she thought, falling against him and returning the fever of his kiss. ''This…this can't, it won't work.''

''Savannah, listen to me!'' His gray eyes were filled with conviction. ''Just trust me. For once in your life, trust me.''

''I already tried that, nine years ago!''

''And I won't hurt you again.'' The honesty in his gaze touched the darkest corners of her soul.

Trust him, Dear Lord.

Without any further questions, Travis lifted her into his arms and carried her to an empty stall at the end of the barn. He tossed his jacket down on the clean hay, and gently lay her upon it. Slowly, he untied the thong restraining her hair. The black curls tumbled free.

The zipper of her jacket slid easily open and he helped her out of it as he kissed her face and neck.

''Travis, I don't think—''

''Good!'' Kissing her hungrily, he molded her body to his, her soft contours fitting against the harder lines of his frame. His breathing was erratic, his heartbeat as wild as her own.

She pressed against him, unaware of anything but the sweet taste of his tongue sliding over her teeth and the warmth of his hands as they pulled the wide neck of her sweater down her shoulder to expose the white skin of her breast.

He kissed her feverishly and she returned his passion, her fingers working on the buttons of his jacket and sliding it down the length of his muscular arms. He tossed it aside and jerked the sweater over her head to gaze at the rounded swell of her breasts peeking over the lacy fabric of her camisole.

Dark points protruded upward against the lace, inviting the warmth of his mouth. He took one soft mound into his mouth, moistening the sheer fabric and caressing the nipple with his tongue. Savannah writhed beneath him, the sweet torment he was applying to her breast a welcome relief. She curled her fingers into his thick hair, holding onto his head as if to life itself.

"I've missed you," he whispered hoarsely, his breath fanning the wet fabric and the throbbing peak beneath.

And I've missed you.

He slid one of the straps of the camisole over her shoulder, baring the firm breast to him, and he gazed upon the swollen mound hungrily before caressing it with his lips.

Savannah shuddered as he lowered the other strap over her shoulder. She was lying half-naked on the straw, her dark hair billowing away from her face, her blue eyes dusky with passion.

Slowly he unbuttoned his shirt.

Savannah stared upward to watch the ripple of his muscles as he tossed the unwanted garment aside. "This time I'll make it right," he vowed, lowering himself over her and watching as her fingers reached upward to caress the dark hairs on his chest.

"And this time I won't expect more than you can give," she whispered, trembling as his lips found hers and his weight fell across her. The hard muscles of his chest rubbed against her breasts, the soft hair teasing her nipples as his hands splayed against the small of her back, pulling her so close that she could hear the erratic beat of his heart. Fingertips brushed past the waistband of her jeans, tantalizing the skin above her buttocks.

Liquid fire began to spread through her body as he touched and caressed her.

"I love you, Savannah," he vowed, his breath fanning the hollow of her throat.

When she didn't respond, he stared into the blue intensity of her eyes. "I love you," he repeated.

"But...but I don't want to fall in love with you," she said, her throat tight. "Not again."

"You're afraid to trust me." It wasn't a question, just a simple, but distasteful, statement of fact. Travis pulled away from her, rubbed his hand behind his neck and muttered a rather unkind oath at himself.

Savannah was left lying on the straw, feeling very naked and vulnerable. "Can't we just leave love out of it?"

He looked disdainfully over his shoulder. "Is that the way you want it? Just sex? No emotion?"

Blushing slightly, Savannah looked away and reached for her sweater.

Travis laughed bitterly and glanced at the rafters. "I didn't think so." He curled his fist and slammed it into the side of the stall next to Mystic. The colt snorted nervously. "Dear God, woman, what am I going to do with you?"

"As if you have any say in my life."

"I sure as hell do," he said. His gray eyes gleamed possessively.

With unsteady fingers, she tugged the sweater over her head, squared her shoulders, jutted her chin and faced him again. "I think it's time to go watch Vagabond. *If* you're still interested."

"Wouldn't miss it for the world," he said, sliding a bemused glance up her body.

Anger surged through her at the insolence of his stare. Plunging her arms through the sleeves of her jacket, she began to stand, but Travis reached for her wrist and restrained her. "I just hope that someday soon you'll get over your bull-headed pride and realize that you still love me."

"Dreamer."

"Am I?" His gaze slid down her neck, to the pulse jumping at her throat. "I don't think so." The confident smile that crossed his face was nearly a smirk. "Let me know when you change your mind."

"I won't."

He lifted a dubious dark brow. "Then I'll just have to convince you, won't I?" He pulled on her wrist, drawing her closer, but she jerked away and raised her hand to slap him, then thought better of it when she recognized the glittering challenge in his eyes.

"You're an impossible, insufferable, arrogant bastard. You know that don't you?" she accused, walking toward the door.

"And you've got the cutest behind I've ever seen."

She twirled and faced him, her face suffused with rage. "That's exactly what I mean. What kind of infantile, chauvinistic male remark was that?"

"The kind that gets your attention," he said, sobering as he stood. He picked up his shirt and held it in his hands, his naked chest a silent invitation. The lean muscles of his abdomen and chest, the curling dark hair arrowing below the waistband of his low-slung jeans and the tight muscles of his thighs and hips, hidden only by the worn fabric of his jeans, all worked together to form a bold male image in the harsh lights of the barn. "I'm just waiting for you to realize that I'm not about to make the same mistake I did nine years ago."

Her blue eyes sparked. "Neither am I!" she said over her shoulder, her small fists balling and her heart slamming wildly in her chest. "Neither am I."

Vagabond was already on the track by the time Savannah met Lester at the railing. It had just begun to rain and Lester was leaning over the top rail of the fence studying a stopwatch as Vagabond raced passed, his graceful strides carrying him effortlessly over the ground. Lester flicked the watch with his thumb and smiled to himself.

"That was a helluva time," he muttered, his gray brows quirking upward in appreciation as his eyes followed the galloping bay. "He's got it in him. Faster than Mystic, he is."

"I thought you were all for selling him," Savannah teased, stuffing her hands into her pockets and hunching her shoulders against the cold drizzle. She knew that Travis had joined them, but refused to look at him or acknowledge his presence. "Or have you changed your mind in the last couple of days?"

"It's controlling him that worries me," Lester remarked.

"Makes your job interesting," Travis observed.

Lester laughed and watched as the colt took one final turn around the track at a slow gallop. "That it does," he agreed, his black eyes never leaving the horse. "That it does." He waved to the rider and called, "Go ahead and take him inside. That's enough for today."

Lester rubbed his hands together and turned toward the stables before hazarding a glance at Travis. "I always wondered why you didn't stick it out, here on the farm."

"Funny," Travis replied, his gaze shifting to Savannah, "lately I've been wondering the same thing myself."

"We could still use you, y'know. Always need a man who knows horses." He walked toward the stables and Savannah felt Travis's eyes on her back.

"Do you think I should take his advice and stay?" he asked.

Savannah's heart nearly stopped beating. "I think it would be the worst mistake of your life," she lied before turning toward the house and walking away from him.

Joshua was released from school early for the holidays. He raced into the house at one-thirty and threw his books on the kitchen table.

"What's the rush?" Savannah asked. She was sitting at the table, trying to balance her checkbook. Deciding that a five-dollar discrepancy with the bank wasn't a life-or-death situation, she stuffed the statement and checks back into the envelope and focused all of her attention on her nephew.

"Don't you remember?" Josh asked. "Travis said we could all go out and cut a Christmas tree today!"

"He said what?" Charmaine asked, walking into the room and frowning at the untidy pile of books on the table.

"That we could go cut a Christmas tree today," Josh repeated, grabbing an apple from a basket on the kitchen counter and biting into the crisp fruit.

"But Grandpa usually buys one in Sacramento," Charmaine said, looking from Savannah to Josh and back again.

"I know," Savannah said. "But Travis did promise."

"When?"

"This morning. Before breakfast at the stallion barn."

"Were you out there again?" Charmaine asked, paling as she turned to the boy.

Josh froze.

"How many times do I have to tell you not to go out there unless you're with Daddy or Grandpa? Those stallions are dangerous!" Charmaine warned.

Travis walked in from the back porch and heard the tail end of the conversation. "It was all right, Charmaine. Savannah and I were out there."

"I don't like it," Charmaine replied. "Mystic almost killed Lester last year, did you know that? And another time he kicked one of his grooms and nearly broke the man's leg."

"He wouldn't kick me, Mom."

"How do you know that? He's an animal, Joshua, and he can't be trusted. Now you don't go out to that barn again without Grandpa. Got it?"

"Got it," Josh mumbled, his eyes downcast and his small jaw firm with rebellion.

"Hey, sport. Come on, let's go get that tree," Travis said, patting the boy on the shoulders. "Want to come?" he asked Charmaine.

Charmaine hesitated, but shook her head. "I'd better not. Someone has to stay with Mother and I've got something

I've got to get done in the studio, if you don't mind me up there, Travis.''

"No, that's fine,'' he replied.

"That's okay, I'll go.'' Savannah said, hoping to ease some of Josh's disappointment.

Charmaine sighed in relief.

A few minutes later, Travis, Savannah, Josh and Archimedes were piled into a pickup and driving along the rutted lane through the back pastures leading to the hills. Snow mixed with rain began to collect on the windshield.

"Maybe it'll snow for Christmas,'' Josh said excitedly, looking out the window as the wet flakes drifted to the ground and melted.

"I wouldn't count on it,'' Savannah said.

"Spoilsport,'' Travis accused, but laughed. "Now, tell me, what's all this nonsense about Mystic nearly killing Lester.''

"He didn't!'' Josh said. "No way!''

"Lester slipped when he was in Mystic's stall and the horse stepped on him. It was an accident and not very serious.''

"You're sure?''

"Lester is and everyone else agrees except Charmaine,'' Savannah said.

"Mom's just freaked out by Mystic, that's all.''

As Travis drove up the lower slopes of the hills, the snow was definitely sticking and Josh's spirits soared.

The boy continued to search the forested hills for the perfect Christmas tree. "There's one,'' he said for the fiftieth time as he pointed to a small fir tree.

"Not big enough,'' Travis thought aloud, but parked the truck to the side of the road near a clearing.

While Travis pulled the hatchet out of the back of the truck, Josh and Savannah, with Archimedes on their heels, scoured the woods. The snow was clinging to the branches of the trees, dusting the evergreens with a fine mantle of white and clinging to the blackened branches of the leafless maples and oaks.

Josh hurried ahead with Archimedes. Travis caught up with Savannah and placed an arm comfortably over her shoulders. "This is how it should be, y'know," he said, watching Archimedes scare a winter bird from the brush. "You, me, a kid or two, a lop-eared dog and Christmas."

Savannah smiled and shook her head. Snowflakes clung to her hair and melted on her face. "The way it should have been, you mean."

"It still could be, Savannah."

Her heart nearly stopped beating. "You're very persuasive, counselor," she said, refusing to argue with him in the wintry afternoon. Snow continued to fall and cling to the branches of the trees. The mountains seemed to disappear in the clouds.

"Along with self-righteous, insufferable, impossible and arrogant?"

Savannah smiled. "All of the above."

"I hope so, lady," he whispered against the melting drops of snow in her ebony hair. "I hope to God that I'm as persuasive as you seem to think."

"Over here!" Josh shouted and they followed his voice until they came upon him almost dancing around a twelve foot fir. "It's perfect!"

"I thought the word was 'awesome,'" Savannah said with a smile and Travis laughed, giving her a hug.

While Travis trimmed off the lower branches and cut the tree, Josh ran through the forest and tossed snowballs at an unsuspecting Archimedes. The spotted sheepdog barked and bounded through the brush.

When Josh's back was turned, Savannah hurled a snowball at him and it landed on his shoulder. Josh whirled and began throwing snowballs at Savannah so rapidly that she had to dodge behind a tree for protection. When she was brave enough to peek around the protective trunk of the oversize maple, two snowballs whizzed past her nose. Travis had gotten into the game and was quickly packing another frozen missile.

"No fair!" she called. "Two against one."

"You've got Archimedes, remember?" Josh taunted with a grin.

"Four-footed allies don't count. Oh!" A snowball landed in the middle of her back and she turned to face Travis, who had sneaked around the maple tree. "Enough already. I give!"

"Don't I wish," Travis murmured, a smile lurking on his lips before he wrapped his arms around her and kissed her feverishly. Josh continued the assault, and Travis had to let go of Savannah. He switched alliances and began hurling snowballs at the boy until Josh squealed and laughed his surrender.

"Okay, let's call it quits and get the tree into the truck!" Travis suggested, dusting the snow from his jacket as he looked at the sky. "It looks like this storm isn't going to let up, so we'd better get back to the farm while we still can."

Josh's brown eyes were shining with merriment, his grin stretching from one ear to the other, as Travis and Savannah loaded the tree into the back of the pickup for the drive back to the farm.

The rutted lane was slippery and the truck lurched, pushing Savannah closer to Travis. She tried to keep to her side of the seat, but the warmth of his thigh pressing against her was irresistible. It even felt natural when Travis's fingers grazed her knee as he shifted gears.

With a sinking sensation, she realized that despite her vows to herself, she was falling in love with him all over again.

Five

The living room smelled of fir boughs, scented candles, burning wood and hot chocolate. Savannah was still helping Josh trim the tree, although Charmaine had already taken Virginia upstairs. The night was peaceful and still, with snow collecting in the corners of the windowpanes and the lights from the tree reflecting on the glass. A fire was glowing warmly in the fireplace. It crackled against the pitchy fir log in the grate.

Savannah set her empty mug on the mantel before stepping on the ladder and trying to straighten the star on the top of the tree.

"I wish Travis would come help us," Josh complained, placing a bright ornament on the bough closest to him.

Savannah slanted the boy an affectionate grin. "He will."

"When?"

She shrugged. "Whenever he's finished."

"What's taking him so long?"

"I haven't the foggiest," Savannah replied truthfully. "He said he had some paperwork to finish." Sighing when the star refused to remain upright on the tree, she climbed down the ladder.

"So why is he locked in Grandpa's study?"

"Good question," she admitted, sneaking a glance through the archway, across the foyer to the locked door of the study. "I guess he needs privacy...to concentrate."

"On what?"

"Look, Josh, I really don't know," she admitted.

"Grandpa doesn't like anyone in his study," Josh said.

"I know, but it's all right for Travis to be in there; he's the attorney for the farm."

"Well, I wish he'd get done."

"So do I." Savannah picked up the empty mugs. "What about another cup of cocoa?"

"Sure!"

"You finish with the tree and I'll be back in a flash," she said with a smile as she walked out of the living room and paused at the door of the study. Travis had locked himself inside nearly two hours before. When she'd asked him to stay and trim the tree after he'd placed it in the stand, he'd shaken his head and told her he had something he needed to do before Reginald and Wade returned. His eyes had darkened mysteriously and Savannah had experienced a feathering of dread climb up her spine.

She knocked softly on the door. Travis opened it almost immediately and she couldn't help but smile at him. A rebellious lock of his chestnut-colored hair had fallen over his forehead and the sleeves of his sweater were pushed over his forearms.

"You're a sight for sore eyes," he said, his voice low.

"So why lock yourself away?" She looked past him to the interior of the room. It was obvious that Travis had been working at her father's desk. An untidy stack of papers littered the desktop and the checkbook for the farm was lying open on a nearby chair.

"Business." The lines between his eyebrows deepened and he frowned slightly.

"Can't you even take time out to see the tree? Josh is dying to show it to you."

"In a minute."

She angled her chin up at him and sighed loudly. "Okay, you win. Go ahead and be mysterious. How about a cup of coffee or some hot chocolate?"

He smiled at her, but shook his head. "I'm just about done in here, then I'll join the rest of the family. Okay?"

"Scrooge," she murmured and he kissed her softly on the nose.

"Be sure to put up the mistletoe," he commanded with a suggestive smile teasing his lips. Then he turned back to the study, entered and closed the door behind him.

"Merry Christmas to you, too," Savannah remarked.

Puzzled by Travis's behavior, she walked into the kitchen and refilled the mugs. Why was Travis looking through the books of the farm? An uneasy feeling stole over her, but she tried to forget about it. The day with Travis and Josh had been too wonderful to spoil with unfounded worries or fears. Travis certainly wasn't hurting anything. Besides, Wade and Reginald were due home any minute. Their arrival was enough of a problem for her to deal with.

Carrying the steaming cups back into the living room, she found Josh returning tissue paper into the packing boxes that had housed the ornaments for the past year.

"It's the best tree ever!" Josh exclaimed proudly as he stood and took a cup from Savannah's outstretched hand.

"I think you're right." Savannah laughed.

"We should go get Travis and Mom."

"In a minute, sport. First let's finish and clean up this mess." She gestured to the empty boxes stacked haphazardly around the tree. "You've done a good job, but we've got a lot of work ahead of us."

The sound of a car's engine caught Savannah's attention, and she felt her pulse jump nervously.

"Looks like Grandpa and your dad finally made it," she said to Josh, who was carrying a load of empty boxes out of the living room to the closet under the stairs in the foyer. "And only three hours late."

"About time," Josh mumbled.

"They couldn't help the fact that the airport's a mess because of the snow. Even the weathermen weren't prepared for a storm like this," she said cautiously when Josh returned. "Come on, let's not borrow trouble, huh?"

"Okay."

Just then the front door opened and Reginald strode into the living room.

"Well, what do we have here?" Reginald asked, eyeing the tree while pulling off his gloves. He unwrapped the scarf from around his neck and tossed both it and the gloves onto the couch.

"You know, Grandpa! It's the tree!" Josh exclaimed with excitement. "Aunt Savvy and Travis and I went to get it today, up in the hills! We even had a snowball fight!"

"Did you now?" Reginald took off his coat and tossed it over the back of one of the wing chairs before patting the boy on the head and admiring the tree. "Who won?"

"Travis and me!"

Reginald glanced at Savannah. "Two on one?"

"Archimedes was on my team," she said wryly. "He wasn't too much help."

"I'll bet not," Reginald said with a hearty laugh.

"So what do ya think of the tree?" Josh asked.

Walking around the Christmas tree, Reginald surveyed it with a practiced eye. "You picked a winner, my boy."

"I found it all by myself, but Travis had to cut it down."

Reginald winked fondly at his grandchild. "Next year you'll probably be able to handle it all by yourself."

"Maybe," Josh agreed.

"So where is everyone?" Reginald asked, facing Savannah.

"Charmaine took Mom upstairs about forty-five minutes ago."

A thoughtful frown pinched the features of Reginald's tanned face and he glanced up the stairs. "Tell me, how's your mother been?"

"Actually, Mom's been a little better since Travis came back to the farm. Having him here seems to have lifted her spirits a bit. She's had dinner downstairs twice and she helped trim the tree until just a little while ago."

"That's good," the older man said with obvious relief. "Maybe I'd better run up and check on her."

"You'd never hear the end of it if you didn't."

As Reginald left the room, Wade entered the house. His leather shoes clicked loudly against the tiled floor of the foyer as he approached the living room. His even-featured face was tight with tension, his taffy-colored hair slightly mussed.

Josh visibly stiffened at the sight of his father.

"Hi, Dad," the boy said. "See the tree? Travis and I cut it down."

At the mention of Travis's name, Wade frowned and tugged on his mustache. "Oh, ah, it looks good," Wade said without much enthusiasm and glanced at the clock. "What're you doing up so late?"

"Josh helped me decorate the tree," Savannah cut in, trying to avoid the argument she felt brewing in the air. "He's done a terrific job, hasn't he?"

"Terrific," Wade repeated without a smile.

"We're just about finished," Savannah explained.

"Good. It's a school night isn't it?"

Josh shook his head and grinned. "School's out for vacation."

Wade scowled. "Doesn't matter. It's late."

"But Aunt Savvy said—"

"No 'buts' about it, son!" Wade snapped, his short temper flaring. "I'm home now and you'll do as I say." Then, feeling slightly embarrassed, Wade gestured toward the boxes still lying on the floor. "You finish up here right away and go upstairs. I've got business to discuss privately with your grandfather."

Josh wanted to argue, but Savannah wouldn't let him. "We'll be done in no time, right, sport?"

"Right," Josh mumbled, bending over to pick up the loose boxes.

Once Wade was convinced that Josh was going to obey him, he took Savannah's arm and pulled her away from the tree, close to the windows. "Where's McCord?" he demanded.

"In the study. He said he'd be here in a minute."

Wade paled a bit and his eyes hardened. "What the hell's he doing in the study? Dammit, he comes back here one day and just takes the hell over! Why is he in Reginald's den?"

"I don't know. You'll have to ask him." She looked over Wade's shoulder and saw Travis striding across the hall, his hands thrust into the back pockets of his cords, his sleeves still pushed over his forearms. His mouth was pinched into a tight, angry line that softened slightly as he met Savannah's worried gaze.

"What do you think?" Joshua asked, stepping away from the brightly lit tree.

"Best tree I've ever seen," Travis said with a brilliant smile for the boy. "Maybe you should go into the business!"

"And maybe he should go upstairs to bed," Wade grumbled, raising his eyebrows at his son. Then, as if dismissing the child ended that particular conversation, Wade turned all of his attention to Travis. "Now, McCord, what the hell's going on? What's all this nonsense about you not running for governor?"

"It's not nonsense," Travis replied, helping Josh with a stack of boxes. "Just the facts." He carried them out of the room and stacked them in the closet under the stairs.

"Great!" Wade muttered, swearing under his breath. He pushed himself out of the chair, walked over to the bar at the end of the room and poured himself a stiff drink.

"Dad," Josh interrupted, sensing the growing tension in the air and trying to find some way of easing it. "Travis cut this tree down all by himself."

Wade looked at his son as if seeing him for the first time. In an obvious attempt to control his irritation with the boy, he gripped his glass so tightly his knuckles whitened. "I think you already said that, son, and I told you I liked it."

"Aunt Savvy says it's awesome."

"Well, she's right, isn't she?" Reginald said, walking

back into the room, picking up Josh and hugging the boy to his broad chest. "The important thing is that I think Santa Claus will be able to find it."

"There is no Santa Claus," Josh replied, wearing his most grown-up expression.

"No!" Reginald expressed mock horror and both Josh and Savannah laughed. "I'm going into the kitchen to look for a snack—why don't you come, too?" he asked the boy.

Josh smiled but shook his head. "Not until I finish the tree," he said.

"Have it your way," the old man said, beaming at his grandson before heading into the kitchen.

Charmaine came down the stairs and entered the living room. "You did a wonderful job on the tree," she said to her son before noticing the hard line of Wade's jaw and the glittering challenge in Travis's eye. "Come on, Josh, I think it's time you went to bed," she suggested.

"Not yet."

"You heard your mother," Wade said, irritably waving the boy off. "Go upstairs."

Josh mutinously stood his ground. "But I'm not done fixin' the tree."

Wade tensed and his eyes turned cold. "It'll wait."

"Please?"

Oh, Josh, don't push it, Savannah thought, searching for a way to avoid the fight that was in the air.

"No, son! You heard me! Get your butt upstairs right now!"

"But, Dad—"

"Don't argue with me!" Wade snapped, color flooding his face, rage exploding in his eyes.

"It's just one night," Savannah protested, instinctively standing closer to Josh, as if to protect the boy. "We're almost finished, aren't we Josh?"

Wade's eyes were as frigid as ice. "This is none of your business, Savannah. Josh needs his sleep and I want to talk to Reginald and McCord alone." His stern gaze rested on the boy. "Now go upstairs and don't push it, Josh, or there just might not be a Christmas this year."

"Wade!" Charmaine whispered sharply, but held her tongue when her husband's eyes flashed angrily in her direction.

"There's always a Christmas," Josh said, holding his ground.

"Not if you're bad," Wade warned the boy.

"I'm *not* bad."

"We know that," Travis cut in. "You're a good kid, Josh. Don't let anyone tell you differently." He turned deadly eyes in Wade's direction, slicing through the blond man's angry veneer. "I'm sure you dad didn't quite mean it the way it came out."

Wade glanced around the room, obviously embarrassed, and then finished his drink in a quick swallow before quickly pouring another stiff shot. Though he attempted to control his anger, his seething temper was visible in the muscle working in his jaw. "Sure," he said unsteadily, smoothing his hair with quaking fingers. "You're a good kid, that's why you'll behave and go upstairs."

"Come on, Josh," Savannah said, offering a hand to lead him out of the room.

"Just butt out, Savannah," Wade exploded. His entire body was beginning to shake with the anger he could no longer contain. "Just butt the hell out of my son's life!"

Travis became rigid. "Benson—"

"This is between my son and me!" Wade growled, turning his furious gaze on Josh and spilling some of his drink. The sloshed alcohol infuriated him further. "Now march yourself up those stairs right now, young man!"

"No!"

"I mean it!" Wade's face was red with fury as he set his drink on a table and advanced toward the boy.

"Leave him alone," Travis warned, reaching forward. He caught hold of the back of Wade's jacket, but the incensed man wriggled free of Travis's grip.

"Wade, don't!" Charmain pleaded, hurrying forward, but she was too late.

"I hate you," Josh said, standing proudly before Wade's wrath.

"You need to learn to respect your father," Wade returned. "And I'll teach you!" Quick as a snake striking, Wade raised his hand and slapped the boy across the cheek. The blow had enough force to send Josh reeling into the Christmas tree.

Savannah gasped. Tinsel and glass ornaments clinked on the wobbling tree.

Travis was in time to stop the second blow from landing. He grabbed Wade by the back of the neck and spun him around. Every muscle in Travis's body was bunched, ready to strike, and the fire in his eyes burned with rage. "You dumb bastard," he growled, looking as if he wanted to kill Wade. His hands tightened powerfully over Wade's shoulders. "Leave the boy alone."

"This has nothing to do with you, McCord."

"It does as long as I'm here. Now leave him alone or I'll give you a little of your own."

"He's not your kid," Wade replied, whirling on his heel, fists clenched as he faced Josh again.

"I wish I was!" Josh shouted, his eyes filled with tears, one hand rubbing the bright red mark on his face. "I know you hate me and I wish I wasn't your son."

"You little—"

"Stop it!" Savannah warned, grabbing Josh and pulling him close to her. "Stop it, all of you!" She felt the warmth of the boy's tears against her blouse. "Josh, oh, Josh," she murmured, kissing his hair. "Don't you ever so much as come near him again," she said, her cold eyes clashing with Wade's.

"You've got no say in it. Josh is my son."

Josh held his cheek and glared upward at his father with open hatred in his young, tear-filled eyes. "You never wanted me," he said between sobs. "But that's okay, because I don't want you either!"

"Josh, no," Charmaine whispered, ignoring her husband and walking to the boy. When Wade took a step toward the child again, Charmaine whirled toward her husband. "Don't you touch him," she threatened. "I mean it, Wade, don't you ever lay one finger on my child!" She straightened and took Josh's small hand in hers. Though she was pale, she managed to square her shoulders and lift her chin proudly. "Come on, Josh. Let's go upstairs." Her lips were white when she added, "Daddy's just tired from his long flight!"

Josh looked at Savannah, and she offered him an encouraging smile. "I'll be up in a few minutes to read you a story...or maybe you can read one to me. Okay?"

"Okay," he whispered, his voice breaking.

Once Josh and Charmaine were out of the room, Savannah, her hands shaking with rage, advanced upon her brother-in-law. All of the worry and anger that had been building over the past few months erupted. "If you ever strike that child again, I'll call the police and have you brought up on charges," she warned, pointing a finger at her brother-in-law and wishing she could strangle him.

"Don't go off the deep end, Savannah," Wade said nervously. He finished his drink, walked to the far end of the room, behind the couch to the bar and poured himself a glass of brandy.

"I'll back her up," Travis said.

"The boy was out of line," Wade pointed out.

"He's just a child!" Savannah said. "A very confused child who feels unwanted and unloved!"

"A lot you know about it," Wade threw back at her.

"I know your boy better than you do," she said in a low voice, accusations forming in her eyes. "And I have enough common sense not to humiliate him in front of his family!"

"He was asking for it." Wade tossed back his drink, but some of his determination seemed to dissolve under Savannah's attack. When he lifted his glass to his lips his hands shook.

"You touch that kid again and I'll personally beat the hell out of you," Travis said calmly, walking over to the bar and pouring himself a drink. He leaned close to Wade, grabbed one of the lapels of Wade's suit and tightened his fingers around the polished fabric before smiling with wicked satisfaction. "And don't think I wouldn't enjoy every minute of it."

Wade had trouble swallowing his drink.

Reginald had walked back into the room and heard the last part of the conversation. "He will, you know," he said, nodding his agreement. "When Travis was about eighteen, I saw him beat the tar out of a kid a couple of years older and forty pounds heavier than he was. I'd listen to his threats if I were you."

"Now wait just a minute," Wade admonished, jerking at the knot of his tie and trying to repair some of his bruised dignity. "Don't tell me you're on his—" he hooked a thumb in Travis's direction "—side!"

"We're talking about my only grandson, Wade," Reginald pointed out as he sat uncomfortably on the corner of the stiff velvet couch. "I know Josh has a mouth on him, but you'd better find a way of dealing with it."

"I am."

"Poorly," Travis said, sipping his drink and smiling to himself.

"I didn't fly two thousand miles to hear about how I raise my kid," Wade said, straightening his vest.

"Then you shouldn't have made a public spectacle of yourself," Travis muttered.

Wade shifted his gaze around the room and cleared his throat. "I think it's time we got down to business."

"Not yet." Travis finished his drink and set it on the bar. "First I think I'll check on *your* kid."

With this pointed remark, he walked across the room to Savannah, took her hand and led her up the stairs.

"Bastard," Travis whispered, his jaw thrust forward and his gray eyes dark with anger.

"You'll get no argument from me," Savannah agreed. When they reached the top of the stairs, Savannah could hear Joshua sobbing in his room. "Oh, no," she said with a sigh. She hesitated before knocking softly on his door. "Josh?"

"Yeah?"

"Are you okay?"

Charmaine opened the door and though she was pale and her eyes were red, she managed a thin smile. "We're okay," she said.

"You're sure?" Savannah looked from her sister to Josh, who looked small and vulnerable beneath the covers of his bed.

"Yes."

"Yeah," Josh agreed, sniffing back his tears.

Savannah's heart went out to the brave boy. "You still want me to read you a story?"

Josh shrugged, but seemed to brighten. "Sure."

"Good. Just give me a few minutes, okay?"

"Okay."

Charmaine had come into the hall and Travis touched her lightly on the shoulder. "Will you be all right?"

She swallowed back her tears. "I think so."

"You don't have to take that kind of treatment, you know."

Rolling her eyes to the ceiling she visibly fought the urge to break down. "Are you speaking as a divorce lawyer?"

Travis shook his head and his shoulders slumped a little. "As a friend. There's just no reason to put up with any kind of abuse—mental or physical."

"It won't happen again," Charmaine insisted, though she couldn't meet Travis's concerned gaze. "Just let me have a little time with Josh alone. And...I'll be able to handle Wade."

"You're sure?" Savannah asked.

"Of course." Charmaine wiped away her tears and forced a trembling grin. "I've got that man wrapped around my little finger."

"Oh, Charmaine—"

"Shh. You go on. Maybe you two can find out what's eating at him."

I wish, Savannah thought hopelessly. She left Josh's room with the feeling of impending doom.

"Has it always been this bad?" Travis asked, placing a comforting arm around her.

"Never," she whispered. "I've never seen Wade hit Josh." She shuddered at the memory. "I didn't think it would come to a physical battle."

"You think it was the first time?"

"It better have been," she said, her anger resurfacing and her blue eyes sparking, "and it had damn well better be the last!"

When they entered the living room again, Wade was standing by the fireplace, one arm poised on the Italian marble of the mantel, his other holding a drink. He seemed somewhat calmer as he looked from Travis to Savannah and frowned.

"Okay, McCord," he said, glancing at Reginald before studying the amber liquid in his glass. "I guess I got out of line. I admit it." Shifting from one foot to the other, he sighed and shook his head. "I'm sorry."

"You're apologizing to the wrong person," Travis said coldly.

"Yes. Well, I'll take care of that. Later. Now, why aren't you running for governor?"

"I'm just not interested."

"You can't be serious."

"I am. I told you that before."

Wade pushed the hair from his eyes and looked to Reginald, who was seated in his favorite chair near the window.

"Why do you care?" Travis asked, leaning against the bar.

Savannah took a seat on the couch, not really wanting to be a part of the conversation, but not knowing how to avoid it.

"Because a lot of time, effort, and money has already been spent toward your candidacy."

"Maybe someone should have cleared all that with me."

"You were too busy—or don't you remember?—playing hero with that Eldridge decision. You were thinking about running. Anyway, that's what you told Reginald."

"And you just assumed that I would follow through."

"A natural assumption, I'd say."

"So you already started collecting campaign contributions, working with my partner on the books of the company and God only knows what else." Travis's jaw had hardened and his eyes glittered angrily.

"Reginald was counting on you."

"Were you?" Travis demanded, sliding a glance in the older man's direction.

"Seems a shame to throw away an opportunity like this," Reginald said. "And yes, I'd say I was counting on the fact that you'd run," he admitted, reaching into the pocket of his vest and withdrawing a pipe.

There was a tense silence in the room as Reginald lit the pipe.

"Even if I did run," Travis thought aloud, "there's a damned good chance that I wouldn't win in the primary, much less take the general election! Why's it so damned important?"

"Reginald has plans," Wade said.

"Well, maybe he should have let me in on them!" Travis walked over and stood in front of Reginald. "Ever since I was a seventeen-year-old kid, I've tried to please you, to the point that sometimes what I wanted got tangled up in what you wanted from me. Well, that just doesn't work anymore."

Reginald ran his fingers around the bowl of his pipe, glanced at Wade and scowled at the brightly lit tree.

Travis sighed loudly and rubbed the tired muscles at the base of his neck. "So, I think we should do something about all those contributions Willis Henderson and the rest of you took in my name. I expect them returned to the people who gave you the money. I want it all over by the end of the year. And I'll pay interest on any of the contributions."

"You don't understand—" Wade said.

"And I don't want to." Travis held Reginald's gaze. "I'm out of it. I don't like the feel of politics any better than I like the feel of corporate fighting, divorces, child-custody hearings or any of the rest of the bullshit that goes with being a lawyer."

"You liked the glory from the Eldridge case," Reginald remarked, puffing quietly on his pipe. The smell of the rich smoke wafted through the room.

"Even that went sour," Travis said, finishing his drink.

"But you can't just drop out," Reginald said, lifting a hand.

"I already have. Talk to Henderson. He knows that I'm serious." Travis stretched and set his glass on the mantel before leaning over the back of a velvet sofa and staring at the Christmas tree. "I don't know exactly why it was so damned important that I run for governor of this state, but I'm really not interested."

"I've worked a long time to see that day when you'd take office," Reginald whispered, as if to himself. Disillusion weighed heavily on the old man's face.

Savannah could almost feel her father's disappointment.

Travis smiled cynically. "I'd like to say that I'm sorry if I interrupted any of your plans, but I'm not. I don't like the way all of you have been doing things behind my back, and I've got to assume that even *if* I had managed to get elected, you'd still be calling the shots. I think it's time the people of the state got the kind of a governor they deserve, one that wants to serve them."

"That's horseshit and you know it," Wade said. "Idealistic words don't work in the real world."

Travis looked at Savannah. "And you thought I was cynical?" He laughed bitterly and shook his head. "That's all I have to say about it."

With those final words, he walked out of the room and into the foyer, where he took his coat off the hall tree. Savannah followed him.

"Come on, let's take a walk," Travis muttered. "I need the fresh air."

"I promised Josh that I'd read him a story." Reluctantly she started up the stairs, but stopped on the second step when he called to her.

"Savannah?"

Turning to face him, she read the passion smoldering in his steely gaze. He was standing at the base of the stairs, close enough to touch. Tense lines radiated from the corners of his mouth and eyes, sharpening his angular features.

The burning stare he gave her seared through her clothes and started her heartbeat racing uncontrollably. The thought flashed through her mind that now that Travis had told Reginald he was dropping out of the campaign, there was no reason for him to stay on the farm. Tonight might be their last together. The realization that he would soon be out of her life again settled heavily on Savannah's shoulders.

"I'll be down in a minute," she said, touching him lightly on the shoulder. "Will you wait for me?"

His mocking grin stretched over his face, softening his ruggedly handsome features. "I've waited nine years, lady, I can't see that a few more minutes will hurt." Then he placed his hand around her neck and drew her head to his, the warmth of his lips pressing urgently to hers in a kiss filled with such passion that she was left breathless, her lips throbbing with desire, her senses unbalanced.

I'm lost, she thought, closing her eyes and wrapping her arms around his neck. *I've never stopped loving him and I never will.*

His arms tightened around her, pulling her body against the taut muscles of his. She fit perfectly in his embrace, her softer contours yielding to the hard lines of his body. "Don't be long," he whispered against her ear.

"I won't," she promised. When she opened her eyes she was looking over Travis's shoulder toward the living room and Reginald was standing in the doorway, watching her eager embrace with a frown creasing his ruddy features. "I'll be right down."

Travis smiled and then walked out of the house, leaving Savannah on the second step, holding onto the rail to support her unsteady legs.

"That's a mistake, y'know," Reginald commented, drawing deeply on his pipe and walking into the foyer. "Gettin' involved with him again will only hurt you, Savannah."

So Reginald did know! Travis had been telling the truth! The knowledge left her exhilarated and disappointed all at once. Though Travis had been honest, her father had been lying to her for nine long years.

"I'm not a seventeen-year-old child any longer," she said, her fingers digging into the wood of the banister. From her position she could see Wade. He was lying on the couch, staring at the fire, his back to the foyer and apparently lost in his own drunken thoughts.

"Maybe not, but you're still my daughter." His bushy gray eyebrows arched. "And Travis McCord is not the man for you."

"Why not?"

"He's always loved Melinda."

Savannah paled and fought the urge to scream and shout that it didn't matter. Instead she said quietly, "But Melinda's gone."

"Maybe to you and me, but never to Travis. She was his first love, Savannah. You'd better face that."

"Why didn't you tell me that you knew I was involved with Travis?" she asked. "You've known for a long time."

Reginald smiled sadly and studied the bowl of his pipe. "Because it was over. He'd hurt you, but it was over."

"And now?"

Sighing, Reginald offered her a fatherly smile. "You're not right for each other. You want to live on the farm, work with the horses, get married and raise a family. But Travis, well, he's…different, cut out of another piece of cloth. He needs the glamour of the courtroom, the glitter of politics—"

"Didn't you hear a word he said?" she asked, incredulous that her father still saw Travis as a politician.

"He's just disillusioned right now. He's tired. Melinda's death and the Eldridge case, they took a lot out of him." Reginald's faded eyes glimmered. "That'll change. You'll see."

"I don't think so."

"Ah, but you have a habit of misreading him, don't you? You thought he and Melinda had broken up nine years ago."

Savannah came down the two steps to the foyer so that she could stand level with her father. "Travis thought she was pregnant," Savannah said. "You backed her up."

"I believed her."

"It was a lie."

Reginald frowned. "I don't know about that—is that what he told you? Well, yes, I suppose he would." The older man sighed loudly. "You have to remember, Savannah, that nobody put a gun to his head and told him he had to marry Melinda, baby or no. He married her of his own volition and they managed to stay married for nearly nine years. Nine years! This day and age that's quite a record.

"Oh, I'll grant you that he was attracted to you. Always has been. But it's just a physical thing—the difference between lust and love, a mistress and a wife." He patted her gently on the arm when he read the stricken look in her eyes. "I'm only looking out for your best interests, y'know."

"Are you, Dad?" she said, barely controlling her anger. "I wonder. The least you could have done is tell me that you knew about Travis and me."

Reginald shrugged. "Why? What would have been the point? Your affair with him was over and he was married. If you're smart, you'll let well enough alone."

"When are you going to understand that you can't manipulate my life any more than you can force him into running for governor?" she said.

Reginald looked suddenly weary. "I'm not trying to manipulate you, Savannah. I'm just trying to help you make the right decisions."

"And the right one would be to forget about Travis?"

"I just don't want to see you hurt again," he whispered, brushing her cheek with his lips. "Isn't one rocky marriage in this family enough?"

"But you and Wade—"

"Are good business partners, don't get me wrong," Reginald said, looking into the living room where Wade was still draped over the couch. "But he should never have married Charmaine and he's a lousy father to his son." He offered her a tight smile. "Just use your head, Savannah. You've got a good brain, don't let it get all confused by your heart."

Reginald turned and went into his study, and Savannah tried to ignore his advice as she climbed the stairs and walked down the short hallway to Josh's room.

Six

The security lights cast an ethereal blue sheen on the white ground and surrounding buildings.

Travis was waiting by the stables. His tall, dark figure stood out against the stark white walls and snow-covered roof of the barns and snow-laden trees.

Savannah pushed her father's warnings out of her mind and approached him, shivering a little from the cold.

"So how was Josh?" he asked once she was in earshot.

"All right, I guess."

"You're not sure?"

She shook her head, disturbing the snowflakes resting in her ebony hair. "How would you feel if your father had humiliated you in front of the rest of the family?"

"Not so great."

"You got it," she said with a sigh. "Josh is definitely feeling 'not so great.'"

Travis took her hand, wrapped his fingers around hers, and pushed their entwined hands into the pocket of his jacket. "You can't solve all the problems of the world, you know."

"Is that what they taught you in law school?"

"No." Shaking his head, he led her around the building to the overgrown path leading to the lake. "Believe it or not, I learned a lot of things on my own."

"And I don't want to solve the problems of the world, just those of one little boy."

"He's not your son."

"I know," she whispered. "That's the problem."

"One of them," Travis agreed.

Frosty branches leaned across the trail, brushing her face and clothes with their brittle, icy leaves as she walked. Both pairs of boots crunched in the new-fallen snow.

The mud at the bank of the lake was covered with ice, and the naked trees surrounding the black body of water looked like twisted sentinels guarding a private sanctuary— a sanctuary where a feeble love had flickered to life nine years before.

Travis stopped near the old oak where he had been sitting so long ago. "It's been a long time," he said, staring at the inky water.

The pain of the past embraced her. "Too long to go back."

"You were the most beautiful woman I'd ever seen," he said. "And it scared me. It scared the hell out of me." He shook his head in wonder at the vivid memory. "I'd just spent two days trying to convince myself that you were off limits, barely seventeen, Reginald's youngest daughter, for God's sake! And then you walked out of the lake, without a stitch of clothes on, your eyes filled with challenge." He leaned one shoulder against the oak. "It did me in. All of my resolve went right out the window."

"You were drunk," she reminded him.

"I honestly don't think it would have mattered." He wrapped his free arm around her and traced the curve of her jaw with his finger. His hand was cold but inviting, and she shivered.

His gray eyes delved into hers, noticing the way the snow clung to her thick, curling lashes. "I was hooked, Savannah. I didn't want to be. God knows, I fought it, but I was hooked." He smiled cynically and added, "I still am."

When his chilled lips touched hers she heard a thousand warnings in her mind, but ignored them all. The feel of his body pressed against hers was as drugging as it had been nine years before, in the summer, in that very spot.

Strong arms held her, moist lips claimed hers and she could smell and taste the man she had never quit loving. She felt pangs of regret as well as happiness build inside.

Lifting his head, he gazed into her eyes. "I want you to stay with me tonight," he whispered, his warm breath caressing her face. "You don't have to promise me the future; just spend one night with me and we'll take it from there."

The difference between lust and love, a mistress and a wife.

"Travis—"

"Just say yes."

Delving into his kind eyes, she swallowed and blinked back her tears. "Yes."

Travis took her hand again and led her back down the path toward the buildings of the farm. He was staying in the loft over the garage, and Savannah didn't argue when he helped her climb the stairs to Charmaine's studio.

After shutting the door behind them, Travis rubbed his hands together and blew on them for warmth. The temperature in the dark room was barely above freezing; Savannah could see her breath misting in the half-light.

Savannah stared at her sister's private domain. Pale light from the reflection of the security lamps on the snow filtered through the windows. Charmaine's draped artwork was scattered around the room, looking like lifeless ghosts propped in the corners of the studio.

"It's changed a little in nine years," Travis observed, not bothering to switch on the lights.

Originally the second story over the garage had been one large apartment, and Travis had lived in the three sloped-ceilinged rooms whenever he was on the farm. A few years before, Charmaine had converted what had been his living room and kitchen into an artist's studio.

The bedroom was still in the back. Travis had been using it since he arrived at the farm and now, in the darkness of the frigid night, he tugged on Savannah's hand and pulled her down the short hallway to what was left of his quarters.

Savannah hadn't been in the room in years. It held too many memories of Travis, too much pain. She leaned against the tall post of the bed and felt the old, angry deception stir in her heart. Looking into his night-darkened eyes she wanted to trust him, but his betrayal was as fresh as it had been on the night he'd left her all those years ago.

"Try to forget the past," he said, as if reading her mind. His hand reached forward and he cupped her chin. "Trust me again."

Savannah's breath caught in her throat when she felt his arms surround her and tasted the warmth of his lips against hers. She told herself to push him away, pay attention to her father's advice, but she couldn't. Instead, her pulse quickened and her blood heated with desire.

He groaned when she responded. "We don't have any more excuses, Savannah," he whispered against her hair. "Tonight there's nothing and no one to stand in our way."

And we're running out of time, she added silently to herself. *Tomorrow you'll probably leave.* Desperation gripped her heart and she wound her arms around his neck, returning the passion of his kiss with the fierce need of a woman who'd been held away from the man she'd loved for far too long.

She felt the warmth of his mouth against her lips, her eyes, her cheeks. His tongue slipped through her parted lips to search and dance with its anxious mate.

His hard body, covered by straining, bothersome clothing, pushed against hers, and she felt the volatile tension of taut tendons, corded muscles and unbridled desire pressing against her flesh. His lips caressed her, his fingers explored and stroked her neck and face.

"I've waited a long time for you," he said, anxiously unbuttoning her coat and pushing it off her shoulders to fall to the floor.

"And I for you," she agreed, her voice low, her fingers working at his clothes.

Slowly the cloth barriers slid to the floor, until finally

there was nothing to separate their bodies but the pain of nine lost years.

He stood before her, a naked man silhouetted in the night. His hand reached upward and his fingers shook a little as he touched one dark-tipped breast.

Savannah quivered beneath his touch. The gentle probe was light at first, a sensual stroking of the breast that made her knees weaken and the warmth within her turn liquid. "Travis," she whispered.

"Shh." His fingers continued to work their magic and Savannah leaned backward against the cold polished wood of the four-poster. Travis pressed harder against her, the warmth of his body contrasting to the smooth, cool post at her back.

His mouth was hungry, his tongue plundering as he tasted the soft skin at the base of her throat, and one of his strong hands reached downward to fit over her buttocks and pull her against his thighs. Hot, tense muscles fitted against her softer flesh, melting away the memory of betrayal.

His hands molded her body as lovingly as those of a sculptor shaping clay, and Savannah's doubts escaped into the night. "I've never wanted a woman the way I want you," he admitted, kneeling and kissing first one ripened breast and then the other. The wet impression left on her nipples made the dark points stand erect, as he stroked them with his thumbs. "God, you're beautiful," he whispered, his breath fanning her navel.

Involuntarily her abdomen tightened, and when he rimmed her navel with his tongue, she moaned and her knees sagged. She would have slid to the floor, but he caught her, forcing her back to the bedpost as he kissed the soft skin of her abdomen and hips. Her fingers twined in his thick hair and dampness broke out upon her skin. The ache deep within her became more intense. She was twisting and writhing with an emptiness that only he could fill.

"Please," she whispered somewhere between pain and ecstasy. "Travis...please..."

"What do you want?" he asked, his tongue and teeth tantalizing her skin.

"Everything."

When he picked her up, letting her knees drape over one arm while cradling her head with the other, she couldn't resist—wouldn't, even if she had the strength. Black hair spilled over his arm as he gently placed her on the bed. The patchwork quilt was ice-cold against her back and goose bumps rose on her flesh, but the fire in her eyes burned brightly.

"I'm glad you decided to stay with me tonight," he admitted, looking into her blue gaze and tracing the pout on her lips with one finger.

Trembling with anticipation, Savannah's fingers wrapped around the back of his neck and she pulled his head to hers. Her eager, open lips fused to his.

The weight of his body fell over her, flattening her breasts with the hard muscles of his chest. His dark, swirling hair rubbed erotically against her nipples. A soft sheen of sweat oiled the corded muscles of his back and chest.

Savannah moaned as Travis's legs entwined with hers. She felt the exquisite torment of his tongue and teeth playing with her nipples before his lips once again claimed hers and he positioned his body above her.

"I love you, Savannah," he admitted, closing his eyes against the truth. "I always have."

Moving below him, she stared into the steely depths of his eyes as he slowly pressed her knees apart and entered her. She felt the heat of his body begin to fill her as his strokes, slow at first, increased in tempo until she was forced to move with him, join him in the ancient dance of love.

She clung to him, tasted his sweat, stared into his fathomless gray eyes as he rocked them both with the fever of his passion until at last the shimmering lights in her mind exploded into a thousand tiny fragments of that very same light and she nearly screamed his name. A moment later he stiffened and fell upon her, cradling her shoulders and resting his head on her breasts.

"God, I love you," he said, still fondling her breast before falling asleep in her arms.

Do. Oh, please, Travis do love me, let me believe you, she silently prayed as tears burned her eyes. *Tell me it's more than just one final night together!*

She listened to the regular tempo of his breathing, thought she should return to the house, but created a thousand excuses to stay with him, and fell asleep entwined in his arms.

Hours later, Savannah awakened. One of Travis's tanned arms was draped protectively across her breasts. She rolled over to kiss him and found that he was already awake and staring at her.

"Good morning," he drawled, his gray eyes delving deep into hers, and his fingers pushing the tousled black hair from her eyes.

Savannah smiled and stretched. "Good morning yourself."

She tried to toss off the covers and hop out of bed, but Travis restrained her by placing his hands over her wrists. "Where do you think you're going?" he asked.

"I realize that you're on vacation, early retirement, or whatever else you want to call it," she teased, "but the rest of us poor working stiffs have jobs to do."

He chuckled to himself. "Your father's back; you can relax."

"Not quite yet," she said, trying to wriggle free, but his hands continued to hold her down and she gave up with an exasperated sigh. "What's so important?" she asked.

"I think we should clear up a few things before you high-tail it out of here."

"Such as?"

"Like what we're going to do if you're pregnant."

Disappointment burned in her heart. There were no options as far as she was concerned; she would bear Travis's child and raise it—alone if she had to. Unfortunately, she didn't even have to worry. "I'm not."

He smiled seductively. "Too early to be sure?"

She did a quick calculation in her head. "Let's just say it would be highly unlikely, counselor."

"Oh?"

"I work with brood mares every day, remember? I think I can figure out when I'm able to conceive and when I'm not. Last night we were lucky."

"Lucky? Well, maybe," he said with a frown.

"Now, unless you have something that can't wait, I've got to get up."

"But that's the problem, don't you see?" he teased, still holding her wrists to her sides and sliding his naked body erotically over hers. "There is something that can't wait, something bothering me a lot."

Her breath caught in her throat. "Travis—"

He pulled her hands over her head and positioned himself over her, softly kissing her lips while rubbing against her.

Savannah found it impossible to think. The warm sensations cascading over her body made everything else seem unimportant.

"I really should go to work—"

"In time," he promised, dipping his head and kissing her gently on the swell of her breasts. He watched in fascination as her nipples hardened expectantly and the fires deep within her began to rage. "In time..."

Travis had fallen back to sleep and Savannah was finally able to slip from the bed, throw on her clothes and head downstairs. It was nearly dawn, sometime after six, and Lester would be arriving at the farm soon.

As quietly as a cat slinking through the night, Savannah sneaked out of the room, through the studio, and down the stairs outside of the garage. The snow had quit falling, but the sky overhead was threatening to spill more powdery flakes onto the earth. She smiled when she noticed that the double set of footprints that she and Travis had made was nearly covered. Snow must have fallen most of the night.

Maybe we'll have a white Christmas this year, she thought with a smile as she pushed her hands into the pockets of her suede jacket and headed toward the stables. *Josh would love it!* This much snow was nearly unheard of in this part of the country.

Her spirits lifted as she walked through the backyard. Spending a night alone with Travis and listening to his words of love had made her think there was a chance that all would be right with the world. Perhaps loving him was the right thing to do, she thought. Even if his words of love had been whispered at the height of passion, he hadn't been forced to say them. So why fight it? She almost had herself convinced that the barriers of the past nine years had been destroyed in one night. Almost.

Humming to herself, she let Archimedes out of the back porch and started on her early-morning rounds. Archimedes bounded along beside her, romping in the snow and breaking a trail in the soft white powder.

Savannah's breath clouded in the air, and her boots crunched through the five-inch layer of snow. Intermittent flakes fell from the sky and clung to her shoulders and hair as she headed toward the stables.

The brood mares, their swollen bellies protruding prominently, snorted and nickered when she arrived. After checking the water and the feed of each of the mares, she walked back outside and crossed the parking lot to the brick path that led to the stallion barn. "That's odd," she thought, noticing the set of footprints leading to the barn from the front of the house. The prints were smaller than her own and softened by a fine dusting of snow.

"What is?" Travis's voice broke through the still morning air.

Savannah nearly jumped out of her skin and turned to face him. He was walking toward her from the direction of the garage. A Stetson was pulled low over his eyes and his hands were jammed into the pockets of his jeans. "Boy, I could use a pair of gloves," he muttered.

"I thought you were still asleep."

"I was, until someone rattled around and made so much noise that I woke up."

"What!" She'd been as quiet as a mouse. She looked into his eyes and saw the sparkle of amusement in his intriguing gaze. "Give me a break."

He leaned over and kissed the tip of her nose. "I missed you, Savvy."

Savannah's heart jumped. *God, how she loved this man.* "Good, I could use the company, as well as the muscle power. You can help me feed the stallions."

"I can think of better things to do."

Savannah laughed merrily. It felt good to throw off the chains of the past. "Not right now, mister," she said. "I told you; I've got work to do." They walked together in the snow. "Speaking of which, are you going to tell me what you were doing in Dad's study last night? Wade nearly fell through the floor when I told him you were in the den."

"I'll bet," Travis muttered, hunching his shoulders against another blast of arctic wind. "I just wanted to do some checking."

"On what?"

"The books."

"Of the farm?"

He nodded and a shiver of dread slid down Savannah's spine. "Why?"

"Curiosity." He kept his eyes to the ground and noticed the other set of tracks in the snow.

"Whose are these?" he asked, then continued without pausing, "Lester's usually the first one around, but they're too small for him." He frowned. "And look at the tread. Definitely not boots. More like running shoes."

Savannah's heart nearly stopped beating. Snowflakes clung to her ebony hair, and her cheeks were flushed from the cold. Her blue eyes darkened with dread in spite of the light from the security lamps and the first hint of dawn.

"Like Josh's shoes?" she whispered.

"Like Josh's," Travis agreed as his eyes followed the arrow-straight path of the footsteps that led from the house to the stallion barn. The crease in his forehead deepened.

A premonition of disaster tightened Savannah's chest and made it hard to breathe. "But what would he be doing here this early?" she asked, as they approached the barn.

"That's what we're about to find out."

Travis opened the door to the barn, flipped on the lights, and began striding down the double row of stalls. Savannah walked more slowly, her eyes scanning the interior of the barn.

"Mornin' fellas," she said, patting Night Magic fondly on his nose as Travis walked down the parallel row of stalls. "It doesn't look like anyone's here," she said. "Just like yesterday morning. Lester heard a noise, but no one was there."

"Strange, isn't it?"

"Creepy," she agreed.

Several of the younger stallions snorted their contempt, while Night Magic whinnied softly. "You're a pushover, aren't you?" Savannah asked, petting the coal-black muzzle again.

Travis stopped at the far end of the stalls. "Where's Mystic?" he asked.

"What do you mean? He's here. The end stall—" The meaning of his question suddenly struck home and Savannah ran down the length of the barn, her boots clattering against the concrete floor, her heart thudding wildly in her ribcage. Once near Travis she stared into the empty box and fear took a stranglehold of her throat.

"Where else could he be?" Travis demanded.

"Nowhere...." Her heart thudding with dread, she slowly went down the double aisle and counted the stallions. All seven stallions and colts were in their proper stalls. Except for Mystic. He was gone, vanished into the night.

"Didn't Joshua say he could ride Mystic?" Travis asked.

Savannah had all but lost her voice. "But he wouldn't... couldn't take him." She leaned against the stall door for support.

"Why not?"

"He's just a boy—"

"An angry, humiliated boy."

Fear tightened her chest. "Oh, God. I don't think Josh would take off like that. Not in the middle of a snowstorm. Not on *Mystic*, for God's sake." But even to her own ears, her protests sounded weak.

"Wade pushed Josh into a corner last night," Travis said. "I know, I've been there myself." He started walking down the row of boxes again, his fists balled at his sides, his jaw jutted forward angrily, and Savannah was reminded of the rebel Travis had been as a teenager. "I'll kill him," Travis swore. "So help me, if that boy is hurt I'll kill Benson and be glad to do it!"

"Wait! Before we go to the house, I think we should check the other barns and the paddocks. Maybe Mystic got out by himself."

"Do you really believe that?" Travis asked, his anger flushing his face.

"Look, I just want to make sure, that's all," she said, nearly screaming at him. "You check the other barns and I'll call Lester."

Travis walked out of the building and headed for the main stables. Savannah used the extension in the stallion barn and dialed Lester's number. While it rang she tapped her fingers nervously on the wall and eyed the interior of the barn.

"Answer the phone," she whispered on the fourth ring.

"Hello?"

"Lester!" she said with relief.

"I was just on my way over," the trainer replied. "What's up?"

"It's Mystic. He's not in the stallion barn."

"What!"

"He's gone."

The old man whistled softly and then swore. "I locked him up myself last night."

"You're sure?"

"Course I am," Lester snapped.

Savannah's knees went weak and she leaned against the wall for support.

"Any other clues?"

"Just another set of tracks coming to the barn. Smaller ones. Maybe Josh might know something about this."

"Well, ask him."

"I will," she promised. *If he's here.*

"I'll be over in about twenty minutes. Have you told Reginald what happened yet?"

"No. Travis is still checking to make sure Mystic didn't get in with the mares or yearlings by mistake...."

"I shut him up myself, missy. If he's gone, it's because someone let him out."

Someone like Joshua, Savannah thought miserably.

Travis came back into the barn just as she hung up the phone. His expression was grim, the set of his jaw determined. "No luck," he said walking back to Mystic's stall.

"Lester locked him up himself."

"Then it looks like Josh took him." Travis slid open the door at the opposite end of the barn. It was used rarely, only for grain delivery. "And this confirms it." In the freshly fallen snow were two sets of tracks: those of a horse and those matching the tracks at the other end of the barn.

"Oh, God," Savannah whispered. Her small fists clenched when she saw the trampled snow and mud where the horse had shied. At that point, near the fence, the rider had to have mounted Mystic. And then the hoofprints became a single file that led through the gate, across the field and toward the hills. "He'll freeze," she whispered, tears beginning to build in her eyes and fear clenching her heart.

"Not if I can help it," Travis said. "Let's go."

After securing the stallion barn, they half ran back to the house. Savannah didn't bother taking off her boots as she mounted the stairs and raced to Joshua's room. She knocked quietly once and then again when there was no answer.

"Josh!" she called through the door.

Charmaine's door opened. Her dark hair was mussed, her eyes still blurred with sleep. "Savannah, what's going on?"

"I don't know," Savannah replied, her hand on the doorknob. Until she was sure of the facts, she didn't want to worry her older sister.

"Savannah?" Charmaine whispered, her eyes widening.

Ignoring her sister, Savannah opened the door to Josh's room and sank against the wall when she saw that the room was empty. The covers of the bed were strewn on the floor. A quick check in the closet indicated that Josh's jacket was missing, as were his favorite shoes and hat.

Charmaine walked into the room. "Where's Josh?" she asked, nearly choking with fear. "Where is he?"

"I don't know," Savannah admitted. Her shoulders slumped in defeat as she thought about the child braving the elements. "But we think he took Mystic."

"*Mystic!*" Charmaine leaned against the dresser for support and knocked over a stack of comic books. "What do you mean?"

"That's a good question," Travis said. "All we know is that Mystic is missing. There're small footsteps from the house to the stallion barn and then it looks like someone took Mystic from his stall, led him outside and rode him into the hills."

"Not Josh," Charmaine whispered, shaking her head. "He wouldn't have done that. He's got to be here on the farm somewhere. Someone else let the horse out of his stall or rode him away but Josh is here.... He's just hiding...."

"He told me he could ride Mystic," Savannah said.

"What the hell is going on here?" Wade demanded, running his fingers through his unruly hair as he entered the room. "Where's the boy?"

"They think Josh is missing," Charmaine whispered miserably.

"Missing?"

"Gone, Wade." She gestured feebly toward Savannah and Travis. "They think he took Mystic."

"Josh took Mystic? That's impossible. That demon of a horse won't let anyone near him...." Wade's angry words died as he surveyed the tense faces in the room. "My God, you're serious, aren't you?" The sleep left his eyes.

"Dead serious," Travis muttered.

"I don't believe it. He's just here somewhere," Charmaine insisted, looking frantically around the boy's room. "Josh? Josh!"

Travis caught her by the arm. "We're pretty certain about this. Otherwise we wouldn't have alarmed you."

Charmaine jerked her arm free. "It's freezing outside. Josh wouldn't go out in the cold...not away from the house. And he wouldn't take the horse...." The reality of the situation finally caught up with her. "Oh, God, it just can't be." She moaned, letting her face fall into her hands and finally releasing the sobs she had been fighting since entering the room.

"Listen, I'll call the sheriff," Savannah offered.

"The sheriff!" Charmaine was horrified. "What good will that do?" Her pale face was terror-stricken and she lashed out at the first person she saw. "Savannah, if what you're saying is true, this is all your fault, you know. You're the one who took him riding, you're the one who planted all those damned horse-loving ideas in his head, you're the one who let him think about riding that horrible horse!"

Travis stood between Charmaine and Savannah. "We're not getting anywhere by pointing fingers! We've got to find Josh."

"We are talking about my son," Charmaine said, tears

sliding down her white cheeks. "My son, dammit! He's gone!"

"This is insane," Wade said, shaking his head as if trying to shake out a bad dream. "Josh wouldn't take Mystic. Why in the world would a boy want a racehorse?"

"Maybe he thought it was the only friend he had," Savannah said, fighting her own hot tears.

"You're wrong!" Wade said, pacing the small room and rubbing the golden stubble on his chin. "Josh is probably just pulling one of his rebellious stunts. No doubt he's hiding somewhere on the farm and having a good laugh over this."

"He's only a nine-year-old boy," Charmaine wailed.

"That you mortified last night!" Savannah said, staring at Wade through tear-glazed eyes.

"Oh give me a break," Wade mumbled, but he was sweating. "Charmaine's right, you know, Savannah. You've been filling that boy's head with all sorts of idiotic ideas. You should never have encouraged Josh to have anything to do with the horses. Especially Mystic. If anything happens to my boy, I'll hold you personally responsible!"

Travis's eyes glinted like newly forged steel. "And if anything happens to either Savannah or Josh, you'll have to answer to me, Benson," he threatened, his voice becoming ruthless. "Now let's quit arguing about it and get to work. Savannah, you call the sheriff. Charmaine will stay here with Virginia in case anyone calls. The rest of us will start searching the farm by following the tracks as far as we can."

"I'm coming with you," Savannah insisted, trying to pull herself together.

"Not on your life. You stay and wait for Lester and the rest of the hands. Someone's got to run the farm and take care of Charmaine. Besides, I want you to talk to that repairman, make sure that the broken wire was just a case of the alarm wearing out. If we get moving now, there's a good chance that we can catch up to the boy by noon."

Travis was walking out of the room and toward the stairs. Wade was only two steps behind him. Before Travis descended, he turned to Wade and his cold eyes bored through Josh's father. "I think you'd better tell Reginald what's happened—that he's missing a valuable colt as well as his only grandson."

Wade nodded curtly and walked toward Reginald's room.

Savannah had followed Travis and Wade. At the top of the stairs she brushed her tears aside and held her chin defiantly while holding Travis's severe glare. "I'm coming with you," she announced. "Josh is my nephew."

"No way, lady."

"You can't talk me out of it."

Travis let out an exasperated sigh and hurried down the stairs. Savannah was on his heels. "Use your head, Savannah. You're needed here," Travis said.

"But I know Josh; I know where he might go."

"We'll find him. You stay with your sister. Whether she knows it or not, she needs you."

"I can't stay here! Not while Josh is out...wherever!"

Travis looked up at the ceiling. "Don't we have enough problems without you trying to add to them?"

"I only want to help."

"Then stay here and be sensible!" he snapped before turning to face her and seeing the tears in her eyes. He wrapped his arms around her and sighed. "Listen, Savannah you're the only one on this whole damned farm that I can count on. Stay here. Help your mother and the police."

"But—"

"And quit blaming yourself! If Joshua left it was because of his father."

"I did encourage him to take an interest in the horses," she whispered, her throat raw.

"Because you're his friend." Travis's face softened. "And right now, Josh needs all the friends he can get. So hang in here, okay? Help me."

The sound of Lester's pickup spurred Travis into action.

He released Savannah and went outside. A few minutes later, Wade and a pale-looking Reginald, who was still stuffing his shirt into his pants, joined Travis and Lester. The men formed a search party on horseback and in four-wheel-drive vehicles.

It had begun to snow heavily again, showering the valley with white powder and making it impossible to see any distance. Finding a nine-year-old and a runaway horse would be difficult.

Savannah stood near the fence by the stallion barn, her arms huddled around herself. She felt absolutely helpless.

"I'll see you later," Travis promised as he climbed into the saddle on Jones. The chestnut gelding swished his tail and flattened his ears impatiently.

Travis's plan was to follow Mystic's footprints on horseback. Reginald and Wade were driving ahead in a Jeep, but Travis insisted on taking the horse just in case Josh rode Mystic through the trees and the vehicle was unable to follow the Thoroughbred's prints in the snow.

Lester and Johnny, one of the stable hands, were searching the other areas of the farm in a pickup. They were hoping to come across Josh's hiding place...if he had one.

Then Travis and the others were gone.

The sounds of engines rumbling up the hills made Savannah shiver inside and she said a silent prayer for the lost boy. *Come home, Josh*, she thought desperately *Please come home!*

Savannah watched the tall man on horseback for as long as she could. Travis rode past the stallion barn, through the enclosed field and up the hillside, carefully following the slowly disappearing tracks in the snow and the roaring Jeep.

Standing on the fence, Savannah squinted and stared after him until he finally vanished from her sight.

With cold dread settling in her heart, she climbed off the fence, turned back to the house and worked up the courage to face Charmaine and call the sheriff.

Seven

Savannah leaned on her father's desk, closing her eyes while trying to hear the voice on the other end of the phone. Listening was difficult as the wires crackled and the background noise in the sheriff's department was nearly as loud as the deputy's voice. Deputy Smith sounded weary, as if he'd been on the job all night, and the words he gave Savannah were far from encouraging.

"It's not that I don't appreciate your problem, Ms. Beaumont," he said in a sincere voice, "and we'll do what we can. But you have to understand that the storm is causing a lot of problems for other people as well as you folks. Several cities are without power and I don't have to tell you about the conditions of the roads. We've got two trucks jackknifed on the freeway and traffic backed up for six miles." He paused for a minute and Savannah heard him talking in a muffled voice to another officer. He was back to her within a minute. "We'll send someone out to the farm as soon as possible."

"Thank you," Savannah said before hanging up the phone and feeling the energy drain from her body. *So Travis and the rest of the men couldn't count on anyone but themselves.* Travis. She should have ignored his anger and logic and gone with him. At least that way she would feel as if she were accomplishing something, doing something useful.

She picked up a cold cup of coffee, took a sip, frowned and set the cup back on the desk.

Taking in a steadying breath, she dialed all of the neighbors within a three-mile radius of the breeding farm. It was another waste of time. No one had seen Josh or Mystic.

"Well, what did you expect?" she asked herself after hanging up and staring through the window at the white flakes falling from a leaden sky. "Oh, Josh, where are you?" She stood transfixed at the window of the study and watched with mounting dread as the small silvery flakes continued to fall. Maybe it was a good sign that none of the neighbors had seen Josh. Maybe he was still on Beaumont property. *And maybe the neighbors were just too busy taking care of themselves in the snowstorm to notice the boy or his horse,* she thought grimly.

Pushing the hair from her eyes, she tried not to think about either Travis or Josh, but found it impossible. No matter what she did to try to keep busy, her thoughts always returned to Travis. He'd been in the storm on horseback for nearly two hours, following a mere shadow of a trail in the snow. The longer the snow continued to fall, the less able he would be to track Mystic. God, how long had Josh been braving the elements? Was he still on the horse or was he curled up in the snow freezing to death?

Tears pricked the back of her eyes, and she leaned her head against the cool panes of the window. "Use your head, sport," Savannah whispered, as if the boy were standing next to her instead of somewhere outdoors in the cold. "Use your head and come home."

Shaking off her fears and fighting back tears, Savannah went into the kitchen and made coffee. When she let Archimedes into the house from the back porch, she eyed the snow. The storm hadn't let up and white powder was drifting against the sides of the stables and garage.

Somewhere out in the near blizzard Josh was alone. And so was Travis. Savannah shivered as she came back inside. Archimedes, from his favorite position under the kitchen table, thumped his tail against the floor.

"You're not worried, are you?" she asked the dog, who lifted his head and cocked his ears expectantly.

She prayed when the lights flickered twice. If the power went out now, running the farm would be nearly impossible. She switched on the small black-and-white television in the kitchen. After listening to the news for a few minutes and discovering that the intensity of the storm wasn't about to let up, she snapped off the set, poured two cups of coffee, put them on a tray and carried them upstairs to Virginia's room.

Knocking softly on the bedroom door, Savannah entered. Virginia was sitting in the bed, her pale hands folded over her lap, her eyes fastened on the floor-to-ceiling window at the far end of the room. Through the glass was a view of the hills surrounding the farm.

"Any news?" Virginia asked quietly.

Savannah shook her head. "Not yet."

With a loud sigh, Virginia slumped lower into the mound of pillows supporting her back. "What about the police?"

"I called the sheriff's department. They're pretty busy right now."

"Yes, I imagine so," Virginia said distractedly. One of her hands lifted and she fingered a small cross hanging from a gold chain at her throat. "And the storm. Who would have thought that we'd get so much snow? It's unusual.... Can't the sheriff come over?"

"The deputy said he would send a man over as soon as possible."

"For what good it will do—"

"Mom," Savannah gently reproached.

Virginia sighed before stiffening her shoulders. "I know, I know. And I haven't given up hope. Really. I...I just can't help but think about Josh and that horse lost in the mountains or God only knows where...." Her voice faded and she swallowed hard. "He's such a dear, dear boy."

"I won't argue with that," Savannah said kindly. "But you know that Travis will find him." Her own throat was nearly swollen shut and the conviction in her voice wavered, so she changed the subject. "Here, I brought you some coffee. What about something to eat?"

Virginia waved the cup aside. "Not hungry," she mumbled shaking her head against the pillows.

"You're sure?"

"Yes."

"Okay. Suit yourself." Savannah left the cup and saucer on the night table near her mother. Then she took the remaining cup of coffee and stood. "I'm going to see how Charmaine is, and then I'll check on the horses. If you need anything, I'll be back in about an hour."

"I won't need a thing," Virginia whispered. "But as for Charmaine..." Pain crossed Virginia's eyes and she raised her hand in a feeble gesture. "Maybe it would be best if you let her alone—let her sort out her feelings."

"She still blames me," Savannah deduced, leaning a shoulder against the wall.

"She's not thinking clearly. Josh is the only thing she has in her life. Even Wade..." Virginia lifted her shoulders. "Well, it's different when you have a child of your own."

"I think I'd better see her."

"Just remember that she's under a horrible strain."

"I will." Savannah started down the hallway to Charmaine's room, but stopped when she came to the open door of Josh's bedroom and saw her sister. Charmaine, still in her bathrobe, was seated cross-legged on the braided rug and softly crying to herself.

"How about a cup of coffee or some company?" Savannah offered, setting the cup on the dresser before folding her arms over her chest and leaning a shoulder against the doorjamb.

"No thanks."

"Charmaine, I know what you're going through—"

Savannah's sister took in a long, deep breath, as if trying to calm herself. "You know what I'm going through," she repeated incredulously. "Do you? You couldn't!" Charmaine lifted red-rimmed eyes and stared at Savannah as if she wanted to kill her. "How could you understand—you don't even have a child!"

Savannah felt the sting of the bitter words, but tried to rise above Charmaine's anger. "But I love Josh. Very much."

Charmaine's throat worked convulsively. "Too much. You treat him as if he were your child, not mine!"

"I just wanted to be his friend."

"Like hell!" Charmaine tossed her head back angrily and her dark hair fell around her shaking shoulders. "You tried to be his mother, Savannah. And you allowed him, *encouraged* him to hang around the horses."

"The same way we were encouraged when we were children."

Charmaine just shook her head, and tears tracked down her cheeks. "You don't understand, do you? Because you don't have a child. Those horses are dangerous, and Mystic...Mystic, he's so mean-tempered that even Lester has trouble handling him. And you let a boy, *my* boy work with him. Now look what's happened. He's out there, with that demon of a horse, probably hurt...maybe...maybe dead. All because you wanted to be his friend." She began sobbing again, raking her fingers through her hair in frustration.

"Have you ever thought that the reason Josh ran away was because of his argument with Wade?"

"Ran away!" Charmaine repeated, her face draining of color. "Ran away?" She shook her head. "Josh did *not* run away! Sure, he was mad at his father, but he just took the horse for a ride, that's all. He didn't have any intention of running away!" Charmaine's fingers trembled when they cinched the belt of her robe around her waist.

"I hope you're right," Savannah whispered, wanting to stand up for herself, but knowing there was nothing she could say in her own defense. Charmaine was beyond reason, too distraught to be comforted, and she was lashing out at the easiest target. In this case, the easiest mark was Savannah.

"Of course I am. I'm his mother.... I...I understand him." She stood on quivering legs. "Now, just leave me alone." Looking around the boy's room, noticing the posters of football players, rock stars and running horses as if for the first time, Charmaine cleared her throat. "I can't stand being in this house another minute. If Travis or Wade gets back, or you hear anything about Josh, I'll be in the studio."

"You'll be the first to know."

Charmaine walked past Savannah without a glance in her sister's direction, and in a few minutes the door to her room closed shut with a thud that echoed in Savannah's mind.

Swallowing against the sense of desperation and fear that parched her throat, Savannah braced herself and walked out of Josh's room. Surely Travis would find Josh and within a couple of hours they would all be together again. It was just a matter of time.

Savannah looked in on her mother again and found that Virginia was sleeping. She removed the cup of untouched coffee from the night table, went downstairs, and placed the cup in the sink. Then, on an impulse, she dialed Sadie Stinson's number. The housekeeper lived several miles away in the opposite direction of Mystic's hoofprints, but there was a slim chance that Josh had sought solace with Sadie. The phone rang several times, but no one answered.

Trying to disregard a feeling of impending doom, Savannah grabbed her coat and continued trying to convince herself that everything would be all right as she walked outside and headed for the brood mare barn. There was work to be done, the first of which was to draw water and make sure that the reserve tank was full. Electricity the farm could do without, but water was another story altogether.

A deputy for the sheriff's department, a young red-haired man with sober brown eyes and a hard smile, made it to the farm later in the morning. After several apologies for not being able to respond earlier, and excuses ranging from jackknifed trucks on the freeway to power outages all over the state, he took a statement from everyone at the house before following Savannah to the office over the foaling shed.

"So you don't think the horse was stolen?" he queried, his dark eyes searching Savannah's. She gave him a cup of coffee and sat at the table near the window.

"No, it looks as if Joshua took the horse."

"Any note from the boy?"

She shook her head and frowned into her cup. "None that we've found."

"And he didn't bother to say goodbye to anyone."

"No."

The young deputy lifted his hat and rubbed his head before scratching a note to himself on his clipboard. "Now, the colt: Mystic. This the same horse that won the Preakness earlier in the year?"

"Yes."

"So he's valuable?"

"Very."

"And insured?"

"Of course." Savannah impaled the young officer with her intense gaze. "What are you getting at?"

"Just checking all the angles. Would you say that this Mystic was the most valuable horse on the farm?"

"No doubt about it."

"And would it be easy for another person, say one that wasn't familiar with the farm, to recognize him?"

"You mean someone that didn't work with him?"

The deputy nodded and took a sip from his cup. "Right."

Savannah thought for a moment. "I don't know. He was pure black, that in itself is striking, I suppose. Most Thoroughbreds are bays or chestnuts."

"How about the other stallions?"

"We have one other black horse, Black Magic, but he's quite a bit older than Mystic; his sire, in fact."

The deputy looked up from his clipboard. "His what?"

"Black Magic is Mystic's sire...you know, father."

"Oh. But could anyone tell them apart?"

"Temperamentally the two are night and day. Black Magic is fairly docile and Mystic is difficult to handle. Magic is slightly larger and has one white stocking. Both horses are registered with the jockey club so their identifying numbers are tattooed inside their upper lips. Anyone who knew what he was doing could make sure that he had the right horse," she mused, "but I don't think we have to worry about that. Josh is missing; he loved the horse, and the boy had a horrid fight with his father last night."

"So you think he just took off in the middle of the biggest snowstorm we've had in fifteen years with the most valuable horse in your stable?" Deputy Smith was clearly dubious.

"He's only nine and he was angry, so, yes."

Scratching the reddish stubble on his chin the deputy stared at the broken wire on the security alarm. "Don't you think it's quite a coincidence that the horse would be taken just when the alarm appeared to be broken?"

"I don't know about that."

"Okay." He shoved the clipboard under his arm and took a final swallow of coffee. "Let's have a look at the barn where the missing horse was taken from."

Savannah led the officer down the path to the barn. Most of the footprints she and Travis had made earlier were covered with snow, just as Mystic's trail was probably covered.

Opening the door of the stallion barn, Savannah stood aside while Deputy Smith peered inside the building, scrutinized every horse and continued to make notes to himself. After searching the barn completely, Mystic's stall thoroughly, and asking Savannah again why Lester thought he'd heard someone in the barn the morning before, he scoured the outside of the buildings. By the time he was finished with his search and was driving away from the house it was almost three in the afternoon, and Savannah felt bone tired and discouraged.

"You'd think they could do more than just poke around

and ask a few questions,'' Charmaine said bitterly when Savannah walked into the kitchen. Charmaine had returned to the house when the young deputy sherrif had arrived, although she hadn't had much to tell him.

"He promised to watch all the roads and inform all the state and county officers about Josh and Mystic,'' Savannah said quietly, shivering slightly as she took off her coat and hung it on a hook near the door to the back porch. "And when they have more men free, they'll be back. I don't know what more they can do.''

"I just thought Josh would be home by now,'' Charmaine whispered.

"So did I.''

Charmaine bit at her lower lip and studied the floor. "I know I've been a bitch, Savannah. I really didn't mean to blame you.''

"I know.''

"I said some pretty awful things earlier.''

"You always do when you get angry.''

"So why do you put up with it?'' Charmaine asked, her chin quivering.

"Because I know you're doing the best you can and you're sick with worry about Josh. And—'' she hesitated, but decided to say what she felt "—and you don't want to blame Wade.''

Charmaine closed her eyes. "You're right,'' she admitted, shaking her head and frowning. "Thanks for understanding.''

Shrugging, Savannah forced a smile. "What are sisters for?''

Charmaine thought a minute. "Well, I don't think they were meant to be whipping posts and I'm sorry that I lost control.''

"It's okay.''

"We all owe you something for holding this place together today.''

"Don't thank me yet,'' Savannah said, watching through

the window as the wind buffeted the wires near the barn.
"We're not out of the woods, not by a long shot." Savannah
gazed out the kitchen window to the stallion barn and beyond. Her thoughts were with Travis and Josh...wherever
they were.

Travis studied the tracks in the snow again and cursed.
Mystic's hoofprints had become less defined until they all
but disappeared in a stand of birch near a frozen creek.

"Son of a bitch," he muttered to himself, dismounting
and eyeing the ground more closely. After tying Jones to a
tree, in order to keep the hoofprints from crossing, he slowly
circled the area again. Keeping his eyes on the frozen earth
and trying to imagine where the kid had decided to go, he
walked carefully, oblivious to the icy wind that cut through
his clothes.

The tracks had faded near the edge of Beaumont land.
On the other side of the ridge the property belonged to the
federal government, and Travis hoped that Josh hadn't been
stupid enough to leave Beaumont property. Dealing with the
government only meant more red tape and more time lost.
"He couldn't have gotten over there," he told himself for
the third time. "No gate, and Mystic is smarter than to attempt to hurdle a fence. At least I hope he is."

Frowning at the dim prints, he thought about the boy. By
now Josh had to be scared out of his wits. "Where the hell
are you?" Travis muttered, as if the boy could hear him.

Maybe Reginald and Wade had found Josh. Two hours
ago, they had doubled back to the house, still looking for
Josh. Lord, he hoped that the boy was already back at the
farm. This was no weather for man or beast. The wind had
picked up and the snow was falling in small, hard crystals,
somewhere between sleet and hail. A nine-year-old kid
wouldn't last long out here.

Travis rubbed the tired muscles of his back and thought
about Savannah. He envisioned her beautiful face and intriguing blue eyes. Less than twelve hours before, she had

been in his arms, naked, warm and filled with passion. She would be devastated if the boy wasn't found.

With a frown, Travis remounted and tried to pick up the trail again. "Josh!" he yelled, cupping his gloved hands over his mouth and listening as his voice echoed through the hills. "Josh!"

The only answer was the whistle of the wind. *Damn it all to hell,* he thought angrily and reined Jones in the direction that Mystic's hoofprints had taken. *If something's happened to Josh, Wade Benson is going to pay and pay dearly.* Travis's steel-gray eyes concentrated on the frozen earth and he tried once again to read the puzzle in the snow.

For several hours Savannah tried to keep herself busy in the house. Fortunately, when Savannah had finally gotten through to Sadie Stinson and told her about Josh, the housekeeper had insisted on braving the elements and driving to the farm. Though Savannah had protested, the housekeeper hadn't been deterred. Now Savannah was glad that Sadie was in the house. Just the familiar sound of clattering pans and the warm scent of Irish stew filling the house relaxed her a bit.

"When that boy get's home, he'll be hungry," Sadie had said when she'd removed her coat and scarf and donned her favorite apron. "And the men, you can bet they'll expect something on the table!"

"You don't have to—"

"Hush, child, and do whatever it is you do around here," the housekeeper had said, shooing Savannah out of the kitchen with a good-natured grin. "And you, too," she'd ordered, when she had spotted Archimedes under the kitchen table. "The kitchen's no place for a sorry mutt like you." Then with a wink, Sadie had extracted a soup bone and handed it to the dog as she'd opened the door to the porch. Archimedes had slid through the portal with his treasure clamped firmly between his jaws.

"Now don't you worry, Savannah," Sadie had cautioned,

when Savannah was almost out of the room. "Josh is a smart lad; he'll be all right. And Travis, you can count on that one. He'll find the boy and the horse."

Though Savannah knew the older woman's optimism was more of a show than anything else, she was grateful for the cheer. The gloom that had settled in the house was oppressive. She was glad for the familiar sight of Sadie's happy face and her constant off-tune whistling as she rattled around in the kitchen.

Savannah glanced outside and noticed that there was a slight break in the weather. *Maybe the storm is finally letting up,* she thought without much hope. The sky was still dark and foreboding, but at least the falling snow had eased. Deciding that it was now or never, she went to the barns and talked to the few hands left on the farm, instructing them to let the horses out of their stalls for a little exercise. "Just keep them in the paddocks close to the barns," she told one of the hands. "I want to give them all a chance to stretch their legs." She glanced up at the cloud-covered sky and frowned. "No telling when this will let up, and if it ices over the horses will be stuck inside."

And what about Josh? she wondered grimly.

Not daring to think about what was happening to the boy, she concentrated on the horses. Watching the yearlings as they came out of the barn made her smile. Most of the young horses had never seen snow before, and they pranced gingerly in the white powder as the stable boys walked them around the paddock. Savannah led a chestnut colt around the small fenced area, and nearly laughed when the sleek animal tried to shake the clinging white flakes from his eyelashes.

"Careful now," she cautioned, leading the frisky colt back to the barn as he tossed his head and pulled on the lead rope.

The sound of an engine splitting the silence caught Savannah's attention, and her heart squeezed in apprehension. *It had to be news of Josh and Travis,* she thought, quickly instructing the stable hands to finish walking each of the horses as she sprinted over the snow-covered parking lot.

A silver Blazer was parked near the house. Savannah didn't recognize the vehicle, but it could belong to one of the neighbors. *Maybe someone had seen Josh!*

She nearly slipped as she climbed up the back steps. Quickly kicking off her boots and sliding into a pair of loafers she kept on the back porch, she hurried through the kitchen and down the hall following the sound of unfamiliar voices.

Her heart was in her throat by the time she rounded the corner by the staircase and walked into the living room. Charmaine was standing nervously near the fireplace, her thin face pale and drawn. She seemed relieved to see Savannah.

Two young men whom Savannah had never seen before were sitting on the couch. One of the men, the shorter blond man, had a camera. The taller man held a tape recorder in his hand.

Charmaine made hasty introductions. "This is John Herman and Ed Cook from the *Register*, Savannah." Both men stood, and John stretched out his hand. "My sister, Savannah Beaumont."

"How do you do?" Savannah responded automatically, her eyes narrowing as she shook the reporter's hand.

"Fine," the tall man replied with a grin. "And the pleasure's all mine, Miss Beaumont."

"They've heard about Mystic and Josh," Charmaine said, her voice barely above a whisper. She was leaning against the mantel for support.

"I don't think there's much we can tell you," Savannah admitted, offering what she hoped would appear a sincere smile. *What the devil was the press doing here and who had sent them?* "Not yet."

"But surely you can confirm the rumor that Mystic is missing," John suggested.

"That's true," Savannah stated, wondering why she felt so nervous. "He's been gone since sometime last night."

"And he was stolen—"

"He was not stolen," Charmaine interrupted. "It looks as if my son, Josh, took him for a ride."

John Herman arched his eyebrows skeptically. "In this storm?" Shaking his head as if he didn't believe a word she was telling him, he adjusted his recorder. "But you must be worried; otherwise you wouldn't have called the police."

"Sheriff's department."

"Yeah." He checked his notes and then looked straight at Savannah. "What's the real story?"

"That's about all there is to it."

"So where do you think your son would take a horse like that?" the reporter asked, turning to Charmaine.

"I have no idea."

"Was he running away?"

"No!" Charmaine said, the features of her white face pinching together angrily. She paced from the fireplace to the window, as if by staring into the dark afternoon she could bring Josh back.

"So who's out looking for him?" Herman asked.

"Some of the people here on the ranch. We've called the neighbors, of course, as well as the sheriff's office."

"Maybe we can help."

"How?"

"If you give us a picture of Josh, we'll run it in the paper. There's a chance that someone who's seen the kid will recognize his picture. As for the horse, we've got a lot of photos on file, don't we Ed?"

Ed nodded. "Yeah, about thirty, I'd guess."

"Good."

John smiled crookedly. "It's a long shot, but worth it, don't you think?"

"Yes," Charmaine said. "I've got a picture of Josh—it's recent; his school picture. It's upstairs, I'll get it." Glad for an excuse to leave the room, and buoyed at the thought of another avenue to locate her son, Charmaine hurried up the stairs.

"I'd appreciate any help you can offer," Savannah said, relaxing a little.

"Good. Then maybe you can explain a few things."

"Such as?"

"Why is Travis McCord back here? This is where he grew up, right?"

Savannah's chest tightened. "He came to live with us when he was seventeen."

"And now he's back. There are a couple of rumors circulating about him."

Savannah felt cold inside and her eyes sparked angrily. "Are there?"

"People are claiming that he's dropping out of the race for governor."

"I didn't know that he'd even announced his candidacy," she replied stiffly, her fingers curling over the back of a velvet chair.

"He hadn't. Not officially. But there's some controversy there, too. A couple of people, especially one lady by the name of Eleanor Phillips, claimed they made contributions to his campaign."

"Even though he hadn't announced his candidacy?" Savannah returned, her voice even, her heart cold with dread. "That doesn't sound too smart. Are you sure you have the story straight?"

The reporter slid her an uneasy smile. "I've got it straight, all right. But I sure would like a chance to interview Mr. McCord."

"He's not here right now."

"Then maybe you or someone else can tell us what the real story is. You know, why he came here from L.A. and threatened to give up practicing law as well as drop out of a primary that he might easily win."

"I can't even guess," Savannah lied. "And I wouldn't

want to. What Travis McCord does with his life is his business.''

"Here it is!'' Charmaine announced, returning to the room and handing the man a picture of Josh. "I really appreciate the fact that you're trying to help,'' she said.

"No problem,'' the reporter replied, meeting Savannah's frosty stare. "And if you change your mind or have anything to add to the story...'' He handed Savannah one of his business cards. "Tell McCord that I'll call him.''

"I will,'' Savannah promised tightly as Charmaine escorted the two men out the front door. After the reporters were out of the house and Savannah saw the silver Blazer slide out of the driveway, she crumpled John Herman's card in her fist and threw it into the fireplace.

Charmaine paused in the archway of the living room before heading upstairs. "Do you think that running Josh's picture in the paper will help?''

"I don't know,'' Savannah said, "but it certainly couldn't hurt. Let's just hope by the time that the *Register* is on the stands, Josh and Mystic are home.''

"Oh, God, yes,'' Charmaine whispered desperately. "If he's not home by tonight...'' She looked out the window to the darkening skies.

"He will be,'' Savannah promised, hearing the hollow sound of her own words.

Lester and the stablehand arrived back at the house at nightfall to report that they hadn't seen hide nor hair of the horse or boy. As Lester checked on the horses, Savannah walked with him and explained about the events of the day at the house.

"Why didn't that blasted repairman show up to fix the security system?'' Lester asked.

"Problems with the weather, or so he claimed when he called,'' Savannah replied.

"Just what we need. How's your mother takin' all this?'' the grizzled trainer asked Savannah.

"Not well," she admitted. "Josh is pretty special to her."

"Ain't he to all of us?" the older man asked, and then scowled. "Except maybe for that dad of his. Y'know, I can't understand it, the way that man treats his kid. If I were Reginald, I'd—" He caught himself and the hard angles of his face slackened. "Well, I suppose your father knows what he's doing. Just because a man ain't much of a father doesn't mean he can't run the farm, and though I'd never have thought I'd admit it, Wade does a passable job."

"But not great. Right?"

Lester's jaw worked angrily. "Like I said, the man was an accountant, and a decent one, I guess. Just never thought he'd want to work with the horses, that's all."

He opened the door to the stallion barn and let out a long sigh. "Why on earth did that boy take Mystic?" Lester wondered aloud.

"That's the sixty-four-dollar question," Savannah replied with a frown.

Lester slapped her affectionately on the shoulders. "Don't you worry about Josh. Travis will find him."

"I hope so," Savannah replied, close to tears again. She patted Vagabond's silken muzzle and stared at Mystic's empty stall. "I hope so."

An hour later Savannah was in the house, looking through the books of the farm and wondering what Travis had been checking into the night before. She never had been one to work with figures, and this day, while her mind was filled with worried thoughts, she couldn't concentrate on the balances. She slapped the checkbook closed and leaned back in her chair.

Just the night before she had slept in the protective circle of Travis's arms. Never had she felt more secure, more loved. And now he was searching the darkness for Josh.

She stood just as a distant rumble caught her attention. Recognizing the sound of her father's Jeep, her heart began to thud, and she grabbed her coat before racing through the kitchen and outside. It was late evening and the sky was dark, and in the distance she could hear the sound of the Jeep as it roared through the fields closer to the house.

Please God, let Josh be with them, Savannah silently prayed as she searched the night for the welcome beams of the vehicle.

Charmaine was standing on the back porch in an instant. "Oh, God," she whispered, just as the Jeep came into view. "Oh, God. Is he with them?" Running out of the porch and down the slippery steps, she hurried to the garage.

Savannah was only a step behind her sister.

Reginald cut the engine and emerged from the truck. He looked exhausted. His weary eyes sought those of his elder daughter. "I guess this means that Josh hasn't shown up."

Charmaine nearly collapsed. "You didn't find him?" she asked, her face ghostly with anguish.

Wade got out of the passenger side of the Jeep and tried to place a comforting arm around his wife, but Charmaine backed away from him. Stiffening, he sent Savannah a silent glare. "Now I suppose you're blaming me," he said to his wife.

"I'm not blaming anyone," Charmaine whispered, her fists clenching as she pounded the fender of the Jeep. "I just want Josh home and safe!"

"What about Travis?" Savannah asked. Her heart was beating wildly with worry for her nephew as well as Travis. *Where were they and why hadn't Travis returned?*

Reginald just shook his head. "Last we saw of him, he'd had no luck. He was going to keep following the tracks as far as he could. We had to turn back when it seemed as if the horse had gone into a thicket of oak."

"I don't even think that was Mystic's trail," Wade said, pulling nervously on his moustache and looking scared. "The damned part of it is, Travis won't find him, not to-night. Those hoofprints were nearly invisible. Now that it's dark, searching any longer would be a waste of time. We'll have to call the police, ask for choppers in the morning."

"No!" Charmaine nearly screamed, shaking her head violently and impaling her husband with furious green eyes. "We've got to find him! Tonight! He'll freeze if he stays out there all night!"

Savannah couldn't help but agree. She was anxious to join the search herself. Travis and Joshua were somewhere in the wilderness, possibly hurt, and she couldn't wait through a long, lonely night just hoping that they would be safe in the morning. She kept her thoughts to herself and just told her father the important facts. "We talked to the sheriff's office earlier today," she said, once they were all walking back to the house.

"I think we'd better call again," Reginald thought aloud.

Once inside the house, Savannah called Deputy Smith and told him that the search party had returned without Josh or Mystic. Charmaine, trying to control herself, told Reginald and Wade about the reporters, the deputy, and the fact that Lester hadn't seen any sign of Josh.

"Where could he be?" Wade asked angrily, stalking to the bar in the living room and pouring himself a stiff drink.

"He's got to be somewhere on the farm," Reginald said.

"We searched every square inch of this place," Wade reminded him, tossing back his bourbon.

"Except where the Jeep couldn't go."

"The rest of it is up to McCord," Wade said, pouring himself another shot. "He and that horse will have to ride down the ravines and through the forests. Like I said, our only hope is police helicopters in the morning."

Savannah walked into the room and heard only the tail-end of the conversation, but she could see from the fear in Charmaine's wide eyes that nothing of consequence had been decided.

"I'd better go upstairs and talk to your mother," Reginald said, looking as if he dreaded the conversation. "How's she been?"

"Remote," Savannah admitted.

"Worried sick, I'll bet," Reginald muttered. "Well, hell aren't we all?"

Sadie came into the living room and tried to liven up the crowd. "Dinner's on. Now, come on, all of you. We'll eat and make some plans about finding the boy. None of us can think on an empty stomach."

"I'm not hungry," Charmaine said, but Sadie only offered her a stern look.

"I've set the dining room table, including a place for Virginia. I think a hot meal would do all of us a world of good!" Sadie reprimanded.

After much cajoling on Sadie's part everyone sat down at the dinner table. The conversation was strained, and though the meal was superb, Savannah barely tasted it. Her thoughts were moving furiously forward, and she nearly jumped when she heard the grandfather clock chime nine o'clock, just as Sadie served an elegant lemon mousse.

Savannah spooned the light dessert into her mouth, but didn't taste it. She was too busy thinking ahead. If Travis didn't return within the hour, Savannah decided, she would go out and find him. Her father would be furious, of course, so she would have to leave the house behind his back and then argue with the security guard posted at the stables. But she couldn't stay cooped up in the house another minute. Come hell or high water, she intended to find Travis and Josh, and she intended to find them before morning!

Eight

At eleven o'clock that night, Savannah was alone. The house was quiet as everyone had watched the ten-o'clock news and then gone to bed, but Savannah's thoughts were screaming inside her head.

Exhausted from the nerve-wracking day, she sat on the edge of her bed and considered trying to sleep, but she knew that despite her weariness she was too restless and worried. Her mind was turning in endless circles of anxiety about Josh and Travis.

Staring out the window, she silently cursed the snowfall then slapped her palm against the cool sill. She was tired of waiting, tired of worrying and had to do something before she went stark, raving mad!

With renewed determination, she walked to the closet, jerked on her warmest riding clothes and silently went downstairs. Once through the hallway she paused in the kitchen at the pantry and grabbed a box of matches, two flares and a flashlight from the small closet.

"What else will I need?" she asked herself and tapped her fingers on the open pantry door. "Lord only knows." With a frown she took a couple of candy bars and stuffed them into her jacket pocket. "So much for nutrition," she muttered wryly.

Going out in this weather is insane, she thought to herself as she pulled on her gloves and wound a scarf around her neck before slipping out the back door. The cold night air cut through her suede jacket as easily as a knife. *Travis will kill you if he catches you,* she cautioned herself, but kept walking, through the backyard, down the path past the garage and across the parking lot to the stables.

The wind whistled and howled through the trees, and the icy snow stung her cheeks, but she had her mind set. She had to find Travis and Josh and there was no time to waste. The news reports indicated that the storm wouldn't let up for several days. *It's now or never,* she thought as she marched through the snow.

"Wait a minute," a male voice called to her just as she reached for the handle on the door to the main stables. "What're you doing?" Johnny, one of the stable hands who had appointed himself security guard when he found out that Joshua and Mystic were missing, placed a hand on Savannah's shoulder. She whirled around to face him and saw the confusion cross his face in the darkness. "Miss Beaumont? What're you doing out here?"

"I'm going looking for Josh."

"Tonight? Are you crazy?"

"Maybe, but I can't stand being cooped up another minute."

The young man was obviously nervous. He dropped his hand from her shoulder and rubbed his jaw pensively. Johnny was used to taking orders from Savannah, but he couldn't believe that she actually planned to light out in the middle of a cold, wintry night like this one. "Reginald said that none of the horses were to leave the stables and no one was to go in."

"I know, Johnny, but Mattie is *my* mare."

Johnny's small eyes moved from Savannah to the cold, dark night and the constantly falling snow. "I don't see that you can do any good out on a horse in the middle of all this," he said, gesturing helplessly at the frozen surroundings.

"As much good as I'll do if I stay in the house."

"Except that tomorrow morning we might have to send a search party after you."

"Tomorrow morning the storm is supposed to get worse."

"I don't know...."

"I'll be careful," she promised, reaching for the door.

"Really, Miss Beaumont—"

She offered him her most disarming smile. "You're off the hook with my dad. I'm taking full responsibility for my actions."

He was wavering, but didn't seem convinced. Savannah pushed a little harder.

"Look, I promise I'll stay on Beaumont land and if the storm gets any worse, I'll come right back. You know Mattie, she could find her way back to the barn in an earthquake."

"It's not the horse I'm worried about."

"Well, don't worry about me. I'm twenty-six. I can take care of myself, and I'll absolutely go out of my mind if I have to stay cooped up a minute longer."

The poor man looked caught between the proverbial rock and a hard place. "You're the boss," he finally admitted. "But I think I should tell Wade or Reginald."

"And worry them further?" she asked. "Because whether they like it or not, I'm going after Josh." Feeling less strong than her words, Savannah turned back to the door of the stables and walked inside the barn without any further protest from Johnny. *Maybe he will tell Reginald,* Savannah thought as she pulled down the saddle and placed it on Mattie's broad back. If Johnny went through with his threat, she'd deal with her father when Reginald came roaring out of the house.

The little bay mare snorted and stamped her foot at the interruption in her sleep and several other horses looked inquisitively at Savannah, their dark ears pricked forward expectantly.

"It's okay, girl," Savannah whispered, tightening the cinch and slipping a bridle over the nervous mare's head. "So far, so good."

Obviously Johnny had decided against waking Reginald with the news that his youngest daughter had her mind set on taking a cold ride through a snowstorm. Otherwise Reginald would already have come storming to the barn in a rage. *Thank God for small favors,* Savannah thought.

Leading the mare out the back door and through the series of paddocks surrounding the stables, Savannah braced herself against the rising wind. She walked Mattie past the stallion barn and heard the quiet whinny of one of the horses that had been awakened by the unusual noises in the night.

The snow all but covered the hoofprints that had been visible earlier in the day. Only the deep ruts of the Jeep remained in the crystalline powder, but even the double tire tracks were disappearing rapidly. Her lips tightening as she tried to read the trails in the soft snow, Savannah climbed into the saddle and pressed her heels into Mattie's warm flanks. "Let's go," she said encouragingly, then wondered if she was talking to herself or the mare.

Deciding to work on intuition rather than fact, Savannah ignored the direction of Mystic's tracks and headed the little mare to the lake. As Mattie slowly circled the dark water, Savannah scanned the darkness and called Josh's name.

No response.

Reining in the horse to a stop and straining to hear over the roar of the wind, she tried shouting again, but still there was no answer.

"Strike one," Savannah muttered to herself. With a deepening sense of dread, she circled the lake and skirted the center of the farm until she came to a field with an old apple tree and a tree house that Josh had constructed the previous summer.

Tying Mattie to the thick trunk of the tree, Savannah climbed up the makeshift ladder of loose boards nailed into the bark and trained the beam of her flashlight inside the rough structure. The interior of the tree house was deserted, snow covering the dirty floorboards as it slipped through the cracks in the roof.

Savannah directed the thin beam of light around the crude shack in the branches and then, from her perch in the doorway, moved the light to the snow-covered earth. Again there was no sign of the boy or his horse.

"Great," she muttered under her breath as she snapped off the flashlight. *This isn't getting us anywhere,* she thought with a sigh. How many times last summer had she had to track down Josh for dinner and found him in his favorite spot, hidden in the branches of the gnarled old apple tree? *But not tonight.*

As Savannah climbed down the ladder, untied Mattie and pulled herself into the saddle, another image crossed her mind. The picture in her mind was of herself as a seventeen-year-old girl, sitting upon a much younger Mattie under the umbrella of the protective apple tree while secretively watching Travis as he strung the wire over a broken fence. *Don't torture yourself,* she reprimanded herself, but thoughts of Travis and Josh spurred her into action. She turned Mattie's head and urged the little mare toward the fields surrounding the stallion barn. Having checked all of Josh's favorite hiding spots, she decided to follow Mystic's almost nonexistent trail into the hills.

As long as the double ruts of Reginald's four-wheel-drive unit were still visible, Savannah was able to follow Mystic's path. The journey was long and cold, but she bent her head against the wind and kept riding, silently promising herself that if she ever saw Travis and Joshua again, she would never let them out of her sight.

Don't think like that, she thought angrily. *Be positive.* But the cold blast of the wind and the silence around her made the doubts in her mind loom like foreboding ghosts that couldn't be driven away.

Travis swore under his breath. *Not one damned sign of the boy!* Where the devil had he gone? Josh couldn't have vanished into thin air. Of course, there was the remote possibility that Josh had returned to the house, but Travis didn't think so. Reginald had promised to send off flares and fire a rifle shot three times in succession if the boy had been located. Neither signal had reached Travis and despite the fact that he distrusted Reginald's politics, Travis was certain the old man would be true to his word and let him know about Josh's safety.

Huddling against the wind, he scowled and considered stopping to build a fire. He was cold to the bone, his face raw from the bite of the frigid air, and Jones, game as the gelding was, needed a rest. Trudging through the snow with a two-hundred-pound man on his back had tired the horse.

"Well, let's see what we've got here," Travis said to himself. Dismounting, he let Jones drink a small amount of water from a near-frozen stream.

His eyes trained on the ground, Travis walked to the edge of the clearing, plowing through half a foot of snow. He stretched his legs and tired back muscles; it had been years since he'd spent so much time in the saddle, and his thighs and lower back were already beginning to ache and cramp.

To Travis, the rest of the night looked bleak. In the morning, he'd have no choice but to return to the farm. Both he and the horse would have to rest. Maybe the roads would be more passable and maybe in the light of a new day, the boy would be found.

The creases near the corners of his eyes deepened as he squinted through the darkened pines. A slight movement caught his eye and he focused all of his attention through the thick curtain of snow.

Nothing stirred. He wondered if he was beginning to imagine things in his desperation to find the child.

Where the hell was Josh? Travis had scoured every inch of Beaumont land and there had been no trace of the boy or the fiery black colt. When Travis had lost Mystic's tracks just before nightfall, he hadn't been able to find any clue as to Josh's whereabouts. He paled beneath his tan when he thought about what might have happened on the more rugged federal land that bordered the farm.

Was the boy lying unconscious somewhere with snow piling over him, or did the kid have enough sense to seek shelter for himself and his horse? The bitter thought that Josh might not be alive crossed his mind again. Travis's jaw hardened with renewed determination. The longer the boy was on his own in the wilderness, the slimmer were his chances of survival.

After walking back to his horse, Travis lifted his Stetson from his head, scratched his head and then replaced the hat. "Let's go," he muttered angrily as he swung into the saddle, lifted the reins and directed the horse across the slippery rocks of the stream before shouting Josh's name into the darkness.

Again he saw a movement through the trees. This time he didn't hesitate, but dug his heels into Jones's sides and took out after whatever was hiding in the shadows.

Savannah's toes felt as if they would fall off. Even though she was wearing riding gloves, her fingers were stiff. *Maybe Johnny was right,* she thought angrily. *Maybe riding out here was nothing more than a fiasco. If I'm not home by morning, Mom and Dad will be worried out of their minds!* Still, the idea of turning back stuck in her throat. At least she was trying to find Josh rather than lying in a warm bed hoping the boy was all right.

She bit at her lower lip as she studied the ground. For over an hour, since the point where the tire tracks had turned back in the direction of the house, she'd seen no sign of Josh or Travis. If there had been hoofprints in the snow, they had long been covered with the drifting white powder. *Travis.* Had it only been last night that she had slept in the strength of his arms? It seemed like an eternity had passed without him. *God, where was he? Was he all right?*

Her voice was raw from shouting Josh's name over the whistle of the wind. Her own words echoed back to her unanswered and the silence filled her heart with dread. "Merry Christmas," she whispered sarcastically, tears from both the stinging wind and her tortured thoughts filling her eyes.

She shivered as she came to the clearing where she, Josh and Travis had cut down the Christmas tree only two days before. Urging Mattie forward, she ignored her pleasant memories of cutting the tree, the snowball fight, decorating the room and making love to Travis.... It all seemed so long ago.

The storm continued to rage, and Savannah bent her head against the wind. Mattie was laboring through the drifts, and snow was falling so thickly that it was almost impossible to see.

Savannah was almost on the verge of giving up her search and starting back to the house when a slight movement in the surrounding trees caught her attention. Mattie shied and nickered nervously, and Savannah's skin crawled in fear before she recognized the big black colt.

"Mystic!" she cried, her heart leaping at the sight of him. "Josh?"

Then she froze as she realized Mystic's saddle was missing, and the reins to his bridle were loose and dragging on the ground. "Oh, Lord," she moaned, dismounting and tying an anxious Mattie to a scrub oak. "Josh! Josh, can you hear me?" *Please let him be all right.*

She approached the black colt cautiously, but Mystic sidestepped, rearing on unsteady hind legs and slashing in the air with his forelegs. He tossed his head menacingly and snorted. His dark eyes were wild looking; rimmed in white from fear. As he reared he stumbled backward and let out an anguished squeal.

"It's all right, boy," Savannah whispered, knowing that the horse was more than frightened. It was obvious from Mystic's erratic behavior that he was in severe pain. She walked up to the colt confidently, hoping to instill some calm into the overwrought animal.

"Be careful!" a voice warned, and Savannah turned to see Travis, leading Jones, step out of the trees. Relief swept through her body at the sight of him. Both he and his horse looked past exhaustion.

"Thank God you're all right!" she whispered, running to Travis, throwing her arms around his neck and warming just at the feel of his arms around her. "I've been worried sick about you!" She couldn't help the tears of relief that pooled in her eyes as she clung to him and kissed his beard-roughened cheek. The smell and taste of him was wonderful, but the feeling of joy was short-lived. "Where's Josh?" she asked, when she felt the restraint in his embrace.

"I don't know," he said softly. "I haven't seen him."

Savannah's heart squeezed in fear. "But Mystic…"

Travis slowly released her and wearily rubbed the back of his forehead. "I know," he admitted, "I thought when I found the horse, I'd find the boy. But I didn't. And right now we've got to catch this one and calm him down." He fixed his eyes on the skittish colt while he tied Jones to a branch of a tree next to Mattie. "And you be careful around him," Travis warned Savannah, keeping his voice low and calm. "He's hurt and scared out of his wits. I've been following him for about a couple of hundred yards. There's something wrong with his right foreleg."

"No—"

"Shh…" Travis continued to advance slowly on the nervous horse. "Steady, boy," he whispered, slowly extending his hand toward Mystic's head.

The frightened animal bolted out of the clearing. "Son of a bitch," Travis muttered. "This is what happened when I came across him a couple of hours ago, but he can't go far…." Travis trained the beam of the flashlight onto the snow, displaying Mystic's tracks as well as bloody splotches where the colt had stood.

"Oh God," Savannah moaned. "What do you think happened? Where's Josh?"

"I wish I knew," Travis replied, starting out after the horse. "Come on. Let's go."

Slowly, with the quiet determination and ruthlessness of

a predator stalking prey, Travis followed the colt. Mystic was standing under a naked maple tree, his ebony coat wet with sweat, his glistening muscles shivering with apprehension. Wild-eyed and ready to bolt, he watched Savannah and Travis as they approached.

"It's all right," Savannah said to the horse.

The colt moaned, tried to rear and finally stood still as Travis, moving with quiet deliberation, took hold of the bridle and wrapped the reins firmly around his right hand.

"Oh, no," Savannah whispered, coming close to the horse and seeing the frozen lather clinging to the big colt's body. She held her breath while Travis ran experienced hands down Mystic's shoulders and legs.

When Travis's fingers touched a sensitive spot on Mystic's foreleg, Mystic reared and jerked his black head upward with such force that the movement nearly wrenched Travis's right arm out of its socket.

"Whoa," Travis ordered, wincing and forcing the colt's head back down in order to continue his examination. "Damn!" He felt the distinctive bump near Mystic's ankle when his fingers touched the horse's foreleg and Mystic tried to rear again.

"What?"

Travis sighed and shook his head. "I think it's broken. The leg's swollen and he's favoring it. When I touch the area over his sesamoid bones, he nearly jumps out of his skin."

Travis tied Mystic's reins to the nearby tree, then trained the beam of his flashlight on the wound. Savannah felt her stomach turn over at the sight of the bloodied gash. She examined Mystic's leg and swallowed back the urge to scream in frustration. "Maybe it's just sprained," she whispered hopefully.

"Maybe." Travis didn't sound convinced.

"So, what now?"

Travis's jaw hardened and his eyes flashed with determination when he turned them upon her. "First we find a way to get him back to the barn, then we find Josh, and then maybe you could give me a quick explanation as to why you're out here.''

''There's no time right now,'' she hedged, eyeing Mystic.

Travis studied the big black colt and sighed when he realized that she was right. They had to work fast to avoid injuring the horse any further. And then there was Josh to find…. ''Okay, you win. For now. But when this is all over, you can bet your hide that I'll want an explanation from you and it had better be good.''

''It will be,'' she said frostily, then turned her attention back to the horse. ''I don't think he should walk any farther than absolutely necessary.''

''Agreed.'' Travis ran a hand over his stubbled chin. ''If you ride Mattie, it will only take an hour, maybe less, to cut through the fields and get back to the house.'' Travis studied the big colt with a practiced eye. ''I'll stay here with him until you can get Lester or Reginald to drive the truck up the federal road…I think it cuts through the land on the other side of the fence, about four hundred yards north.''

''It does.''

''Then bring wire cutters. We'll have to cut open the fence to get Mystic through.''

Savannah hesitated. ''I don't want to leave you.''

Travis managed a weary, but rakish smile. ''Just for a little longer,'' he promised, ''until we can get the horse back to the farm. Oh, and call the vet.''

''I will.''

''And bring up a fresh horse and a couple of rugs for these two.'' He motioned toward Mystic and Jones.

''Why the extra horse?'' she asked, dreading the answer.

''Jones is tired.''

''And you want to keep looking for Josh?'' she surmised, not knowing whether to feel glad or worried.

''I found the horse, didn't I? The boy couldn't be far away.''

''Only miles,'' she speculated.

"Not if he fell off when Mystic hurt his leg. I can't believe that Mystic would try to travel that far when he was in as much pain as I think he feels. Anyway, let's hope not, for Josh's sake."

There was logic to Travis's thoughts and for the first time that night, Savannah felt a glimmer of hope that they would be able to find Josh and bring him home. *Unless he was dead,* she thought, her heart fluttering with panic.

"Don't think like that," Travis said, his gray eyes delving into hers as he seemed to read her morbid thoughts. "We'll find him and he'll be all right."

"Oh, God I hope so."

Travis's arms surrounded her. "Come on," he urged, pressing his cold lips to her forehead and hugging her fiercely. "Don't lose the faith; not now. Josh, Mystic and I are counting on you."

"Okay," Savannah whispered, then sniffed, pushing her worries aside and bracing herself for what promised to be a long, tiring night.

"I knew I could count on you," Travis said, slowly releasing her.

She mounted Mattie reluctantly, unable to tear herself away from Travis. There was something in the cold night air that seemed to warn her that leaving him would cause certain disaster.

Travis noticed her hesitation and he looked up and forced a tired smile. "Buck up, will ya? It's only a little while longer," he whispered, reaching up and stroking her trembling chin with his gloved hand. "And then it will be over."

"And Josh?"

"I'll find him," Travis promised, hoping that he sounded more sure of himself than he felt. "I won't give up until I do."

His fingers wrapped around the nape of her neck, and he pulled her head slowly downward until his lips brushed hers. "Don't you know there's nothing that can keep me away from you?"

Savannah's raw throat went dry. "I hope so," she whispered as he kissed her chilled lips, and she realized how desperately she loved him. Her heart seemed to bleed at the prospect of leaving him.

"Now, go on. Get out of here," he commanded, once the kiss had ended. He squared his shoulders and looked directly into her eyes. "You'd better hustle because I'm going to give you about a forty-minute head start and then I'm going to fire rifle shots into the air. That should wake everyone up at the house. Then I'll send up my flares. By that time, you should be getting back and everyone will be ready to go. Have Lester bring the truck with the fresh horse."

"And the wire cutters."

"Right."

"I'll throw in a thermos of coffee and a sandwich," she said, and then as a sudden thought struck her, she dug into her pockets for the candy bars. "It's not much, but here." She tossed him the snack.

Travis smiled and caught the candy. "You're an angel of mercy."

"I doubt it," she said, her eyes scanning the darkened landscape as she thought about Travis staying up there alone. "Do you really think that staying out here tonight looking for Josh will do any good?"

Travis stared straight into her eyes, his face suddenly solemn. "I don't think I have any choice. Do you?"

"No, I guess not," she admitted, gazing longingly into his eyes before reining Mattie toward the farm.

Travis watched her leave the clearing before striding through the snow to Jones, taking off the horse's saddle and blanket and placing the blanket over Mystic's quivering shoulders.

"I don't know how much good this will do, old boy, but it's better than nothing." He patted Mystic and then walked back to Jones and frowned, rubbing the gelding's neck. "Hardly seems fair, does it? Unfortunately, that's the way life is."

* * *

Savannah reluctantly left Travis, calling Josh's name as she started back to the farm. She listened but heard nothing other than the steady crunch of Mattie's hooves in the snow. The wind whipped at her face and pushed her hair away from her neck while her thoughts lingered on Travis standing guard over Mystic.

"Josh," she screamed again, cupping her gloved hands to her mouth. "Josh! Where are you?" There was no response other than the rustle of the wind through brittle leaves and the mournful cry of a winter bird disturbed from his sleep. *"Dear Lord, let me find him,"* she whispered to herself. Where was he? Was he still alive, or lying half-frozen somewhere nearby?

Mattie came to an unexpected halt and sidestepped.

Savannah's eyes pierced the darkness, but she saw nothing. Knowing it was futile, she called one last time to Josh and waited for a response.

Somewhere in the distance, she heard a faint reply, a small groan in the darkness. Savannah's heart skipped a beat, and she told herself that she was probably just imagining what she'd heard. As loudly as possible, she called again. Not daring to breathe, she waited. This time the reply was more distinct.

Her heart in her throat, she urged Mattie forward, following the sound of Josh's voice and calling to him continually. "I'm coming," she yelled over the shriek of the wind, praying silently that Josh could hear her. To her relief, she saw Travis riding Jones through the trees.

"I heard you," he said, "I would have been here sooner but I had to resaddle old Jones here." Then he shouted Josh's name as loudly as possible.

The boy's groans sounded closer.

"He's alive," Savannah whispered, tears of relief threatening her eyes as Mattie plowed through the snow until they came to the edge of a steep ridge and they could ride no farther. "Josh, where are you?" she called, her voice echoing in the snow-drifted canyon.

"Here…help me…." The boy's feeble voice came from somewhere below.

"I'm here, Josh," Savannah replied, nearly jumping off Mattie and racing to the edge of the ravine. *Oh God, it was so dark and so far down.* She could barely make out Josh's inert form in the snow. "We'll get you out of there in no time," she said, with more conviction than she felt. "You just hang in there."

Travis was at her side, his narrowed eyes surveying the snow for the quickest path to the boy. "I think I'd better handle this," he said.

"But he needs me," she protested.

"And how're you going to carry him?" Without waiting for her response, he took a rope from his saddle bag and anchored it around the trunk of a sturdy pine.

"Let me go after him," she pleaded.

"Just this once, Savannah, do as you're told, okay? If I need help, I'll yell, but the last thing I need is to have you get yourself hurt trying to help the boy. Now, I don't have time to argue with you."

Gritting her teeth, Savannah backed down. "Just get him up here."

"I will."

After securing the other end of the rope around his waist, Travis carefully picked his way down the steep hillside. Savannah watched from the top of the ridge.

The boy was huddled under the relative protection of a small pine tree. "How're ya doin'?" Travis asked, once he was near enough to talk to Josh.

Josh didn't answer. His teeth were chattering, and he was shaking from head to foot.

"Come on, let's check you out and see if I can carry you out of here." Carefully Travis examined the boy, feeling for any broken bones. "I know this is going to hurt, Josh, but we've got to get you home. Can you make it?"

Josh nodded weakly, but he didn't attempt to stand.

Travis threw his coat over the boy and gently lifted him

from the hard ground. He considered his options. Either he could take the boy out of there now, or wait until Savannah went for help. But that could take hours. "Look, Josh, I'm going to try and carry you out of here. Do you think you can make it?"

"Don't know," the boy admitted, and groaned as Travis shifted his weight.

"It won't be long now," Travis encouraged, starting up the steep hillside, the boy pressed to his chest.

Savannah watched as Travis slowly climbed up the snow-covered incline. It seemed to take hours. He slipped twice and she gasped as she watched him fall, then regain his footing, until he finally made it to the top of the ridge.

"Oh, Josh," she whispered, kissing the boy on the head and crying softly. "Thank God you're alive." Tears were streaming down her face as she touched Josh's cold skin. "He's freezing."

"We've got to get him back, but I don't think he can ride alone, and Jones is too worn out to carry two of us. Can you hold him in the saddle with you?"

"Of course."

"Good." After Savannah mounted Mattie, Travis helped Josh into the saddle.

"Where's Mystic?" Josh asked faintly once they were moving. He was pressed against her body, quivering from pain.

"I've got him tied; we'll send a truck for him when we get down the hill," Travis assured the boy.

"Shh. Don't worry about Mystic," Savannah said, her voice soothing as she helped hold Josh in the saddle. "We'll get him home. You just take care of yourself."

The journey back to the house seemed to take forever. Savannah's arms ached from the strain of holding Josh while trying to balance on Mattie. Josh didn't talk, but only groaned during the ride.

Savannah could hardly take her eyes off Josh, and she held him until she thought her arms might break. By the time the buildings of the farm came into view, the first streaks of dawn were lighting the sky, and Savannah recognized Lester's pickup in the parking lot.

They had barely gotten into the paddock near the stables when Lester spotted them. His grizzled face spread into a wide grin, and he told Johnny to wake everyone in the house to let them know that Josh had been found.

"You're a sight for sore eyes, child," Lester said to Josh as he and Travis carefully got the boy out of the saddle.

Charmaine and Wade met the ragged party just as they approached the house. Charmaine was dressed in her nightgown, bathrobe and boots. "Josh," she called, tears streaming down her face. "Oh, honey are you all right? Let me look at you."

"I think I'd better take him inside," Travis said.

"No. Give him to me." She took the boy in her arms and held him tightly to her breast before raising tear-filled eyes to Travis. "Thank God you found him!"

"You'd better call an ambulance," Travis replied. "He's hurt and nearly frozen."

"Oh, baby," Charmaine whispered, turning to the house. Josh clung to his mother as if to life itself. Charmaine was sobbing and Savannah felt her own tears tightening her throat.

"Let's get him inside," Wade suggested, unable to do anything other than appear worried. "What the devil were you doing out there?" he asked Savannah, but she didn't bother to respond.

"What about Mystic?" Lester asked.

"We've got to go back to get him," Travis said, watching as Charmaine walked through the back door with Josh. "He's hurt and it looks bad. Right foreleg, probably his ankle."

Lester scowled. "I'll get the truck." He was off in a minute.

Travis turned to Savannah. His countenance was grave, his silvery eyes narrowed with worry and shadowed from lack of sleep. "I've got to go back for the horse, but you take care of Josh. Make sure an ambulance is on the way, and don't forget to call the vet."

"I won't," she said, running to the house.

Slipping her boots off on the back porch, she entered the kitchen and smiled at the sight of Archimedes under the table. "Sadie will skin you alive if she catches you," she murmured to the dog, who responded with a sigh.

The warmth of the house made her skin tingle, and she jerked off her gloves with her teeth and set them on the counter.

Rubbing her hands together, she walked through the kitchen and down the short hallway to the den. Wade was just hanging up the phone.

"Ambulance?" she asked.

"It's on its way."

"Good. What about Josh?"

Wade frowned. His blond hair was stringing over his eyes and his skin was white with worry. "Charmaine's got him upstairs in his room. He...he doesn't look all that good," Wade said nervously.

"He was thrown from a horse, fell down a mountainside and spent over twenty-four hours outside in a snowstorm the likes of which we hardly ever get around here. He probably feels terrible!"

"I hope he'll be all right."

Savannah's eyes narrowed on her brother-in-law, and all of her anger and frustration exploded. "He'd be a lot more 'all right' if you'd treated him like your son, like you care about him, instead of acting like he's just one big bother!"

"I try—"

"Bull!"

"I don't relate to children very well."

"He's your son, dammit. Don't give me any excuses, Wade, or college buzzwords like 'relate.' Just give the kid a chance; that's all he wants. The bottom line is he needs your love!"

"I know, I know," Wade admitted, his fingers rubbing anxiously together. "But I can't help it if he gets on my nerves."

"My God, you almost lost a child and all you can say is that he gets on your nerves. That's disgusting, Wade. Think of what he's been through! Maybe it's time you showed him some compassion!" Savannah's cheeks were flushed, and she didn't bother to hide the rage and loathing she felt for her brother-in-law.

Wade paled slightly but didn't move. He had no response to her outburst. "God, Savannah, this is no time to get angry. What about Mystic? Where is he?"

"Still on the mountain. Travis and Lester are going to get him." She turned away from Wade in disgust, grabbed the telephone receiver and punched out the number of the local veterinarian, Steve Anderson. When he answered, Savannah explained about Mystic's condition and the vet assured her that he'd be over as quickly as possible, considering the conditions of the roads.

Just as she hung up, Reginald entered the room. He looked as if he hadn't slept all night. "What's this I hear about you taking off last night?" he asked.

"I couldn't sleep."

Reginald paled and ran his fingers over his head. "I was just up in Josh's room with Charmaine. That boy's been through hell and back. And you, taking off in that storm; that was a foolish thing to do. Good Lord, Savannah, we could have lost you, too!"

She shook her head and waved off her father's fears. "But you didn't and Josh is safe."

"Thank God. I think I need a drink."

"Me, too," Wade agreed, starting for the liquor cabinet.

"Why aren't you with your son?" Reginald demanded.

Stopping dead in his tracks, Wade turned to face his father-in-law. "I just got through calling the ambulance."

"Hmph."

Wade's back stiffened. "I'm as worried as you are about

Josh, but I thought it would be better if he spent a little time alone with his mother.''

Savannah didn't want to hear any of Wade's feeble excuses. She sighed and faced Reginald. "Travis and Lester are going to get Mystic.''

"I'll go with them," Reginald decided.

"You should know something first," she said quietly. "Mystic's injured, Dad.''

Reginald went ashen at the grim expression on her features. "Seriously?''

"I don't know, but it's his foreleg, around the ankle...well, you can judge for yourself. I've already called the vet.''

"The horse will be all right," Wade said, looking to Savannah for support.

"I hope so," she replied, before walking toward the foyer. "I want to see Josh before the ambulance gets here.''

"And you'll look after your mother, won't you?" Reginald asked, as he walked into the foyer, grabbed his coat from the closet and placed a warm cap on his head. "She's been worried sick about the boy.''

"Of course.''

"Tell Josh that I'll be up in a minute," Wade said, following Reginald. "I just want to see that they've got enough men to get the horse.''

"Sure," Savannah said with a weary sigh. *Put your kid last again,* she thought as she hurried up the stairs to Josh's room. He was lying in bed, Charmaine huddling over him.

"How're ya feelin', sport?" Savannah asked.

Josh tried to smile, but couldn't.

Savannah's heart wrenched for the child. "The ambulance will be here in a minute. They'll fix you up, good as new. I promise.''

Josh's worried brows drew together and when he spoke his voice was only a rough whisper. "What about Mystic?''

"Grandpa and Travis are going to get him right now,''

Savannah said. "Now don't think about him, you just take care of yourself, okay?"

Josh turned away from her and closed his eyes, letting exhaustion carry him away.

Am ambulance arrived a little later, and two attendants put Josh on a stretcher before carrying him downstairs. Savannah watched as Wade nervously paced the foyer between the den and the living room.

"Aunt Savvy?" Josh whispered to her as the attendants stopped in the hallway.

She walked over to the stretcher and took hold of the boy's hand. "What is it?"

"Will you come with me?"

"Of course I will," she answered, but Wade held up his hands in protest.

"No dice, Savannah," he whispered loudly. "I want you to leave Josh alone. If you hadn't encouraged him to ride that horse in the first place, we wouldn't be in this position, would we?"

"Dad—"

Savannah gave Josh a silent glance that warned him to be quiet. "I only want what's best for Josh."

"Please," the boy begged, his voice cracking. "Come with me."

Swallowing back the urge to cry, Savannah looked at Josh's drawn face and shook her head. "I'll come visit you later, but right now I think I'd better made sure the vet gets here to check on Mystic."

"Is he hurt?"

"We don't know, but he's had a pretty wild twenty-four hours. I promise to let you know how he is, okay?"

"Okay," Josh replied with obvious effort, wincing at a stab of pain.

"Good. And the minute you get home, we'll have Christmas."

"But Christmas is tomorrow."

"We'll wait for you," Savannah said.

"Promise?"

"Promise!"

She let go of Josh's hand and fought her tears.

"We'll be at the hospital," Charmaine told Savannah as she came hurrying down the stairs with an overnight bag. "I'm riding with Josh, and Wade will bring the car."

"Not alone he won't," Virginia stated from the top of the stairs. She was dressed and holding on to the banister as she slowly descended. "I'm coming, too."

"You don't have to be there," Charmaine said.

"I know I don't, but Josh is my grandson and I intend to be at the hospital with him."

"Lady?" One of the attendants prodded Charmaine.

"I'm coming," Charmaine replied. "You two fight this out," she said to Wade and Virginia, as she followed the attendants outside and shut the door behind her.

"There isn't going to be a fight and that's that," Virginia stated evenly.

"Mom?" Savannah asked, but saw the look of defiance in Virginia's proud stare.

"Are you sure you're up to this?" Wade asked skeptically. "I think you should rest—"

"I'm going to the hospital. I think this is a good chance for you and me to have a little talk about your relationship with Josh."

"I don't think—"

"That we have much time," Virginia finished for him. "Let's go."

"All right," Wade said tightly, but turned his eyes to Savannah. "I want you to call me when the vet examines Mystic."

"And I'll expect the same from you when the doctor checks Josh."

Wearing a pained expression, Wade walked briskly out the door after Virginia, leaving Savannah to wait for news of Mystic.

* * *

Travis and Lester returned within the hour.

Steve Anderson, the local veterinarian for the farm, was already waiting in the office over the stables when the big truck slowly drove into the stable-yard.

"Well, let's see how bad it is," the vet said, getting up from the table and setting down his coffee cup. He and Savannah quickly put on their jackets before going outside to meet the truck.

Travis was the first man out of the cab, and from the expression on his face, Savannah guessed that returning Mystic to the farm had been more difficult than expected. The strain was obvious in his eyes.

"It doesn't look good," Travis admitted, placing a strong arm around Savannah's shoulders for support. "Lester agrees with me; he thinks Mystic's broken his sesamoids."

"Maybe not," Savannah said hopefully, but grim lines deepened beside Travis's mouth.

Lester and Reginald had opened the back of the truck and were attempting to lead Mystic outside.

The horse was in a state of shock. Wild-eyed and flailing his hooves at anything that moved, Mystic tried to bolt when the veterinarian bent to look at him.

"I think he's broken his leg, sesamoid bones," Lester said as Steve tried to examine Mystic's ankle. The vet frowned at the sight of the frenzied animal's wound.

"Maybe." He shook his head and worked to place an inflatable cast on Mystic's leg, but the frightened colt tried to thwart all Steve's attempts to help him.

Savannah felt her insides shred at the sight of Mystic. Unless the veterinarian was able to calm him, the horse would be his own worst enemy and wouldn't survive the effects of the anesthesia.

"We'd better take him right to the hospital," Steve thought out loud. "I'll need X rays and I'll probably have to perform surgery—unless we get lucky."

"He's not stable enough for surgery," Savannah said.

Steve nodded. "I'll sedate him and maybe we'll get lucky

and nothing'll be broken. But I think that's being optimistic. It looks like Lester is right.''

Savannah felt herself slump, but Travis's arms tightened around her shoulders.

"We'd better get moving," Steve said.

"Then let's do it," Reginald replied, looking at the agonized colt and shaking his head. "Travis, can you drive the truck?"

With a frown, Travis nodded. "Sure."

"I'm coming, too," Savannah said firmly. "This time you're not leaving me here alone."

"Don't you think you'd better get some rest?" Travis asked.

"No."

"You have to stay here," Reginald pointed out.

"Why?"

"Don't ask foolish questions," her father said irritably. "You need your rest."

"I'm fine!"

Reginald's face flushed with anger. "Okay, so you played the heroine and helped find Josh; now let it lie. You're needed here. Think about it. What if Charmaine calls about Josh? He's not exactly out of the woods yet, you know. Won't you want to take the message?"

Savannah looked helplessly from her father to Travis and then to Mystic as Lester led him back into the truck. "I suppose so," she agreed reluctantly. "But this has shades of a conspiracy, you know."

"Nothing all that sinister," her father assured her. "I just need someone I can depend upon to stay here and look after things. As soon as we know Mystic's condition, we'll call."

Steve was already walking to his van. Reginald and Lester had climbed into the cab of the truck.

Travis looked dead tired and his eyes held hers in silent promise. "I'll be back," he promised, "and soon."

She forced a weary smile and caressed the stubble on his chin. "I'll be waiting."

Managing a smile he said, "That makes it all worthwhile, you know." Then, as if to make up for lost time, he climbed into the truck, started the engine and drove out of the frozen stable-yard to follow the path of Steve Anderson's van.

Savannah watched as the truck rumbled out the drive, and she felt more alone than she had in years. Josh was on his way to the hospital with the rest of the family, Travis and Lester were taking Mystic to a fate she didn't want to think about and she was left with the responsibility of the farm.

Shivering, she walked back to the house and let Archimedes inside for what little company he could provide. "Well," she said, making a cup of hot chocolate, "I guess all we have left to do is wait."

Looking out at the early-morning light she shook her head sadly and silently wished for the strength of Travis's arms.

Nine

Time had never moved so slowly for Savannah as she waited for word on Josh and Mystic. It was nearly dark when the phone finally rang. Savannah answered and heard the exhaustion in Charmaine's voice.

"Josh will be all right," Charmaine assured her.

Savannah sank against the wall of the kitchen in relief. "Thank God!"

"But he has to stay here a few days. He's got a broken collarbone and several fractured ribs, as well as a lot of cuts and bruises. Fortunately there's no evidence of internal bleeding or damage to any of his organs. He should be out of the hospital in two or three days."

"I'm just glad it wasn't any worse," Savannah said.

"My sentiments exactly." Charmaine hesitated and then sighed. "So...have you heard anything about Mystic? Josh keeps asking about that damned creature."

Savannah winced at Charmaine's harsh words, but managed to hold her tongue. Charmaine was under a lot of strain. "There's nothing to tell him yet. The vet was here and he took Mystic to the equine hospital near Sacramento. Everyone, including Steve, seems to think that Mystic may have broken the sesamoid bone in his right foreleg."

There was a pause at the other end of the line and Charmaine sighed. "What bone? I think you'd better talk in layman's terms, okay? Even though I've lived on the farm all these years, I've tried to avoid most of the talk about horses—especially when it came to anatomy," she admitted. "How serious is it?"

"Serious."

"I see," Charmaine whispered. "But he will pull through, be all right even if he can't race again, right?"

"I don't really know. Lots of horses do," Savannah thought aloud. "It all depends upon the horse, his mental condition at the time of the surgery, the skill of the vet and luck, I guess. The problem is that Mystic's temperament is against him and he was overwrought before the surgery. That's not good."

"But surely they can save him," Charmaine persisted.

"I hope so, for all our sakes," Savannah said, knowing that if Mystic didn't survive, Josh would be devastated with guilt.

"I guess we can only hope for the best. Look, I'll call you if our plans change," Charmaine said. "But at least for tonight, Wade and I are staying in town."

"How's Wade taking it?" Savannah asked.

"Not too good. Josh admitted that he took the horse because he was angry with his father. He also said that he had intended on running away. And, oh, that's how the security wire broke. Josh was using a key he had 'borrowed' from his father one morning when he wanted to see Mystic, and the wire snapped."

Savannah let out a weary sigh. Josh had managed to dig himself into a deeper and deeper hole of trouble.

"And now Josh is petrified that Wade will punish him—not let him see Mystic again. It's a horrible mess."

"Is there anything I can do?"

"Not now."

"I'll call Josh in the morning, when he's feeling better," Savannah said.

"He'd love it."

"How's Mom doing?" Savannah asked.

"Fine. She's staying here with us."

Savannah thought about her mother's frail health. Worrying about Josh and Mystic wouldn't help Virginia's condition. "How's she taking all this?"

"Like a trooper. Hard to believe, isn't it?" Charmaine replied, and then she rattled off the name and number of the hotel in which she and Wade were staying. "Call me if you hear anything about Mystic."

"I will," Savannah promised. "And give Josh my love."

After hanging up the phone, Savannah glanced at the clock. Four-thirty. She'd spent the past six hours making sure that all the horses were comfortable and cared for, especially Mattie and Jones, and that the stalls had been cleaned, the water was running and the heat was working.

Exhaustion had finally taken its toll on her. Even a quick snack of cheese and crackers didn't give her the energy to stay on her feet.

Worried about Mystic and Josh, she went upstairs, took a long, hot shower and then tumbled into bed and fell asleep just after her head hit the pillow.

When Savannah awoke it was completely dark. A glance at the bedside clock told her that another four hours had passed. Still tired, she forced herself out of bed and was about to call the veterinarian's number when she heard the sound of familiar voices drifting up the stairs. Travis's low voice made her heart leap expectantly. *He's home! Maybe Mystic was already in the stallion barn!*

Shoving her arms through the sleeves of her robe, Savannah hurried down the stairs, through the hall and into the kitchen where Travis and Lester were talking. Both men looked as if they hadn't slept for over a week.

Travis was sitting on the counter, his long legs dangling down the cupboards, his elbows supported by his knees. The lines of strain on his rugged face had become deep grooves and his gray eyes had lost their spark. His wrinkled shirt was stretched tautly over his broad shoulders, which were slumped in defeat, and his jaw was dark with his unshaven beard. All in all he looked completely worn out.

Lester, too, appeared fatigued. The wiry little trainer seemed bent with age as he sat at the kitchen table slowly sipping coffee and smoking a cigarette. His eyelids folded over disenchanted dark eyes and his cheeks were hollow. Gray smoke curled lazily to the ceiling.

Instinctively, Savannah prepared herself for the worst.

"How's Mystic?" she asked without preamble as she walked over to Travis and stood next to him.

The men exchanged worried glances and then Travis looked at her with pained gray eyes. "He's gone," he said. "Never had a chance." With a sound of disgust, he lowered himself from the counter and angrily tossed the dregs of his coffee into the sink.

"Gone?" she echoed blankly but she knew exactly what he meant. Steadying herself against the refrigerator she fought the dryness in her throat. "Oh, no...."

Lester stared into the black liquid in his cup. "Your father had him put down, missy. It was the only thing to do." Taking a drag from his cigarette, he blew out the smoke and then crushed the cigarette out in disgust.

"But why?" she asked, slowly sinking into one of the chairs at the table and staring at the little old trainer.

"It wasn't anyone's fault and Steve, he tried his damnedest to save Mystic's leg," Lester said, rubbing his chin and fishing into his jacket pocket for another crumpled pack. "I thought he'd do it, too, but..." The old man shook his head and lit up again, blowing smoke through his nose. "Mystic, he just couldn't handle it."

"What happened?" she asked, though it really didn't matter. Mystic was dead and that was that. But the thought of the proud black colt brought tears to her eyes. Mystic had been the finest horse ever bred at Beaumont farms. A hellion, yes, but also a gallant Thoroughbred with the speed and endurance of the best. Savannah had to clear her throat against a painful lump that blocked her voice.

Travis stretched his shoulders and rubbed his hands over his dark chin. "The way I understand it, the operation on his ankle was a success. After Mystic had been sedated, Steve had been able to clean the wound, remove some of the bone chips, repair the torn ligaments, set the bones and put a cast on the leg.''

"Then what went wrong?'' Savannah asked, but knowing Mystic's high-strung temperament, she had already guessed the answer.

"Mystic was in a frenzy when he came out of the anesthesia,'' Lester explained, drawing on his cigarette and staring through the window into the black night. "We couldn't control him.''

"He was frantic, kicking and rearing. No one could hold him down. He managed to kick off his special shoe as well as his cast and he even landed a blow on Lester's thigh.''

Lester just shook his head and stared blankly through the window.

"So couldn't Steve have set the leg again, put him in a sling? They do wonderful things these days.''

"Maybe,'' Lester admitted, "but your dad, well, he did the most humane thing possible. The horse was out of his mind as it was; more anesthesia and surgery would have been too traumatic for him. It was doubtful if he would have survived a second operation. It's a shame,'' Lester said softly. "A goddamned shame.''

Fighting the constriction in her chest Savannah stared at her hands. "So what about Josh? What're we going to tell him?''

"I don't know,'' Travis said. "Your father went straight from the equine hospital to Mercy hospital, where Josh is, but I don't think he's going to tell the boy about Mystic until Josh is on the mend.''

"Do you...do you think that lying to him is a good idea?''

Travis took the chair next to her and took hold of her hands. "I wish I knew. I've been asking myself a lot of questions today, and I haven't had much luck finding any answers.''

"Well," Savannah said, taking in a steadying breath and telling herself not to grieve for the big, black colt. At least Mystic was out of pain and there was nothing she or anyone else could do for him now. And Josh was going to be well. She explained about Charmaine's phone call to both Lester and Travis. As she told the men of Josh's condition and prognosis, both Travis and Lester relaxed a little. "Now, how about something to eat?" she asked, forcing false cheer into her voice. "I made some soup earlier."

"Not for me, thanks," Lester said, stubbing his cigarette in an ashtray on the counter. "It's been a long day. I think I'll go home."

"You're sure?"

"As sure as I am about anything, missy." He reached for his hat, which was sitting on the corner of the table, pushed it onto his head and walked out the back door. A few minutes later his pickup rumbled down the drive toward the main road.

"What about you?"

"I'm starved," Travis admitted, gazing affectionately at her. But his gray eyes were clouded with a silent agony. "I just hope I don't have to go through another day like this one," he admitted, stretching his tired back muscles. "There just wasn't a damned thing anyone could do to help the horse."

"Then it's over."

"Except for Josh."

"Except for Josh," she repeated hoarsely. "It won't be easy for him."

Seeing the defeat on her soft features, he squeezed her shoulders and then placed his larger hands over hers. "Well, we'll just have to help him through it, won't we? Now, didn't you promise me something to eat?"

"Oh. Yes. It'll only take a few minutes to warm."

"Do I have time for a shower?"

"Sure." She tried to shake off her black mood and offered him a tentative smile.

Still holding her hand in his, he pulled her closer to him, so that his face was just a few inches from hers.

"It's been one helluva thirty-six hours," he said, his voice low, a finger from his free hand reaching forward to the point where the lapels of her robe crossed. The finger brushed her skin and her heartbeat accelerated rapidly.

His eyes lowered to the seductive hollow of her breasts. "And throughout it all, the one thing that kept me going was the thought that eventually, when it was all over and the smoke had cleared, I'd be with you."

The lump in Savannah's throat swelled. "I've been waiting a long time to hear just those words, counselor," she admitted with a weary sigh.

His hands drifted downward to the belt cinching the soft velour fabric together and his long fingers worked at the knot.

Savannah's breath caught in her throat as his fingers grazed the sensitive skin between her breasts.

"There's one thing I'd like better than a hot shower," he admitted, his voice rough, his eyes meeting hers in a silent, sizzling message.

Savannah's blood was already racing through her body in anticipation. "And what is that?"

"A hot shower *with you*."

The robe slid open to reveal Savannah's scanty silk and lace nightgown, and Travis, his teeth flashing beneath the dark stubble of his beard, smiled wickedly. "Looks like you were expecting me."

She laughed unexpectedly at the seductive gleam in his eyes. "You're flattering yourself."

"I deserve it."

Smiling shyly and observing him through the sweep of dark lashes, she had to agree. "Yes, I suppose you do," she said, gasping when his fingers slid downward to outline the point of her nipple beneath the pink silk.

His other hand slipped upward, behind her neck, and his

strong fingers twined familiarly in the black silk of her hair as he gently drew her face closer to his.

Savannah's heartbeat quickened. When his warm lips molded to hers hungrily and a gray spark of seduction lighted his gaze, she felt warmth spread through her body in rippling waves of desire that started deep within her and flooded all of her senses.

Travis groaned and buried his rough chin against her neck as the breast in his hand swelled, and the firm dark peak pressed taut beneath his palm. He felt Savannah quiver beneath his touch. His loins began to ache with the need to make love to her, the desire to wipe away the strain of the past two days by burying himself in the soft, liquid warmth of her and the yearning to be comforted by her tender hands.

He squeezed his eyes tightly shut and kissed her almost angrily, as if by releasing his leashed fury in passion he could forget that he had just spent two days in the wilderness to save a boy and a horse and that he had failed.

"Just love me, sweet lady," he insisted, wanting to think of nothing other than the yielding woman in his embrace, the smell of her hair, the feel of her pliant muscles, the taste of her skin. "Make love to me until there's nothing left but you and me."

Her answering moan was all the encouragement he needed. Without another word, Travis picked her up and carried her lithely up the stairs to her bedroom.

Then he placed her on the bed and stared down at her with night-darkened eyes that studied every curve of her body.

The pink silk shimmered in the semidarkness. Beneath the fragile cloth, dark nipples stood erect. Her tousled ebony hair splayed against the white pillow, framing the oval of her face in billowing, black clouds. A soft flush colored her creamy skin and her deep blue eyes, glazed with longing, delved deep into his soul.

A powerful swelling in Travis's loins pressed painfully against his jeans as he watched the gentle rise and fall of her breasts. It was all he could do to go slow, take it easy, draw out the sweetness of making love to her.

"I couldn't forget you," he admitted roughly, slowly unbuttoning and removing his shirt only to let it fall onto the floor.

She watched in fascination as he started on the wide buckle of his belt.

"I tried, y'know," he admitted, as if remembering an unpleasant thought. "For nine years I tried to tell myself that you were just a summer fling, one night in a lost world that didn't really count." He slid the jeans off his hips, and kicked his boots into the corner of the room. "But I couldn't. Damn it, I couldn't forget you."

"And you regret that?"

A crooked smile slashed white across his face. "Never!" Sliding next to her on the bed, his fingers fitting familiarly around her waist, he let out a long, ragged breath. "We should have stayed together; it would have saved everyone a whole lot of grief."

"We're together now," she whispered.

"And that's all that matters," he said with that same wicked smile, his fingers inching upward to stroke the underside of a breast through the lace and silk.

"You're so right," she agreed with a sigh as she arched upward, fitting her body against his and kissing him passionately, her tongue slipping familiarly between his teeth.

Travis moaned and slid one hand under the hem of her nightgown as he moved against her. "About that shower?" he asked.

"Later…" she whispered, listening to the thudding of his heart and feeling the wiry hair of his chest brush against her cheeks. "Much later."

Vaguely aware of someone saying something to her, Savannah woke up. She rolled over in the bed and groaned before she felt a warm hand reach over and brush her hair away from her cheek.

"Merry Christmas," Travis whispered.

Opening her eyes and blinking as she stretched, Savannah smiled into Travis's silvery eyes. "It is Christmas morning, isn't it?"

"Christmas afternoon."

Savannah's groggy mind snapped, and she levered herself up on one elbow in order to see the clock on the nightstand. Twelve-thirty! Without another thought she swung her legs over the side of the bed. "Oh my God! The horses—"

Travis's long arm encircled her waist. "Hold on a minute, will ya? Lester's already been here and looked in on them. Everything's fine. Even Mattie and Jones survived without you. Lester said he'll be back later this afternoon."

"And I slept through it?" she asked, unbelieving.

"Like a baby."

"I can't believe it!" She pushed the hair out of her eyes and let out a sigh. "I haven't slept like that in years."

"Nine years, maybe?" he asked softly, nuzzling her ear.

She remembered back to that morning long ago. She had woken late and learned that Travis was going to marry Melinda without even offering an explanation. The old needle of betrayal pricked at her heart and she had to ignore the painful sensation. "Maybe," she admitted, her voice rough.

"Well, lady, you'd better get used to sleeping in, I guess," Travis said with a twinkle in his eye. "Because I never intend to let you get away from me again and I expect that last night was just a preview of what's ahead."

She blushed a little as she thought about the shameless passion that had overtaken her just hours before. Her hunger for Travis had been all-consuming to the point that she had finally fallen asleep from sheer physical exhaustion.

Looking at him lovingly and affectionately stroking his chin, she asked a question that had been in the back of her mind for the past two days. "What is ahead, for you and me?"

"Before or after we're married?"

Her heart nearly stopped beating. *Married? To Travis?* It was almost too good to be true.

He nibbled at her ear, but she pushed him away. She needed to clear her mind and force him to become serious.

"Both," she finally replied, thoughtfully.

"You're no fun," he accused. Then when his thoughts revolved back to what had occurred between them just hours before, he grinned roguishly. "At least you're not much fun this morning."

"And you're ducking the issue."

"Make me some breakfast and I promise to confide in you," he suggested, burying his face in her hair and playfully running his fingers up her spine. "Or maybe you have a better idea...."

She laughed as his fingers slid against her skin, tickling her lightly. "Okay, okay, I guess it's the least I can do," she muttered, realizing that he hadn't eaten much for the better part of two days.

She slid out of bed and started dressing in front of the bureau, aware that his eyes never left her as she took her clothes out of the drawers. Though she was facing away from him, she could see his reflection in the mirror. After tugging her sweater over her head and pulling her thick hair out of the neck opening, she shook the black strands away from her face and arched a brow in his direction. He was still draped across the bed, the sheets covering only the lower half of his body.

"I'm not about to bring you breakfast in bed, you know," she pointed out.

"Like I said, 'no fun in the morning.'" He reached behind his head, grabbed one of the plump pillows and hurled it across the room.

Savannah sidestepped, managed to dodge the soft torpedo and laughed merrily. "Watch it, buster, or you'll end up with dry toast and water instead of crepes and salmon pâté," she warned.

He arched a thick, dark brow and smiled. "Thank God."

"You'll be sorry," she warned.

"I don't think so. As long as I'm here with you, I really don't care." His gray eyes were serious.

"Give me a break," she muttered, but smiled all the same as she left the room.

A half hour later, the kitchen was filled with the tantalizing scents of sizzling bacon, warm apple muffins and hot coffee. Travis was pulling a sweater over his head as he walked into the kitchen. He eyed the table with a Cheshire-Cat-sized smile.

"For me?" he asked, looking at the small table decorated with brass candlesticks, a Christmas-red cloth and dainty sprigs of holly.

"For you, counselor," Savannah admitted, pouring two glasses of champagne and setting them on the table near the plates before lighting the candles.

"Champagne?"

"It's Christmas, isn't it?"

"Maybe the best one of my life," he thought aloud.

She was standing at the sink cutting fresh fruit, when he came up behind her and rested his chin against her shoulder, his long arms wrapping possessively around her waist, his fingertips pressed against her abdomen. "I love you, you know."

Savannah felt tears of joy build behind her eyes. "And I love you."

"I can't think of a better way to spend Christmas than with you," he said, his voice low, his clean-shaven cheek warm against her skin. "Domesticity becomes you."

"Does it? I'm not sure I like the sound of that."

"It's a compliment, and you'd better get used to it," he suggested. "I think I want to wake up with you every morning to pamper me."

"I'm not pampering you." She slid him a sly glance, but grinned at her obvious lie.

"No?"

Smiling, she thought for a minute. "Well, maybe a little.

But I really just wanted to say thanks for finding Josh. If you hadn't been out there looking for him…'' Her voice drifted off and she shivered.

Travis's strong arms tightened around her. "But I was," he remarked. "I just wish we could have done something to save Mystic."

"So do I," she whispered, thinking of Josh and how devastated the boy would be when he learned that Mystic had been put down.

She'd called Charmaine with the bad news while Travis was still upstairs. Charmaine had been adamant that Josh wasn't to be told about Mystic, at least not right away. When Savannah had spoken to Josh, she'd found it difficult to sidestep the truth about his beloved horse. Josh had sounded tired, but anxious to come home to celebrate Christmas and see Mystic. Savannah had hung up with mixed feelings.

Now, she frowned and pushed those unhappy thoughts aside. It was Christmas, she was alone with Travis and she wouldn't let the rest of the world intrude. Not today. "Come on, let's eat and then I intend to put you to work."

"That sounds interesting," he drawled, kissing the back of her neck.

"Not that kind of work," she quipped. "I'm talking about the back-breaking work on the farm."

"Even on Christmas?"

"Especially on Christmas. No one else is here."

"Precisely my point," he said, his lips brushing her ear sensually.

She trembled beneath the gentle assault of his tongue on her ear. He smelled so clean and masculine and the feel of his fingers moving against the flat muscles of her abdomen started igniting the tiny sparks of passion in her blood all over again. It was all she could do to concentrate on the apple she was slicing.

"Travis," she whispered huskily, "if you don't stop this, I might cut myself…or you."

"Spoilsport," he accused with a soft chuckle, but kissed the top of her head and finally released her.

The meal was perfect. They ate in the kitchen and finished the bottle of champagne in the living room between a warm fire and the decorated Christmas tree.

"Two nights ago I never thought I'd be warm again," Travis said, setting his empty glass on a nearby table. He was lying on the thick carpet and lazily watching Savannah.

"And I wondered if I'd ever see you again."

"Well, that's behind us," he said, propped on one elbow near the tree and staring up at her as she sat on her knees and adjusted a misplaced ornament. "And now you'll have one helluva time getting rid of me."

"Promise?" she asked.

"Promise!" He leaned closer to her and kissed her neck until she tumbled willingly into his arms.

They spent the rest of the day taking inventory of the feed and supplies in the barns. It was tiring work and coupled with the usual routine, Savannah was dead tired by the time she returned to the house.

Sadie Stinson had come by earlier in the day and put a stuffed goose in the oven, a platter of cinnamon cookies on the counter and a molded salad in the refrigerator.

"It's not much," the older woman had said as she was leaving.

"What do you mean? It's a feast and it'll save my life! I didn't have anything planned," Savannah had replied.

"Well, I'd rather have stayed and helped."

"Forget it!" Savannah had waved off the older woman's apologies. "I won't hear any excuses! You have your family to worry about. It's Christmas!"

The housekeeper had finally agreed and left with a gift from Savannah tucked under her arm and a promise to return and fix "that child the best Beef Wellington this side of the Rocky Mountains" when Josh was released from the hospital.

"I'll hold you to it," Savannah had replied, waving as Sadie drove carefully down the snow-covered lane.

Now, hours later, as Savannah opened the door to the kitchen, the scent of roasting goose filled her nostrils. "Thank you, Sadie Stinson," Savannah murmured to herself while kicking off her boots and walking through the kitchen in her stocking feet.

She dashed upstairs for a quick shower and hurried back down to the kitchen to put the finishing touches on the meal just as Travis returned from the barns.

"I'd forgotten what it's like to work with the horses," he said, raking his fingers through his hair. "I've spent so many hours behind a desk or in the law library that I can't remember the last time I cut open a bale of hay."

"And how did it feel?"

"It felt good," he admitted with a bemused frown as his eyes searched hers. "But maybe that was because of the company. What do you think?"

"I think you're addled from overwork, counselor." She laughed.

Travis built a fire in the living room while Savannah set the table. They ate by candlelight in the dining room and finally had brandied coffee in the darkened living room. The flickering fire and lighted Christmas tree cast colorful shadows on the walls and windowpanes.

Savannah sat with Travis on the floor, her back propped against the couch, Travis's head resting in her lap. He had taken off his shoes and was warming his stocking feet by the fire while her fingers played in the dark chestnut curls falling over his forehead.

"I want you to marry me," he said at last, moving slightly to get a better view of her face.

She arched a slim, dark brow. "Just like that?"

He chuckled. "This isn't all that quick, you know. I've known you most of my life—well, at least most of yours," he said with a smile. "I don't think we're exactly rushing into it, do you?"

"No…"

"But?"

"A lot of 'buts,' I guess," she admitted.

"Name one."

"Melinda."

Savannah felt the muscles in Travis's back tighten. "Melinda's gone," he said, his jaw clenching and anger smoldering in his eyes.

"But if she were still alive?"

"That's a tough one," he admitted, rolling over and sitting up so that his eyes were level with hers. "And it's not really fair. While she was alive I tried to be the best husband I could to her. Maybe I failed, but I damned well gave it my best shot. Now it's over. She's gone. Don't get me wrong, I didn't wish her dead, but I can't bring her back, either."

Savannah's throat felt raw. "You loved her."

"Yes," he admitted, his eyes seeming distant as he gazed into the fire. "I did. It was a long, long time ago. But I loved her very much."

Even an admission that she had expected tore a hole in Savannah's heart. She tried to tell herself that what happened in the past didn't matter; it was the future that counted, but doubts still nagged her mind. Loving Travis as much as she did, she couldn't bear the thought of him having cared for another woman.

"But I fell in love with you," he said, his lips twisting downward at the corners as if he had read her thoughts. "I think I fell in love with you on the very day I saw you riding Mattie in the fields. You were watching me from under the apple tree and trying to look very grown up and sophisticated. Remember?"

How could she ever forget? "I remember."

"From that day on I couldn't get you out of my mind." He turned his solemn gaze in her direction, and his eyes caressed the soft contours of her face. "You have to believe that I would never have married Melinda, never, except that

I believed she was carrying my child. I couldn't very well marry you knowing that Melinda was going to have my baby, could I?"

"I suppose not. But Dad seems to think… Oh, I guess it doesn't matter."

He became rigid and his back teeth ground together in frustration. His thick brows drew downward over his eyes. "Of course it matters. Tell me, what does Reginald think?"

"He warned me to stay away from you, that you weren't the man for me, that you've always loved Melinda and she'll always be between us."

Travis's face hardened. "Do you believe that?"

"No…"

"Then?" he snapped.

"I just wanted to be sure."

"Good Lord, Savannah," he said with a loud moan. "Haven't you heard a word I've said this past week? Don't you know that your father is still trying to manipulate us both?"

"That, I don't believe. My father is only concerned about my happiness."

"Is that why he didn't tell you that he knew about our affair?" he argued.

Savannah's temper flared. "You mean our one-night stand, don't you? It was only once, by the lake, remember?"

Travis softened a little. "Oh, I remember all right. That night has haunted me for the past nine years, and for the first time since then I'm going to do something about it. I'm going to marry you, lady, and you're not going to come up with any more excuses."

The argument should have ended there, but Savannah couldn't let it lie. Instead, she got to her feet, walked to the fireplace and turned to face him. "Suppose we do get married Travis. What then?"

"We'll move to Colorado."

"Colorado!" she repeated. "Why Colorado?"

"I have some land there; my parents left it to me. I

thought we could make a clean, fresh start away from everything and everyone.''

"You're talking about running away and dropping out, right?"

The corners of his mouth twisted downward. "No. What I mean is that we could raise horses, if that's what you want to do. But we wouldn't have Reginald looking over our shoulders, and I'd be rid of the law practice for good.''

She could feel her stomach quivering, but the anger in his eyes gave her pause. "Is that what you want?"

"What I want is you. It's that simple. I've got enough money to get started somewhere else and I want to get away from lawsuits, political schemes and the past.'' He looked her squarely in the eye. "I'm not running away from anything, Savannah, I'm running *to* a home, a private, safe place for my wife and my children and I'm asking you to come with me.''

"I want to, Travis, but I have a family here, a family that I love very much. My mother's not well, my father depends on me, my sister needs me and then there's Josh. He's more than a nephew to me, he's almost like my own son.''

"I'm not asking you to give them up, not entirely.''

She raised her hands in the air and let them fall to her sides. The argument was futile, but couldn't be ignored. "I understand that you're dissatisfied with your work and your life, but I'm not. I love it here. It's my home. Working with the horses is what I do. I tried working and living in the city once and it didn't work out. This house, this land, these horses...'' She gestured around the room and toward the windows. "They might belong to Dad, but they're mine.''

"You're not coming with me, are you?" he asked.

She felt the tears threatening her eyes. *Why was she arguing?* All she ever wanted was to be with Travis, and he was offering her a lifetime of love, if only she could give up the family that meant so much to her. "You know that I love you," she said. "I always have. But I need a little time to think about all this.''

"I can't wait forever," he said slowly.

"And I wouldn't expect you to." She shrugged her shoulders and tried to think clearly. "Would it be possible for you to stay here on the farm?"

"Live here with your family?"

"Yes."

"No," he replied tersely. "I'm not about to live my life like Wade and Charmaine. I want my own place, my independence, my own home. I came here to cut the ties with Reginald, Savannah, and I still mean to do it."

A slow burn crept up her cheeks at Travis's ingratitude to her father. "You're going to forget that he raised you?" she asked, sarcasm tainting her words. "When no one wanted you because you were such a problem, my father gave you a home!"

Travis pushed himself upright and his shoulders bunched angrily. "I'll always owe your father a debt, no doubt about it, but I'm not paying for it with my life. I'm going to try and forget that he's tried to run my life—to the point of going behind my back with my partner, Henderson. I'm not about to be anyone's pawn, not even Reginald Beaumont's!"

"You'd better watch it," she snapped, her blue eyes sparking. "Or that chip you're wearing on your shoulder might just fall off and create another grand canyon!"

"Cheap shot, Savannah."

"But true."

A glimmer of revenge flickered in his eyes. "Then while we're taking shots..."

"Be my guest."

"At least I'm not afraid to face the past or take a chance and be my own person. I'm not tied like a calf ready for branding to a father and mother because I'm afraid of stepping out on my own for fear of failure."

"I haven't failed!"

"Because you haven't even tried. We all fail, Savannah."

She was so angry her fingers curled around the edge of

the mantel. "The only time I've ever failed was when I trusted you nine years ago," she said, shaking with raw emotion. "I trusted you and loved you, and you made a mockery of that love. And you! You were such a coward that you didn't even bother saying goodbye before you married another woman!"

Stripped of all pretenses, alone in the house, Travis walked over to Savannah and gripped her shoulders. His eyes were bright with challenge, his jaw hard with anger. "I made a mistake," he said between clenched teeth. "And I'll be damned if I'll make another. I've lived with the love I felt for you burning my skin, ruining my wife's self-worth, and I've paid over and over again. Now I'm through paying and lying, and so are you. You can hide from me, Savannah, but I'll find you, and sooner or later you're going to have to face the fact that the past is dead and gone. Buried, just like Melinda and Mystic. We've got a future, damn it, and we're going to have it together."

He pulled her roughly to him and kissed her angrily, his lips hard and bruising, his tongue plundering. She tried to resist but couldn't. Traitorous desire burned brightly in her breast, and she leaned against him and let her tears of frustration run down her cheeks.

"Tell me you love me," he demanded, his hands spreading on the small of her back, pushing her tight against the hard evidence of his desire, possessively claiming her as his.

"You know I do—"

"Say it!"

"I love you," she whispered, her voice catching.

His glittering eyes softened a little. "Then don't let all the bullshit get in our way. I love you and I'm not about to let anything or anyone stand between us!" His shoulders slackened a little as the fury seeped from his body. "Oh, Savannah, we've come too far to turn back and hide. We're going to face the future and we're going to face it together!"

He kissed her again, more gently this time, and she

wound her arms around his neck. And then, by the warmth of the fire, with the colored lights from the tree winking seductively, he slowly undressed her and made love to her long into the night.

Ten

For the remainder of the week, Savannah and Travis lived with an unspoken truce. The subject of the future was pushed aside while Savannah concentrated on keeping the farm running smoothly.

The snow had finally begun to melt the third day after Christmas, and life on the farm returned to a more normal schedule.

Travis seemed to thrive on the physical labor of the farm, and Lester was pleased to have him around. From time to time, Savannah caught the trainer smiling to himself and nodding as he watched Travis working with the animals.

Saturday afternoon, Lester was watching Vagabond and a few other other colts stretch their legs in the paddock when Savannah and Travis joined him. Only a few patches of snow remained on the ground, and the horses were making the most of their freedom.

Vagabond, his tail and head held high, raced from one end of the field to the other while snorting and bucking.

"Sure beats all that Perry Mason law business, doesn't it?" Lester remarked, watching the frisky colt's easy strides.

Travis threw back his head and laughed aloud. "If only my cases were as interesting as Perry's. If they had been, I might not have given up law." He leaned against a fence post and rubbed his cramped shoulders. "Most of the time I was in the library reading decisions regarding corporate law."

Lester's older eyes sparkled. "Not exactly your cup of tea."

"Not exactly," Travis commented dryly, his lips thinning as he watched the animals romp.

"But you've got a way with the horses," Lester pointed out.

"That's right," Savannah added, smiling slyly in Travis's direction. "You've got Vagabond eating out of your hand."

"That'll be the day," Travis replied, cocking his head in the direction of the bay colt. "Just yesterday he tried to take a piece out of my arm."

"He's a little temperamental," Savannah admitted with a teasing smile.

"High-strung," Lester added.

"Temperamental?" Travis echoed. "High-strung? I'd call it downright miserable and mean," Travis said before chuckling to himself.

"But you've got to admit he's got charisma," Savannah said.

"And speed," Lester added, watching the bay colt kick up his heels in the west pasture. The bay's smooth coat and rippling muscles glistened in the pale morning sunlight. "Let's just hope he has a little luck as well!"

"That, we all could use," Savannah agreed.

Later in the morning Charmaine called to say that Josh was about to be released from the hospital. Reginald and Virginia as well as Wade, Charmaine and Joshua would be home late in the afternoon.

"Worried?" Travis asked, resting on the handle of the pitchfork in the hayloft over the stallion barn and staring into Savannah's troubled blue eyes.

"A little," she admitted. "These past few days I'd forgotten about all the problems, I guess." She smiled faintly and climbed down the ladder to find herself standing in front of Mystic's empty stall. It had been cleaned and now was waiting for another one of Beaumont Breeding Farm's colts to claim it as his own. She felt empty inside at the loss of Mystic.

"And now all the trouble is coming home?" Travis followed her down the ladder and hopped off the final rung.

"Yeah, I guess."

"Don't worry about it," he suggested with a patient smile.

"Easier said than done." Leaning over the gate to Mystic's stall, she thought about the magnificent black colt.

"You can't bring him back, y'know," Travis said softly.

Savannah sighed and nodded. "I know, but I can't help but worry about Josh and Wade...."

"Wade is Josh's father."

"Unfortunately," she whispered. "I wish to God that I could take that kid away from Wade Benson."

"He's the boy's father whether you like it or not."

Her throat ached and her frustration made her angry. She turned around to face the tenderness in Travis's eyes. "Is it as simple as all that?" she asked. "Is the law so cut-and-dried that a man who should never have become a father in the first place can browbeat a child until he has no self-esteem left?"

Travis tugged pensively on his lower lip. "Unless you can prove abuse—"

"Physical abuse, you mean," she snapped, her jaw jutting forward angrily. "But it doesn't matter what kind of mental cruelty a child like Josh is put through."

"That's Charmaine's problem," Travis pointed out, steadying Savannah with his hands by placing his palms firmly over her shoulders.

"According to the law! But I feel responsible for that child. It's just so damned unfair!" She crossed her arms over her chest and tried to turn away from him.

"Hey, slow down. Come into the house.... I'll buy you a cup of coffee. Josh will be home soon and you can shower him with all that pent-up auntly love."

"Auntly?"

"That's what you are, aren't you?" he asked, pulling on her shoulders and hugging her body next to his before kissing her tenderly on the top of the head.

She had to smile despite her anger. "I suppose so."

"And I'd guess that you bought out the stores with all sorts of those ugly creatures and robots that he likes."

"Not quite."

Travis laughed. "Then buck up, will ya? Josh's coming home tonight and you promised him that we'd celebrate Christmas together. So you'd better put on one helluva show or you'll disappoint that nephew you love so much. I've got to run into town for a while, so you can fiddle in the kitchen with Sadie."

"She'd kill me. When she's here, the kitchen is her domain. Even Archimedes isn't welcome."

"Then go and string popcorn, hang mistletoe, sing carols or whatever it is you do around this time of the year, and while you're at it put a smile on that beautiful face."

"Sing carols?" she repeated, laughing a little. "I don't think so."

He sobered slightly and squeezed her shoulders. "Just be happy, love; that's all."

The depth of her feelings for him was reflected in her eyes as she forced a small grin. "And where will you be?"

He winked broadly. "I'm gonna get Josh a present that will knock his socks off."

"Are you?" Savannah was delighted.

"You bet."

"So who's going to take care of the horses while I'm, uh, singing carols?"

"I will, when I get back."

"You?"

"Sure, what's wrong with that?"

"Nothing," she said with a wicked twinkle in her eyes. "You're on." She chuckled as she handed him a bucket and a brush. "First you can clean the stalls and then—"

Setting the tools aside, he glared at Savannah in mock

anger. "And then I'll come into the house and show you who's boss."

"Promises, promises," she quipped as she slipped out of his arms, through the door of the stallion barn, running back to the house with Travis on her heels.

"I thought you were going into town," she laughed when he caught up with her and jerked her roughly against him.

"I am, but when I get back…" He pressed warm lips to hers and held her as if afraid to let go.

"What?" she coaxed with a knowing smile.

"I'll deal with you then."

"I can hardly wait." She extricated herself from his arms and heard him swear under his breath as he started toward the pickup in the parking lot.

Savannah, her head bent while tucking a pin in her hair, started down the stairs. After helping Sadie in the kitchen, she'd spent the past hour showering, dressing, pinning her hair into a chignon and wondering when Travis would return. Josh would be home any minute and Travis hadn't come back from town.

The doorbell caught her by surprise.

"I'll get it," she called downstairs toward the kitchen, where Sadie was still fussing. She hurried down the remaining steps and across the foyer.

Jerking open the door, Savannah found herself face to face with the reporter from the *Register*. Her heart nearly stopped beating and her smile froze on her face. *Not now,* she thought wildly, *not when Josh is due home within the hour!*

"Good afternoon," John Herman said, extending his hand.

"Good afternoon. What can I do for you?" she asked warily.

"I'd like to talk to you about Mystic for starters," the reporter responded, a full smile sliding easily over his face.

"I'd like to do a story about a great horse, you know, from the time he was a foal to the present."

She blocked his passage into the house and met his inquiring gaze. "I thought the *Register* already ran an article on Mystic."

"Right, but I'd like to do a bigger piece on the horse. You know, more of a human-interest story. I'd need to find out where he was raised, who worked with him, interview his trainer and the jockey who rode him, bring up all of his races, especially the Preakness, and slant the story for the local readers."

"I don't think so."

"It could be good publicity for the farm," John Herman persisted. "We'd be glad to include anything new, say, about the other horses. You've got another horse, a—" he checked his notes "—Vagabond, isn't it?"

"Yes. He's a two-year-old."

"I've heard people compare him to Mystic."

"The same temperament," Savannah said, forcing a tight smile. "But that's about it. And, as for Mystic, I'm not ready to give you a story about him, not yet, anyway." *Not until Josh is told the truth.* "I'm sorry you made the trip for nothing, maybe next time you'll call," she apologized, when she heard the sound of a pickup coming down the lane and realized with a sinking feeling that Travis had finally returned.

"Then maybe I could speak to Mr. McCord," the reporter persisted.

"He's...he's not here at the moment."

The screen door to the back porch banged shut. Savannah heard Travis walk through the kitchen and toward the hall.

"I'll tell him you were here to see him," she said hurriedly.

"Savannah," Travis called out, stopping when he walked into the hall and saw her wedged between the door and the doorjamb. "What the devil?"

"Mr. McCord!" John Herman said with enthusiasm, looking over Savannah's shoulder and smiling broadly.

There was nothing she could do about it. Reluctantly Savannah let the man inside. It was obvious from the spark of interest in John Herman's eyes that the main purpose for his visit to the farm had been to question Travis.

"John Herman," the reporter said, extending his hand. Travis took the man's outstretched palm, but didn't hide his skepticism. "I'm a reporter for the *Register*."

"I see." Travis smiled cynically. "Why don't you come into the living room where we can talk?" He glanced at Savannah and mildly inquired, "Savannah?"

Stunned at Travis's polite reaction to the press, Savannah realized she had completely forgotten her manners. "Yes, please come into the living room and I'll get some coffee." Casting Travis a I-hope-you-know-what-you're-getting-yourself-into look, she went to the kitchen, grabbed the blue enamel coffeepot and several empty cups and quickly explained to Sadie what was happening.

"Lord have mercy," Sadie prayed, rolling her eyes to the ceiling before preparing a tray of cookies. "Just make sure that reporter is gone before the boy arrives. His folks haven't told him about the horse, you know."

"I know," Savannah muttered angrily.

Sadie noticed Savannah's trembling fingers and placed her hand over the younger woman's wrist. "You go in there and keep Travis out of trouble. I'll bring the coffee in when it's brewed."

"You're sure?"

"Go on...go on."

"All right," Savannah replied as she walked out of the kitchen.

There was something about John Herman's attitude that rankled and unnerved her. The reporter tended to write a biting column that was filled with sharp wit, a smattering of truth and more rumors than fact.

Don't worry, she told herself as she started back to the

living room, *Travis can handle himself. He's a lawyer and was almost a politician. He can deal with the press.*

"So you really are dropping out of the race?" Herman asked, his tape recorder poised by his side on the arm of the couch.

Travis, looking calm and nearly disinterested, leaned against the fireplace. Only the tiny muscle working in the corner of his jaw gave any sign of his inner tension. "I was never in it."

"But you did take contributions?"

"Never."

Herman's mouth tightened and he quickly scanned his notes. "There are several people who would dispute that. One of the most prominent is a Mrs. Eleanor Phillips. She charges that she gave you five thousand dollars."

"She didn't give me a dime," Travis replied. "And I wouldn't have taken it if she'd tried to give it to me."

"She claims she has a cancelled check to prove it."

"If so, I've never seen it."

John Herman held out his hand, as if to prevent Travis from lying. "Mr. McCord—"

"There may have been a few people working for me who were...overzealous in thinking that I would run. And they may have taken contributions in my name, but they did it without my knowledge, and I've instructed them to return the money with interest."

"So you're saying that you can't be persuaded to run for governor."

"That's right."

Flipping his notebook to a clean page, and making sure that his recorder was working properly, the reporter turned to Savannah just as Sadie brought in the coffee.

"Now, what can you tell me about Mystic?" he asked, while accepting a cup of coffee from a cool Sadie.

"Nothing you don't already know."

Herman wasn't about to be dissuaded. "We got the official story from the veterinarian, Steve Anderson, but we'd like to know exactly what happened to the horse to cause the break in his leg."

"I really don't know," Savannah replied.

"Well, how did he get out? Did the kid really take him?"

"Joshua took him," she admitted.

"But why? Where was he going? Did he have an accomplice?"

"I think that's enough questions," Travis cut in, the smile on his face deadly. "Josh took the horse out for a ride and got caught in the storm. Subsequently, Mystic was injured and unfortunately couldn't be saved. It was a very unfortunate and tragic situation for everyone involved."

"Yes, but—"

"Now, if you'll excuse us," Travis said calmly. "Ms. Beaumont and I have work to get done."

Begrudgingly taking the hint, John Herman stood from his position on the couch, shut off his recorder and stuffed it, as well as his notepad, under his arm.

"It's been a pleasure, Mr. McCord," he said and nodded curtly to Savannah. "Thank you, Ms. Beaumont."

"You're welcome," she lied.

Travis escorted the reporter to the door and Savannah sank into the cushions of the couch.

"Vultures," Travis muttered once the reporter was gone. Taking a cup of coffee from the table, he balanced on the arm of the couch and patted Savannah on the knee. "The good news is I don't think he'll be back."

"Impossible," Savannah replied, threading her fingers through Travis's strong ones. "You know what they say about bad pennies?"

Nodding, Travis waved off her worries. "Well, we can't be too concerned about John Herman; he writes what he wants to. We'll just have to hope that the editor of the *Register* makes him stick to the facts." He cocked his wrist and checked his watch before finishing his coffee. "Everyone will be home soon and we still have Christmas to celebrate."

"Speaking of which, what did you get Josh?"

A broad smile crept over Travis's face. "Something that he'll positively adore."

"I hate to ask."

"Then don't. I'm going to get cleaned up and then I have some work I have to finish in the den," Travis said.

"Again?" Savannah's fine brows drew together in confusion.

"It wont take long," he promised, kissing her lightly on the cheek.

"What is it you do in there?"

"Accounting," he replied cryptically.

"Why?"

His smile grew. "For peace of mind."

"I don't believe you."

"You asked," he said, standing and stretching, "and I told you. Now, why don't you get this couch fixed up for Josh? That way he can be down here with the tree before we have to put him in his room for the night."

"That's a good idea, even if you only offered it because you wanted to change the subject."

"Stick with me," he said, his eyes gleaming seductively and his voice lowering as he touched her cheek. "I've got lots of good ideas, some of which I'll be glad to personally demonstrate later."

She laughed in spite of herself. "That's a terrible line, counselor," she said, chuckling. "It's a good thing I love you or I'd never let you get away with it."

Deciding to bring down warm blankets and a thick quilt for Josh, she left the room and smiled to herself. The love in her heart swelled until she could almost feel it.

Josh looked so small. He was pale and in a brace that covered most of his upper body. His usually bright eyes were dull, and his hair had lost some of its sheen.

"You look like you've been to the wars and back," Savannah said as she finished tucking the blankets around the cushions of the couch.

"I feel like it, too."

"Tell me about it," Savannah suggested, helping the boy onto the sofa and tugging a Christmas quilt around his slim pajama-clad legs.

"I'm okay, I guess," he said bravely looking at the room full of adults.

"Are you ready for Christmas?"

"You bet," he replied, his eyes dancing a little and color coming back to his cheeks.

"Good. Just wait here, and I'll move this table in front of the couch, and you can eat right in here."

"Will you eat with me?" he asked shyly.

"Wouldn't hear of anything else," she agreed, smiling fondly at the boy and pulling up a chair near him.

While the rest of the family changed for dinner, Savannah spent her time spoiling Josh. "I missed you around here," she said, once the small table was covered with more food than an entire battalion of soldiers could eat.

"Really?"

"Really."

"I missed you, too," Josh admitted. "And I missed Mystic. Do you think you can take me out to see him?"

Savannah had thought she'd prepared herself for the question, but her carefully formed response felt like the lie it was and it stuck in her throat. She forced herself to meet Josh's worried gaze. "No, Josh, I can't. You know that. You've got to stay in the house and rest. At least until the brace is off."

"That might be weeks," he whined.

"Well, for the time being the stables and the stallion barn are definitely off limits." Turning to her plate, Savannah made a big show of starting the meal, hoping Josh would follow her lead and quit asking about Mystic.

Josh studied the platter of food before him but didn't

touch it. "I think something's wrong with Mystic," he finally said.

Savannah's palms had begun to sweat. "Wrong? Why?"

He eyed her speculatively, with the cunning of a boy twice his age. "Everyone gets real jumpy when I talk about him."

"It's just because we're worried about you."

He shook his head and winced at a sudden stab of pain. "I don't think so," he said paling slightly. "Dad and Mom, even Grandpa, they act like they're hiding something from me."

"Maybe they're just sharing Christmas secrets."

"Aunt Savvy?"

Here it comes, she thought.

"You wouldn't lie to me, would you?"

Savannah felt her heart constrict, but she managed to meet his concerned gaze. "I wouldn't do anything to hurt you, Josh."

"That's not what I asked."

"Have I ever lied before?"

He was quiet for a moment. "No."

"Then why would I start now?"

"Because something bad happened. Something that nobody wants me to find out about."

Savannah forced a smile. "You know what I think, don't ya?"

"No, what?" Earnest boyish eyes pierced hers.

"That you've been lying in that hospital bed with too much to think about and too little to do. Well, sport, we're about to change all that right now. Eat your dinner and we'll open some presents, what do ya say?"

"All right!" Josh exclaimed enthusiastically, but slid a questioning look through the window toward the stallion barn.

Josh went to bed early, and he was so besotted with the cross-breed cocker spaniel puppy that Travis had given him, he didn't ask about Mystic again.

The evening had been strained and Savannah was grateful that it was over. *But there's still tomorrow and the next day,* she thought angrily to herself. *Sooner or later someone will have to tell Josh the truth!*

Savannah and Travis were just pushing the used wrapping paper into a cardboard box when Charmaine came back down the stairs. She was dressed in her bathrobe and slippers and she looked tired enough to drop through the floor.

"I just came down to say good-night," she explained, leaning one shoulder against the archway between the foyer and the living room. "And to say thanks, Travis, for the puppy."

"I figured that Josh might need a special friend when he finds out about Mystic."

"I know, I know," Charmaine said, shaking her head. "I should have told him before now, but I just couldn't. Strange as it was, he loved that foul-tempered horse. It'll kill him when he finds out that Mystic's gone."

"He'll know sooner or later," Travis said. "Reporters were here earlier today. There's bound to be another story in the paper. Even if that doesn't happen, one of Josh's friends might call and ask him about the horse."

Charmaine paled. "You're right, of course, but it's just not that easy."

"It's better if he hears it from you," Savannah said, pushing the last piece of paper into the box before straightening. "That way the lie will seem smaller."

"Maybe we'll tell him tomorrow," Charmaine said. "I just can't think about it right now, I'm too tired." She smiled sadly and left the room.

"Someone's got to tell him," Savannah said, crossing her arms over her chest.

"But not you, remember?" Travis reminded her. He took her hand and pulled her into the archway. "That's a job for his parents."

"Then they'd better do it and soon."

"I've got no argument with that," Travis said, "but let's trust Charmaine and Wade to handle it their way. Like it or not, you're not his mother."

"So you keep reminding me. But I am his aunt and his friend, and I can't stand lying to him."

"Then don't. Just avoid the subject of Mystic."

"That sounds like a lawyer talking," she said caustically. "And even if I do avoid the subject, it won't matter. Josh can read me like a book."

"Come on, lady," he cajoled, unplugging the Christmas tree and then pinning her against the wall with the length of his body. "You can worry about that tomorrow. Tonight you've got enough on your hands just keeping me happy."

"Is that so?" she asked.

The darkened room cast intriguing shadows over Travis's handsome features. His eyes stared deep into hers, and the kiss he gave her made her insides quiver. "There is something else I've been meaning to discuss with you," he murmured into her ear.

"Such as?"

"Something I've wanted to do for a long time." He reached into his pocket and extracted a white-gold ring with a large, pear-shaped diamond. The exquisite stone shimmered in the firelight, reflecting the red and orange flames. "Merry Christmas," he whispered against her hair.

Savannah stared at the ring and fought the urge to cry. "But when did you get this?"

"It came with the dog."

"Sure." She laughed, tears gathering in her eyes.

"Honest."

"I never dreamed..." she whispered.

"Dream. With me." His lips brushed over hers and his slumberous gray eyes looked past her tears and deep into her soul. "Just know that whatever happens, I love you."

"What's that supposed to mean?"

"Just that the fireworks are about to begin."

She swallowed hard. "You're going to confront Dad again, aren't you?" she accused. "Oh, Lord, Travis. What is it? What have you found out?"

"Nothing," he said. "Nothing yet."

"But you expect to."

"Just trust me." He placed the ring in her palm and gently folded her fingers around it. "I'm giving this ring to you because I love you and I want you to marry me. No matter what else happens, remember that."

"You act as if you're going to leave," she said.

"I am, for a little while. But I'll be back."

"And then?"

"And then I'll expect you to come with me."

"To Colorado," she guessed, feeling a weight upon her slim shoulders.

"Wherever. I really don't think it will matter."

Savannah sensed that things were about to change, that all she had known was about to be destroyed by the one man she loved with a desperation that took her breath away. "What're you going to do?" she asked, her fingers clutching his shirt.

"Bait a trap," he said with a sad smile.

"And you're leaving tonight?"

"In the morning." Travis saw the anxiety in her eyes and kissed her forehead. "Don't worry. I'll be back, and when I am, you'll be free to come with me."

Ignoring the dread that feathered down her spine, she responded to the gentle pressure of his hands against her back and the warmth of his lips over hers.

"We only have one night together for a while," he murmured. "Let's make the most of it." Without waiting for her response, he gently tugged on her hand, led her through the kitchen to collect their coats, and out the back door, to the loft.

As she had worried it would, Savannah's life changed drastically the next morning.

"What the hell is all of this about?" Reginald roared as he kicked off his boots on the back porch. He'd already made his rounds and had come back into the kitchen with the morning paper tucked under his arm. Seeing Travis and Savannah together obviously made his blood boil.

He slapped the open paper onto the table. Bold black letters across the front page of the *Register* made Travis's withdrawal from the governor's race official.

"I told you I wasn't planning on running," Travis said, a lazy grin slanting across his face.

"But I thought you'd change your mind. A man just doesn't throw away an opportunity like this! We're talking about the governorship of California—one of the most powerful positions on the West Coast! Why in God's name wouldn't you want it?" Reginald looked stunned and perplexed, as if Travis were a creature he couldn't begin to understand.

"I explained all that before."

Reginald slid into the nearest chair and Savannah poured him a glass of orange juice. "I thought you'd change your mind, that you just needed a change of scenery to recover after the Eldridge case as well as Melinda's death."

"I haven't and I won't."

"You should have waited before you told the press," Reginald said dejectedly.

"No reason."

"But there's a chance you will reverse your position."

"No way. I'm out." Travis finished his glass of juice and reached for a cup of coffee.

"So what do you plan to do? Willis Henderson said you wanted to sell your half of the law partnership to him."

"That's right. I'm going back to L.A. today to sign the papers and tie up a few loose ends."

"And then?"

"And then I'll be back. For Savannah." The smile on Travis's face hardened around the corners of his mouth. "I've asked her to marry me."

"You what!" Reginald paled. He slumped lower in the chair and sighed before looking at Savannah. "You're really not seriously thinking about marriage are you?"

Savannah laughed. "I'm twenty-six, Dad."

"But your feelings for him are all turned around. They have been since that summer that he came back to the farm." He rubbed a tired hand over his face and then impaled Travis with his cold eyes. "And after the marriage, what then?"

"Colorado."

"Colorado? Oh, God, why?"

"A new start."

Reginald reached into his jacket pocket for his pipe. "Well, I can't say as I blame you, I guess," he said wearily. "From the looks of this," he tapped his pipe on the paper, "you'll need one."

Savannah picked up the paper and her stomach twisted as she read the article. Though most of the facts were accurate, the slant of the report was that Travis was leaving the race because of a reported scandal in which he had been accused of taking contributions for a nonexistent campaign.

Later in the article it was mentioned that Travis may have been involved in the controversy surrounding Mystic's death.

Savannah, white and shaking after reading the article, lifted her eyes to meet the concerned gaze of her father. "What controversy?" she asked.

"There are those who think Mystic could have been saved," Reginald said. "I heard about it when I stayed in Sacramento to be near Josh."

"But Steve did everything possible."

"There are always some people who will second-guess." Reginald studied his pipe. "I considered another surgery on the horse, but it just didn't seem fair to Mystic. The odds that he would have survived were minimal and we—Lester, Steve and I—agreed it would be best to put him out of his agony. I explained that to the press, but of course, other people, including some in the racing industry, disagreed.''

"So what does that have to do with Travis?"

"Nothing, really," Travis explained with a grimace. "But right now it makes for an interesting story, especially since I've been staying here at the farm and was involved in finding Mystic."

"You should stay here and fight," Reginald said, his face suddenly suffusing with color. "You should run for the governorship and win, damn it. That would stop all the wagging tongues...."

Travis took a seat opposite Reginald at the table. "But that's not what you're worried about is it? You have other reasons for wanting me involved in politics."

"Of course I do."

"Name one."

"I think it would be a great accomplishment for you."

"I said, 'name one' and I meant a real reason."

Reginald's eyes flickered from Travis to Savannah and back again. "You know it would be a feather in my cap," he said nervously.

"How?" Travis leaned forward on his elbows and stared straight at Reginald with a look that could cut through steel.

"I practically raised you as my own son and— "

"And that has nothing to do with it except for the fact that you've always tried to use me." He pointed one long finger on the table and tapped it against the polished wood. "Now, give me specifics."

"I don't have any."

Travis frowned and settled back in his chair, crossing his arms over his chest. Then he smiled cynically and his eyes remained cold.

"What's this all about?" Savannah asked, surveying the confrontation between the two men with mounting dread.

"I think it all started with a piece of property just outside of San Francisco."

"You mean Dad's land?" Savannah asked, noticing that Reginald's stiff shoulders fell. "I don't understand."

"You would if you snooped through his office and did some digging in the checkbook."

"Oh, Travis, you didn't," she murmured.

"Why don't you let your father explain?"

Reginald's thick brows lifted. "Wade was worried that you'd been looking where you shouldn't have."

"He had good cause to worry," Travis said angrily.

"What's wrong with the property?" Savannah asked.

"Nothing. Not yet. But plans are already being made."

"What kind of plans?" she asked, leaning against the counter and staring at her father with wide, disbelieving eyes.

"It's not all that big a deal," her father said with a frown. "You know, I've always thought that Travis should go into politics."

Savannah nodded and Travis's eyes narrowed. "Go on," Savannah coaxed.

"Two years ago I had this opportunity to buy some land near San Francisco at a good price. The company that owned it was going bankrupt. I heard of the distress sale and bought the acreage. It was just a case of being in the right place at the right time. Anyway, I had it surveyed and decided that I'd want to build a racetrack, a kind of memorial to myself and the horses we've raised, name it Beaumont Park." His eyes slid to Travis. "There's no crime in that, is there?"

"I didn't know this," Savannah said incredulously. "So what does that have to do with Travis?"

"Red tape," Travis explained. "The land was zoned all wrong and there was bound to be some protest from the farms bordering Reginald's land if he decided that he wanted to build a racetrack."

"But Travis wasn't even elected," she said to her father.

"I know. It was kind of a long shot, but when I couldn't get a straight answer from Travis, I talked to Melinda and she told me that he was setting his sights for the next governor's race. I knew that as governor he could be influential and help me build the park.''

''As well as make a ton of money,'' Travis cut in.

''That, too, of course.''

''Of course,'' Travis repeated. ''You know, Reginald, that's taking a helluva lot for granted. Especially since I hadn't announced any intention of running.''

''But I knew Melinda and how influential she was in your life.'' Reginald looked at his daughter. ''She managed to get you to marry her, when you were attracted to Savannah, didn't she?''

Savannah felt her face color in the ensuing silence.

''And she held on to you, helped you make career decisions as well as personal ones. I knew that you relied on her judgment, Travis, and if she said you were going to run, it was good enough for me.''

''All behind my back.''

''You were busy.''

''So what happened when Melinda died?'' Travis wanted to know.

''There was the Eldridge case, which you won with flying colors. You were the hero of the hour after winning that decision against the drug company....''

Travis glared at the older man. ''What if I had run and lost? That was a distinct possibility, you know.''

''Not according to the pollsters.''

''A lot could have happened between now and then; besides, the public does happen to change its mind on occasion.''

''I'd considered that,'' Reginald admitted. ''I could still sell that land at a substantial profit. But of course, it would be a lot less than I'd make if I sold to a consortium of investors who were interested in building Beaumont Park.''

''I don't believe this,'' Savannah said.

''There's more,'' Travis thought aloud. ''You expected me to appoint you to the board, didn't you?''

Reginald frowned thoughtfully. "I'd hoped," he admitted.

"You expected one helluva lot, didn't you?" Travis said, swearing angrily. "Good God, man, not only did you bet that I'd win a race I wasn't running in, but then you wanted personal favors from me as well." Travis's face colored as he became more incensed. "I just want you to know here and now, for the record, if I ever decide to go into politics, I'll never owe any man anything!"

"This is insane," Savannah thought aloud. "Travis hadn't even announced his candidacy!"

Reginald offered his daughter a humbling grin. "I still have dreams, you know, dreams I haven't fulfilled, and I'm running out of time. I'm not the kind of man who can just retire...." He lifted his palms, hoping she would understand.

"But you don't have to."

Lighting his pipe, Reginald shook his head. A thick cloud of scented smoke rose to the ceiling. "I'm afraid I do. I need to move your mother into town, so she's closer to the things she likes to do. She needs to be near a hospital, but I'd be bored to death in the city. You know that."

"Yes," Savannah replied, remembering her own brief career in San Francisco. All the while, she'd been itching to return to the farm. Working outside with the horses was in her blood, as it was in her father's.

Reginald stood and walked to the door. "Then try and understand and be patient with me."

She watched in disbelief as Reginald, attempting to straighten his shoulders, walked out the door. "So you were right," she whispered to Travis. Through the window Savannah watched her father walk through the wet grass toward the stables. Archimedes was tagging along behind him.

"Does that change things?" Travis asked.

She offered a faltering smile. "A little I guess."

He looked down at her hand and the diamond sparkling on her finger. "Come with me to L.A."

"I can't." She shook her head and smiled. "Too much

is unsteady here at the farm. Josh is still laid up, Charmaine's worried, Dad's still despondent about Mystic and Wade…''

"Yeah, I've noticed. He's holed himself up with a bottle every night.'' Travis sighed wearily and looked deep into her eyes. "So what happens when I come back for you? Will you be able to leave with me?''

"I hope so,'' she said, her eyes sliding over the familiar rolling hills and fields that were so dear to her.

"But you can't say for sure.''

"No, not yet.''

"I was afraid it would come to this, but maybe I can help you make up your mind.'' His smile became hard. "Like I told you last night, I'm going to L.A. to bait a trap and when I come back, maybe this whole mess will be straightened out.''

"I don't see how,'' she whispered.

"Trust me,'' he said, kissing her softly on the lips. "I told you that I wasn't about to let you go again and that's a promise I intend to keep!''

Eleven

Travis had been gone for over a week and Josh was beginning to heal. So far, Charmaine had been able to screen Josh's friends' calls, and no one had let Josh know that Mystic had been destroyed.

Savannah was more on edge with each passing day, afraid that she or someone else on the farm would experience an inadvertent slip of the tongue around the boy. She'd even tried to talk to both Wade and Charmaine, but no amount of persuading could convince Josh's parents to tell their son about the dead colt.

She missed Travis more than she thought was humanly possible and reluctantly agreed that he had been right all along. It was time for her to make a life for herself, a life with him. But walking away from the family she loved and the farm she held dear would be like tearing a huge hole out of her heart and leaving a dark empty chasm in her life.

"Don't be foolish," she'd told herself, but couldn't fight the pangs of regret she was already feeling.

She walked slowly from the main stables toward the stallion barn and wondered when Travis would return. Though he'd called once, their telephone conversation had been brief and stilted.

The engagement ring around her finger continued to sparkle and remind her that soon, after so many years apart, she would be Travis's wife, able to start a new life, perhaps have a child of her own. *Travis's child.*

With that warming thought she hurried to the stallion barn

but stopped dead in her tracks when she saw Josh near the barn door.

"Hey, sport," she called and Josh jumped and whirled to face her. "What're you doing out here?" she asked softly. "I thought you gave up your early-morning rounds."

"I just wanted to see Mystic," Josh replied, turning earnest eyes upward to meet her loving gaze.

"Does your mom know you're here?"

Josh pushed his toe into the mud. "No."

"Or your dad or grandpa?"

"No one but you, Aunt Savvy. You're not going to tell on me, are you?"

Savannah shook her head and smiled. Bending her head to be on eye level with the boy, she winked at him. "I wouldn't dream of it."

Josh took advantage of her good nature. "Then you'll let me into the barn?"

She leaned a shoulder against the door and weighed the alternatives. In another week Josh would get his brace off and would be returning to school. He needed time to adjust and grieve for the horse he'd loved before he faced his friends.

"I'd be in big trouble with your folks," she said.

"They'll never know," Josh pressed.

"They'd know." Her smile slowly fell from her face.

"How?" His question was so innocent. It ripped through her heart.

Breathing deeply, she placed a comforting hand on Josh's shoulder. "First of all, let me explain something."

"Why?"

"For once, you just listen, okay?"

The boy swallowed and stuck out his chin. "Okay."

"You know that we all love you very much." When he tried to interrupt, she held up her hand and kept talking very quickly. "And everything that we've done is to protect you and keep you safe."

"Like what?"

"Josh, I really don't know how to tell you this, but I wish I'd done it a long time ago. Come on." She pushed open the door to the barn. It creaked on old hinges and let a little daylight into the darkened interior. Several stallions nickered softly as Savannah snapped on the lights and braced herself for Josh's despair.

"What's wrong?" Josh asked, his gaze wandering to Mystic's empty stall. "Where's Mystic?"

"He's gone, Josh," Savannah said softly, touching the boy on the shoulder.

"Gone?" he repeated, his face pinching with fear as he twisted away from her. "Gone where?" The boy raced down the aisle and stood at Mystic's empty stall. "Where is he?" he asked, tears in his eyes. "Grandpa didn't sell him did he? He wouldn't!"

"No," Savannah said calmly. "But Grandpa did have to have Mystic put down. He was hurt and the vet couldn't help him."

"Hurt!" the boy screamed, losing all of his color, his eyes widening in horror. Several of the horses began to shift warily within their stalls. "What do you mean?"

"His leg was broken," she said as calmly as possible.

Josh's small features contorted in grief, and tears drizzled down his cheeks. "Because of when I took him away from here during the storm, right?"

Savannah's stomach knotted painfully. "That's when it happened."

"Then it's all my fault!"

"Of course not." Slowly she advanced toward her nephew, offering him an encouraging smile as well as her understanding gaze.

"How can you say that?" Josh demanded, his voice cracking. "I took him, didn't I? I rode him when I wasn't supposed to! Oh, Aunt Savvy, I killed him! I killed Mystic!"

"Mystic hurt himself. It was an accident."

"Then why didn't anybody tell me?" Josh asked, wiping his eyes with his sleeve.

"Because the doctors were afraid that you'd be upset. Once you got home it was difficult to tell you about Mystic because you loved him so much."

"I should never have taken him," he said, sobbing.

"That's right, you shouldn't have. But it happened and you can't blame yourself for the accident. You loved the horse; no one blames you for his death. Now, come on. Let's go into the house and I'll fix you some breakfast."

"No!" Josh stepped away from her and angrily pushed her arm away from his shoulders. "You lied to me! All of you lied to me! You let me think that Mystic was alive and all the time he was dead!"

Josh began to run from the barn.

"Josh, wait!" Savannah yelled after him, and watched as he disappeared through the door. "Damn!" Her fist balled and she slammed it against the top of the gate to Mystic's stall. Vagabond snorted and tossed his head, but Savannah, her thoughts centered on her nephew, ignored the horse. "You made a fine mess out of this, Beaumont," she chastised herself before running after Josh to the house.

When she walked into the kitchen, she found that the entire household was awake.

"You told him about Mystic, didn't you?" Wade demanded. He was sipping from a cup of coffee and impaling her with his cruel eyes.

"Josh was already at the barn. What else could I do?"

"March him back here and have him talk to me. I'm his father."

"Then I suggest you start acting like it and quit lying to the kid. You had plenty of opportunities to talk to him about Mystic."

"And since I didn't you took it upon your shoulders to handle the situation."

"Don't push this off on me, Wade. Face it, you blew it." She started through the kitchen in an effort to go up to

Josh's room and try to console him, but Wade's hand restrained her.

"Stay away from him, Savannah. He's with Charmaine. She'll handle him. As far as I'm concerned you can leave my boy alone and just butt the hell out of my life."

"I love Josh, Wade."

"But he already has a mother." He dropped her arm and ran an unsteady hand through his hair. "And as for Travis McCord, you can tell him to leave me alone as well."

Savannah bristled. "What's Travis got to do with you?"

Eyeing her speculatively, Wade pressed his fingers against his temples as if trying to forestall a headache. "Nothing. Forget it."

"Forget what?" she asked. "Have you talked to him?"

"Of course not!" Wade snapped.

"Then—"

"I said, 'forget it,'" Wade grumbled, taking his coat from a peg near the back door and storming out of the house toward the garage.

"What was that all about?" she whispered to herself as she watched Wade walk angrily to his car. A few minutes later he drove away from the farm at a breakneck speed.

Knowing that something had happened between her brother-in-law and Travis, she tried to dial Travis's apartment in L.A. Though she let the phone ring for several minutes, Travis didn't answer. "Where are you?" she wondered aloud, hanging up the receiver and realizing just how much she depended upon him.

Taking a deep breath, Savannah climbed the stairs and found Charmaine walking out of Josh's room.

"I let the cat out of the bag," Savannah admitted.

"I know. It's all right. I should have told him when it first happened," Charmaine said with a weary smile. "He just wants to be left alone for a while."

"Do you think that's okay?"

"Yeah. He's okay. And Banjo's with him."

"Thank God Travis gave him the puppy."

Charmaine slid a conspiratorial glance in her sister's direction. "I had to do some fast talking to get Wade to agree to the dog," she admitted.

"I imagine. Wade just left."

"I heard," Charmaine said as if it didn't really matter one way or the other.

"How're things...between you two?"

"No worse than they ever were, I suppose, but it's hard to say. He's been a basket case ever since Travis showed up here a few weeks ago, and I'm about ready to call it quits." She ran a trembling hand over her eyes.

"Charmaine—"

"I'm okay. Really. I just don't understand Wade anymore. And his reaction to Travis...it's scary, he almost acts paranoid."

"Because of the governor's race?"

Charmaine shook her head and bit pensively on her lip. "There's more to it than that, I think. I just don't exactly know what it is." Looking Savannah squarely in the eye, she said, "But the whole thing scares me; it scares me to death."

"Why?"

"I don't know. I feel like Wade is worried about something—something big. But he won't confide in me."

"Maybe you're just imagining it," Savannah offered. "We've all been on edge ever since the accident with Mystic."

"I wish I could believe that was all it was," Charmaine replied grimly. "But I don't think so."

Two days later Travis returned to the farm. Savannah was standing near the exercise track with Lester when she heard footsteps behind her. She turned and found Travis, his eyes sparkling silver-gray in the morning light, walking toward her.

"I was beginning to think that you'd changed your mind," she accused with a laugh.

"About you? Never!" Travis took her into his arms and twirled her off the ground. "God, it's good to see you," he said, lowering his head and capturing her lips with his.

"You could've called," she accused.

"Too impersonal. I didn't want to waste any time. The faster I got done in L.A., the quicker I could get back to you!" He kissed her again, and this time the kiss deepened, igniting the dormant fires in her blood and sending her senses reeling.

Savannah blushed when she looked up and saw Lester staring at her.

"Don't mind me, missy." Lester grinned. "I always knew you two were right for each other."

"How?"

The older man grinned. "I was younger once myself, y'know. Had myself a wonderful lady, but things didn't work out."

Savannah was dumbfounded. "Why not?"

The older man smiled wistfully. "Turned out that she was married. And to a good man, too." He shrugged. "Water under the bridge. But with you two, that's a whole other story."

Vagabond finished his workout and Lester studied the colt with narrowed eyes. "This one, he might just do it this year."

"Do what?"

"Win 'em all!"

Savannah laughed and shoved her hands into her pockets. "That's what you said about Mystic."

"Ah, well, some things just don't work out as ya would have liked, don't ya know?" he said wistfully.

Lester walked over to the horse and Travis and Savannah turned back to the house.

"You think you can ever really leave this place?" Travis asked suddenly.

"With you? Yes."

"But you wouldn't be happy." It was a simple statement

and one Savannah couldn't really deny as she looked at the wet, green hills and the carefully maintained buildings of the farm. In a few months the brood mares would be delivering their foals and the spindly-legged newborns would get their first breath of life on the farm.

"I'll miss it," she admitted.

"Even if we start again?"

"In Colorado?"

"Wherever."

She angled her head and looked up at him. Light from a wintry sun warmed her face. "This farm is special to me. For you it represents my father and the fact that he tried to mold you into something he wanted. So, to you, it's a prison. But to me, it represents freedom to do exactly as I please."

"Which is work with the horses."

"And be near my family."

"I see," he said tersely, his teeth clenching together just as they reached the back porch. "I think it's time I talked to Reginald in person."

"Oh, God, haven't you quarreled enough already?"

"That's behind us."

"I don't understand."

"Oh, but you will. I've been doing a lot of thinking lately and I've talked to Reginald every day."

"You called here and didn't talk to me?" she demanded, confusion clouding her eyes. *What was going on?*

"Guilty as charged," he conceded with a rakish smile.

"I'll get you for that, you know."

A grin sliced across his tanned face. "I can't wait."

They walked into the den and found Reginald, his glasses perched on the end of his nose, sitting at his desk and carefully making marks on invoices as well as ledger entries.

"So you finally got here," Reginald said, all the old animosity out of his voice.

"Just a few minutes ago."

"You knew he was coming?" Savannah asked in surprise.

"Didn't you? Oh, I see." Reginald pushed the papers on his desk to the side and motioned for Savannah to take a seat in his recliner. "Well, I thought you'd want to know that I've decided to retire."

"Right away?"

"Yes. As soon as possible."

"*What!*"

He tapped a pencil to his lips and smiled at his daughter. "I've given a lot of thought to it, ever since the tragedy with Mystic and then with what Travis has discovered, it just seemed like the right time to turn over the farm to you."

"To me?" Savannah repeated, stunned. "Wait a minute. What about Wade?"

Reginald frowned and looked at Travis. "So you haven't told her anything, have you?"

"I figured it was your responsibility."

"What responsibility?" Savannah demanded. "What's been going on?" Then Travis's cold words came back to her. *I'm going to bait a trap.* What had happened?

"I've decided to sell that piece of property near San Francisco, take your mother and move to a warmer climate, somewhere south near San Diego, I think."

"But why now?"

"I told you that your mother needs to be closer to town and a hospital, and I'd been giving some thought to retiring anyway. When Travis discovered that Wade had skimmed money from the farm, I double-checked. Unfortunately, he was right. In the past six years, Wade has taken Beaumont Breeding Farm for nearly a quarter of a million dollars."

Savannah blanched and dropped into the nearest chair. "No!" But the expression on her father's face remained grim.

"Yes," Travis interjected. "Also, much to my partner, Willis Henderson's embarrassment, Wade has been skimming money out of the law firm with phony invoices and receipts."

"Same here," Reginald said, gesturing to a stack of bills. "Dummy companies who supposedly charged us for anything from paper clips to alfalfa to stud services." Reginald picked up his pipe and began cleaning the bowl. "I guess I'm getting too old to oversee everything. A few years ago this never would have happened. I would have caught it." He sighed heavily. "I just can't afford to make mistakes like that, not even for my own son-in-law."

"I can't believe any of this," Savannah whispered, but Travis's stony gaze convinced her that it was true. *Wade? A thief?*

"So I'm counting on you to keep the farm going," Reginald said with a sad smile. "Charmaine has no use for the horses, but you, you've had a feel for them ever since you were a little girl."

Savannah looked from her father to Travis. "You knew all about this, didn't you? And yet you let me think we were still going to Colorado."

"Just checking," he replied, his eyes lighting mischievously. "I had to know that you were serious about marrying me."

"Nothing will ever change my mind," she vowed, standing next to the man she loved with all of her heart.

"What the hell's going on here?" Wade demanded, bursting into the room. His face was flushed, his eyes wild and he was shaking from head to foot. "Charmaine just gave me some cock-and-bull story about you retiring and leaving the management of the farm to Savannah."

"That's right," Reginald said quietly.

"But—" His voice dropped when he saw the stack of invoices on the corner of the desk.

"I think you'd better call a good lawyer," Reginald said. "We've found you out, Wade."

"And don't bother contacting Willis Henderson," Travis added. "He's on to you."

"What's that supposed to mean?"

Travis sighed loudly. "Give it up, Benson," he suggested, his voice cold. "Not only do we know about the phony receipts and how much money you've embezzled to the penny, but we also know about the gambling debts that you've had to repay."

Wade blanched and stumbled backward, leaning against the wall for support. "Lies," he choked out. "All a pack of lies."

"I don't think so."

Gesturing wildly, Wade pointed a condemning finger at Travis. "And I suppose you've spread all these lies to Charmaine, haven't you! Haven't you?"

"She knows all about it. If you want, you can try and explain your side of the story," Travis said. "But she's got all the facts and figures."

Wade's eyes narrowed and his fist curled at his side. "This is all your fault, McCord. You've spent the last few weeks of your life trying to destroy me. Well, I'm going to fight it. Tooth and nail. Just because you're a big hotshot attorney, you're not going to force me into going to jail for something I didn't do!"

He stomped out of the room and thundered up the stairs.

"Well, that's that," Reginald said wearily. "Can't say that I like it much." He lit his pipe and sighed as the smoke billowed around his face. "It will probably kill your mother."

"She's stronger than you think," Savannah whispered.

"I hope so." Reginald shook his head and put his hands on the desk to rise to his full height. "Oh, and Savannah, you may as well know that I told Travis I expect him to help you with the farm."

"That's right," Travis said. "The old man is still trying to manipulate me."

"And you let him?" Savannah asked.

Travis's smile stole from one side of his face to the other.

"Maybe it's because he told me he wanted us to fill this house with his grandchildren."

She lifted her confused eyes to her father. "Wait a minute. Are you saying that after all your warnings you *want* me to marry Travis?"

Reginald snorted. "I would have preferred him to become governor; I wouldn't even have opposed having a daughter who's the first lady of this state, but I guess I'll just have to settle for a son-in-law who will run this farm with care and integrity."

"And what about Wade?" Savannah asked.

"I don't know," Reginald said, obviously tired. "But he's made his own bed; now he'll have to lie in it." Reginald walked out of the room and trudged up the stairs to talk to Virginia.

"So what happens to Wade now?" Savannah asked.

"I suppose Wade will be prosecuted, if Willis Henderson and your father have their way," Travis replied.

"And Charmaine?"

"She's taking it in stride, but she could probably use a little support from you."

Savannah's heart twisted and her voice was only the barest of whispers. "And what about Josh?"

"Charmaine's already talked to him. The boy seemed to handle it fairly well. Remember, he and his father didn't get along very well, anyway."

"He and Charmaine have become a lot closer since Mystic's death," Savannah said.

Travis leaned against the desk with his hips and drew Savannah into the circle of his arms. "The way I figure it, we'll live here until we can build a house of our own. And your father has promised not to try and run our lives."

"I can't believe you've buried the hatchet."

"Face it, the man is your father. I'm stuck with him and he's stuck with me. Because of you, we're trying to work things out."

"Unbelievable," she murmured. "Now, tell me what's wrong with this house."

"Nothing, except that it belongs to Reginald and Virginia. Charmaine and Josh will probably stay here."

"So what was all this song and dance about filling up this house with children?" she asked, turning to face him, a sparkle lighting her blue eyes.

"Just that. The house I intend to fill with children will have to be twice this size just to hold them all."

"You're out of your mind, counselor," she said, but tossed her hair away from her face and laughed at the thought.

"Only with love for you." He pulled her closer, so that her ear was pressed to his chest and she could hear the steady pounding of his heart. "Don't worry about anything, we can have it all."

"And Wade?"

"He'll probably be sent to prison and I think that's a good place for him. He won't be around for the next few years, and by the time he gets back, if Charmaine doesn't decide to divorce him, Josh will be old enough to stand up for himself."

"You've got it all figured out, don't you?"

"Except for one thing."

"Oh?" She lifted her head and traced the seductive curve of his lips with her finger. "What's that?"

"How I'm going to get you to marry me before tonight."

"Impossible."

"Reno's not that far away...."

She laughed merrily. "Oh, no, you don't. I'm not settling for a quick ten-minute speech in front of some justice of the peace I've never met before. You're going to have to go the whole nine yards on this one. You know, big church, long white gown, stiff uncomfortable tuxedo and at least four attendants."

Travis squeezed her. "You're really out for blood, aren't you?"

"I've waited a long time."

"And it was worth it, wasn't it?" Without waiting for a response, he pressed his hungry lips to hers and deftly swept her off her feet. "Don't answer that question," he whispered against her ear. "We have much more important things to do right now."

Without a word of protest, Savannah stared into his eyes and locked her arms around his neck. "And for the rest of our lives," she added.

Travis smiled and carried her out of the den, down the hallway and into the kitchen.

"Hey, where are you taking me?" she asked.

"To some place where we can be alone." He crossed the parking lot to the garage and climbed the stairs to his loft. Once inside, he set her on the floor, kicked the door shut and locked it. "Now, Ms. Beaumont," he said, with a twinkle in his eyes. "I think it's time we spent the next few days locked away from the rest of the world."

"Is that possible?" she asked.

"Probably not, but we can try." Grinning wickedly, he extracted a gold key from his pocket and dangled it in front of her nose. "Face it, lady, you can't get away from me."

"I wouldn't have it any other way," she agreed, as he folded her into his arms and carried her into the bedroom.

From *New York Times* bestselling sensation

HEATHER GRAHAM

Comes an unforgettable holiday story

A powerful heiress, a mysterious stranger…
Against their wills, Jillian Llewellyn and Robert Marston
are drawn together as they try to unlock a centuries-old
secret of passion and betrayal that has come back
to haunt them. In this season of magic and
miracles, two lost souls have been given
a second chance—one that will not
come around again.

"An incredible storyteller!"
—*Los Angeles Daily News*

A SEASON OF MIRACLES

*On sale mid-October 2002
wherever books are sold!*

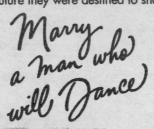